CRITICAL ACCLAIM FOR

'A million readers can't be wrong... take a deep breath, order in for the day, sit back and enjoy a bloody good read'

'Taut and compelling' **Peter James**

'Leigh Russell is one to watch' **Lee Child**

'Leigh Russell has become one of the most impressively dependable purveyors of the English police procedural' *Times*

'DI Geraldine Steel is one of the most authoritative female coppers in a crowded field'
Financial Times

'A brilliant talent in the thriller field' **Jeffery Deaver**

'Brilliant and chilling, Leigh Russell delivers a cracker of a read!' **Martina Cole**

'A great plot that keeps you guessing right until the very end, some subtle subplots, brilliant characters both old and new and as ever a completely gripping read' *Life of Crime*

'The latest police procedural from prolific novelist Leigh Russell is as good and gripping as anything she has published'
Times & Sunday Times Crime Club

'A fascinating gripping read. The many twists kept me on my toes and second guessing myself'
Over The Rainbow Book Blog

'Well paced with marvellously well-rounded characters and a clever plot that make this another thriller of a read from Leigh Russell' **Orlando Books**

'A well-written, fast-paced and very enjoyable thriller' **The Book Lovers Boudoir**

'An edge-of-your-seat thriller that will keep you guessing' **Honest Mam Reader**

'Well paced, has red herrings and twists galore, keeps your attention and sucks you right into its pages' **Books by Bindu**

'5 stars! Another super addition to one of my favourite series, which remains as engrossing and fresh as ever!' **The Word is Out**

'A nerve-twisting tour de force that will leave readers on the edge of their seats, Leigh Russell's latest Detective Geraldine Steel thriller is a terrifying page-turner by this superb crime writer' **Bookish Jottings**

'An absolute delight' **The Literary Shed**

'I simply couldn't put it down' **Shell Baker, Chelle's Book Reviews**

'If you love a good action-packed crime novel, full of complex characters and unexpected twists, this is one for you' **Rachel Emms, *Chillers, Killers and Thrillers***

'All the things a mystery should be: intriguing, enthralling, tense and utterly absorbing' **Best Crime Books**

'A series that can rival other major crime writers out there...'
Best Books to Read

'Sharp, intelligent and well plotted' ***Crime Fiction Lover***

'Another corker of a book from Leigh Russell... Russell's talent for writing top-quality crime fiction just keeps on growing' ***Euro Crime***

'A definite must read for crime thriller fans everywhere'
Newbooks Magazine

'Russell's strength as a writer is her ability to portray believable characters' ***Crime Squad***

'A well-written, well-plotted crime novel with fantastic pace and lots of intrigue' ***Bookersatz***

'An encounter that will take readers into the darkest recesses of the human psyche' ***Crime Time***

'Well written and chock full of surprises, this hard-hitting, edge-of-the-seat instalment is yet another treat... Geraldine Steel looks set to become a household name. Highly recommended' ***Euro Crime***

'Good, old-fashioned, heart-hammering police thriller... a no-frills delivery of pure excitement' ***SAGA Magazine***

'A gritty and totally addictive novel'
New York Journal of Books

Also by Leigh Russell

Geraldine Steel Mysteries

Cut Short
Road Closed
Dead End
Death Bed
Stop Dead
Fatal Act
Killer Plan
Murder Ring
Deadly Alibi
Class Murder
Death Rope
Rogue Killer
Deathly Affair
Deadly Revenge
Evil Impulse
Deep Cover
Guilt Edged
Fake Alibi
Final Term
Without Trace
Revenge Killing
Deadly Will

Ian Peterson Murder Investigations

Cold Sacrifice
Race to Death
Blood Axe

Poppy Mystery Tales

Barking Up the Right Tree
Barking Mad
Poppy Takes the Lead
Poppy's Christmas Cracker

Lucy Hall Mysteries

Journey to Death
Girl in Danger
The Wrong Suspect

Leigh Russell

THE STAKES HAVE NEVER BEEN HIGHER

COLD JUSTICE

NO EXIT PRESS

First published in the UK in 2025 by No Exit Press,
an imprint of Bedford Square Publishers Ltd,
London, UK

noexit.co.uk
@noexitpress

© Leigh Russell, 2025

The right of Leigh Russell to be identified as the author of this work has been asserted in accordance with the Copyright, Designs and Patents Act 1988. All rights reserved. No part of this book may be reproduced, stored in or introduced into a retrieval system, or transmitted, in any form or by any means (electronic, mechanical, photocopying, recording or otherwise) without the written permission of the publishers.

Any person who does any unauthorised act in relation to this publication may be liable to criminal prosecution and civil claims for damages.
A CIP catalogue record for this book is available from the British Library.
This is a work of fiction. Names, characters, places, and incidents either are the product of the author's imagination or are used fictitiously, and any resemblance to actual persons, living or dead, businesses, companies, events or locales is entirely coincidental.

ISBN
978-1-83501-280-2 (Paperback)
978-1-83501-281-9 (eBook)

2 4 6 8 10 9 7 5 3 1

The manufacturer's authorised representative in the EU for product safety is Easy Access System Europe, Mustamäe tee 50, 10621 Tallinn, Estonia
gpsr.requests@easproject.com

Typeset in 11 on 13.9pt Times New Roman
by Avocet Typeset, Bideford, Devon, EX39 2BP
Printed and bound in Great Britain by
CPI Group (UK) Ltd, Croydon CR0 4YY

To Michael, Joanna, Phillipa, Phil, Rian and Kezia.
With my love.

Glossary of acronyms

DCI   – Detective Chief Inspector (senior officer on case)
DI   – Detective Inspector
DS   – Detective Sergeant
SOCO – scene of crime officer (collects forensic evidence at scene)
PM   – Post mortem or Autopsy (examination of dead body to establish cause of death)
CCTV – Closed Circuit Television (security cameras)
VIIDO – Visual Images, Identification and Detections Office

Prologue

THE YOUNG WOMAN LAY flat on her back, blood pooling on the ground beside her. After so much careful preparation, the struggle hadn't lasted long. It never did. One minute the girl was alive, the next minute she was dead. The blade had entered at exactly the right spot, in the middle of her chest, and death was swift. With practice, a quick death had become almost assured. It was better that way, reducing any risk of discovery before the job was done, and less messy. The victim had barely attempted to struggle or even remonstrate. As long as they were caught off guard, victims put up no resistance, which was crucial. Killers had been caught by traces of DNA under the fingernails of corpses, a needless blunder.

It was a pity to leave the body so exposed, only half hidden in the bushes, but the longer the delay, the greater the danger that someone would chance to appear. Regret was a waste of energy. So negative a response was as pointless as indulging in a feeling of pride that everything had gone according to the plan. That could come later. All that mattered now was to slip away unseen.

A shaft of sunlight caught The Knife which seemed to glow with a mystical red light, but there was no time to linger, lost in wonder at the beauty of the blade. A cool head and deft reactions were essential: wrap The Knife in a plastic bag, shove it in the backpack, grab the body under the arms and drag it completely out of sight before hurrying home to clean up, all before anyone came along. There was no point in taking chances. However confident the police might be, the negligence of criminals resulted in more arrests than any cunning detective work. With care, the police could be dodged at every step and any unpleasantness avoided.

Attempting to heave the body into the overgrown weeds bordering the waste ground was hazardous. One tiny scratch from a bramble and it would all be over, a trace of DNA left behind like a calling card. Staring blindly up at the sky, the dead woman's eyes jolted horribly when she was moved. It soon became obvious that any hope of concealing the body would be thwarted by the difficulty of manoeuvring it across uneven ground. It would be too risky to spend time trying to shift it any further. At least it wasn't lying in the street and it might not be found straight away.

Sunlight penetrating the clouds illuminated a trail of blood that seemed to glow on the ground like crimson arrows pointing the way to the body. Terror struck, transforming an invulnerable killer into a fugitive. It was surprising the power one death could have, even though there had been others.

A fine drizzle began to fall. Slowly it might wash away the blood but, in the meantime, the body could be discovered. Glancing furtively around to make sure no one was watching, the killer fled lightly across scrubby grass.

The Knife dropped on the kitchen worktop with a faint clatter. It rolled over, leaving a smear of blood on the pale grey surface.

Human blood.

Irritated, the killer seized the murder weapon and flung it in the sink, before searching in a cupboard for an old rag and a bottle of bleach and setting to work, scrubbing at the bloodstained table and floor. The smell was repulsive but eventually the marks completely disappeared. Next, The Knife had to be scoured repeatedly until every trace of blood had been removed before it went in the dishwasher.

Having showered and changed, it was time to put on fresh rubber gloves, conceal them beneath thin woollen ones and take a carrier bag of clothes to the laundrette before depositing them at a charity shop. No one there was going to test garments for stray vestiges of human blood stains. A light plastic raincoat and a rag used to clean the kitchen were ditched in a bin somewhere in the centre of the city, hidden under a mess of food wrappers and cigarette packets, bottles and cans. Confident that every trace of the murder had been successfully erased, the killer felt physically and emotionally cleansed. All things considered, it had been a successful day.

That evening, there would be a steak for supper to mark the occasion. Even that served a purpose. After going through the dishwasher several times, The Knife might still retain traces of blood. Cutting raw beef would hopefully obfuscate any lingering evidence. It was very satisfactory knowing The Knife would help to prepare the celebratory steak. Everything was working out well. This run of luck couldn't continue indefinitely, but it wasn't over yet. All the same, it made sense to move on; more than two fatal attacks in any one location would be rash. Gratifying though it was, soon it would be time to think about bringing this killing binge to an end. But not yet. Having grown up in York, that seemed a fitting place to draw matters to a close. With the next victim in mind, it was time to go home and finish the job.

1

A LOURING SKY HAD been threatening rain for several days but, apart from a few brief showers, it had remained dry. Even though they were well into May, the weather remained dull.

'I wish it would hurry up,' Geraldine muttered at breakfast, as a radio presenter promised 'a warmer front' was on its way.

Ian looked up. 'What's that?'

'They keep saying the weather's going to improve, but I can't see any sign of it,' she replied. 'This time last year we were having breakfast out on the veranda.' She glanced out of the kitchen window and scowled. The sky was overcast and it looked as though it might rain at any moment.

'The forecasts are usually quite accurate these days,' Ian replied, waving his toast in the air. 'And didn't your mother ever tell you not to pull faces. If the wind changes, you could be stuck like that.'

Geraldine laughed. 'I wish the wind would change. And stop dropping crumbs on the floor.'

They smiled at one another and finished their breakfast in a companionable silence broken only by Tom's spoon banging on the tray of his high chair.

'What's happened to our summer?' Geraldine grumbled as she bundled the baby into his blue one-piece padded waterproof and pulled up the hood. By the time they reached the car, his mittens were already dangling from their string and his hood had been pulled back. When she asked him where his mittens were, he wriggled his tiny fingers at her and giggled. Geraldine dropped him off at his childminder's house in Maple Grove, barely five minutes' walk from the police station in York.

Lisa was holding a girl of about two in her arms when she opened the door. With accustomed ease, she shifted the girl on to one hip so she could carry Tom on the other. Geraldine was about to turn away when Lisa detained her. Afraid of hearing that the childminder could no longer look after Tom, Geraldine hovered anxiously on the doorstep, but Lisa seemed unexpectedly tongue-tied.

'What is it?' Geraldine asked after a moment, hiding her impatience. Clearly something was bothering the childminder. After waiting a few more seconds, Geraldine prompted her. 'Is something the matter?'

'Well,' Lisa began, and hesitated, a troubled expression on her usually cheerful face.

Geraldine tensed, expecting bad news. 'What's wrong? Is this about Tom?'

'No, no, it's nothing to do with Tom. Nothing's wrong. Everything's fine,' Lisa hurried to reassure her.

As if to agree with her, Tom gurgled happily and both women smiled. The little girl began wriggling to be put down, but Lisa ignored her and she settled down again.

'It's just that I have a question, if that's all right,' Lisa resumed, repeating that her question was not related to Tom in any way.

'Go on,' Geraldine said, with a slight feeling of dismay. If this had nothing to do with Tom, then she had an inkling of what might be coming.

'You work for the police, don't you?' Lisa went on, her dark eyes peering uneasily from her plump face.

Geraldine nodded and stifled a sigh. Lisa knew she was a detective inspector investigating serious crime. 'I try to keep my private and professional affairs separate,' she said gently.

'Oh, this isn't for me,' Lisa replied, as though that justified any imposition. 'It's for my niece, Alice. She needs help. Please wait and listen to me,' she added, as Geraldine took a step backwards. 'She really needs your help.'

Geraldine hesitated. 'Tell me what the problem is,' she replied. 'But please be brief. I need to get to work.'

'Have you got time to come in? I called her and told her you'd be here. She'll be here any minute. Please. You've met her here,' she added with an air of desperation. 'You remember her? My niece, Alice.'

Geraldine recalled meeting a woman of around twenty on Lisa's doorstep. She was slim, with fair hair cut in a short bob, and a long fringe that reached her widely spaced pale eyes. Under her raincoat she had been wearing faded jeans. Geraldine had noted nothing remarkable about her appearance, but remembered thinking that she had seemed like a pleasant girl.

Lisa smiled eagerly at Geraldine. 'You remember her, don't you?'

'I can't stay long,' Geraldine replied. Seeing Lisa's dashed expression, she added apologetically, 'I have to get to work, but I can wait for a few minutes.'

Hoping that the childminder would tell her it wasn't really important, she was disappointed when Lisa's frown cleared. 'That would be wonderful,' she cried out. 'Thank you so much. She should be here any time now.'

Geraldine was slightly irritated, but the childminder was reliable and Tom was settled with her, so she was reluctant to upset her. After living for so long as an independent woman, her peace of mind was now completely dependent on her son's happiness. Lisa handed Tom to Geraldine who removed his outer clothing and lay him on a mat where he gurgled happily and reached out to her. She bent her head and pretended to nibble his fingers and he squealed with delight.

'I don't know what's happened to Alice,' Lisa said uneasily after a moment. 'She isn't answering her phone. I left her a message earlier, insisting she come round. She should be here soon.'

Geraldine shifted in her seat.

'I'll call her again,' Lisa said, and hit a speed dial button on her phone. 'The friend I told you about is here and she needs to get to work,' Lisa said. 'Are you coming round or not? Please, call me back right away.'

Lisa rang off and turned to Geraldine, her eyes darting around the room, as though searching for reassurance. She was clutching the arm of her chair so tightly her knuckles turned white.

'Alice refuses to talk to me about her boyfriend, but—' She began and hesitated. 'The fact is, I think he's abusing her physically.'

Geraldine considered what Lisa had said. 'Would she be prepared to make a statement? These situations can be dealt with discreetly, but they are always difficult to investigate, and it's almost impossible when the victim is unwilling to come forward.'

'What if she's in danger?' Lisa blurted out.

'What makes you say that? Lisa, in what way do you think she may be in danger?'

Lisa drew in a deep breath before answering. 'What if things get out of hand and he kills her?' she murmured.

'Do you really believe that's going to happen? If you're genuinely concerned, you have to persuade her to report him to the police. Or she might want to talk to someone? Perhaps her GP might be able to help?'

Lisa shook her head. She seemed close to tears. 'I don't know what to do. This is driving me to distraction.' She sounded desperate. 'Alice is a nurse,' she added, failing to repress a faint note of pride. 'She works in intensive care, so she's not one to panic or become hysterical. But she's seemed – oh, I don't know – overwrought lately. And she refuses to talk to me about her boyfriend.'

The bell rang and Lisa leaped to her feet.

'That'll be her now,' she cried out. 'At last!'

Lisa hurried out of the room and the two-year-old girl followed her. Geraldine heard voices in the hall and a moment later, Lisa returned. She was alone, apart from the little girl toddling behind her.

'It was the postman,' she said, flopping down on a chair with a sigh. 'I don't know what's happened to Alice.'

'She should take her concerns to the police station,' Geraldine said gravely. 'If she has a violent partner, a few words from one of my colleagues might be all it takes to calm the situation down. And if that's not enough, we can advise her about keeping herself safe. If necessary, she can apply for a restraining order against her partner. But if she's suffering abuse, I would strongly advise her not to ignore it, not if there's a chance she could be at risk. I don't want to prejudge anything, but these things can sometimes escalate.'

Lisa lowered her voice, although no one but Geraldine could hear her. 'What if she won't do anything? What can I do to protect her from him?'

Geraldine hesitated. If this was anything other than a vexatious claim, such an accusation needed to be investigated properly, through the right channels. It was not something to chat about in private behind closed doors. But it was possible Lisa simply didn't like her niece's boyfriend. There could be several reasons why she might hold a grudge against him. Perhaps she was possessive over her niece. Clearly devoted to her, she might think no one was good enough for her. Even if the boyfriend was treating her niece badly and was making her unhappy, that did not mean he was abusing her. So far, this was all very vague.

'You are making a serious allegation,' she said quietly. 'Do you have any evidence to support your suspicions?'

Lisa shrugged and shook her head. In spite of her reservations, Geraldine was bothered. Lisa had not struck her as someone who was prone to exaggeration.

Lisa leaned forward in her chair. 'Can you help her?' she asked.

Geraldine spoke very carefully. 'I'm afraid I won't be able to instigate an official investigation unless your niece chooses to come forward. If she does, she needs to take any proof she has to the police station so we can look into this properly. But it's unlikely anyone will do anything about unsubstantiated accusations you report.' She sighed. 'There's nothing we can do if your niece herself denies your allegations. You'd be surprised how often that happens and there's nothing we can do. I'm sorry, but I need to hear this from her.'

Lisa looked at her, dismayed, and Geraldine stood up and took her leave.

Apologising profusely, Lisa followed her to the front door. 'I shouldn't have mentioned this to you,' she said. 'It wasn't appropriate, I know, but I'm desperate.'

Geraldine reassured her that she had done nothing wrong; it was understandable that she would want to help her niece.

'The thing is,' Lisa added, 'she's usually such a level-headed girl. Nothing spooks her. Like I said, she's a nurse and she works in intensive care, so she's not one to get hysterical about anything. But this boyfriend...' Her voice petered out. 'I can tell the situation is bothering her. And she's such a lovely girl.' She was close to tears again.

'I wish there was something I could do,' Geraldine said. 'If you can persuade her to take her concerns to the police, hopefully that will help. I'm sorry, but there's nothing I can do.'

Lisa nodded miserably and Geraldine left, feeling dissatisfied. Ian noticed her deflated mood when she arrived home that evening, and asked her what was wrong. When she told him about her conversation with the childminder, he shook his head, frowning, and his fair hair flopped forwards.

'She had no business thrusting her niece's problems at you like that,' he said.

'She didn't thrust anything at me,' Geraldine protested. 'I said I'd listen to her.'

'And you did,' he replied. 'But that's all, and even that was more than she should have expected. We pay her to take care of Tom, not to use you as a private police force for members of her family. If she comes on to you like that again, tell her in no uncertain terms that you can't listen to any more domestic problems.'

Geraldine was tempted to laugh at his overreaction. He had a point, but she couldn't shake off a nagging anxiety about Alice. Lisa was a sensible woman and it was hard to believe she would throw out accusations against her niece's boyfriend without good reason. Still, so far the allegations were nothing more than speculation on Lisa's part and, besides, the police were powerless to take any action unless Alice herself came and asked for help. With a sigh, she tried to dismiss what she had heard as a domestic falling-out.

2

GERALDINE WAS HAVING LUNCH in the police station canteen with two of her colleagues, dark-haired Ariadne and blonde Naomi. Geraldine enjoyed mulling over issues at work, and swapping rumours about colleagues, with two women she considered her close friends. She had worked with her sergeant, Ariadne, for several years. Almost the same age, they had developed a strong bond. Naomi, the youngest of the three, was also a detective sergeant. While Ariadne was happily married and readily admitted she had never wanted to rise above the rank of sergeant, Naomi was ambitious, and Geraldine and Ariadne were both confident their young colleague would do well. Geraldine had become an unofficial mentor to her and the young sergeant was quietly devoted to her.

'How's Tom?' Ariadne asked, brushing her long, loose curls off her face.

'Tom's fine,' Geraldine replied, smiling. 'He's settled down well with his new childminder, thank goodness.'

'I couldn't think of anything worse than spending all day looking after other people's children.' Naomi pulled a face, making Geraldine and Ariadne laugh.

'Yes, spending time with little children must be far worse than questioning vicious criminals,' Ariadne said, laughing. 'I think you may have been working here too long and it's warped your perception of humanity.'

Chatting about how pleased she was with Lisa, Geraldine held back from mentioning the childminder's concerns for her niece. After all, what sounded like nothing more than a family disagreement was hardly a matter for the police to discuss. They began talking about their holiday plans. Ariadne told them she was keen to go back to Greece, where her mother had grown up. She still had family there. Naomi fancied a trip to Cuba and Geraldine encouraged her to travel while she was still young and childless.

'That's assuming I want to have children,' Naomi replied, with a grin. 'We're not all born with a maternal instinct.'

Geraldine nodded. 'To be honest, I wasn't either. We never actually planned to have Tom. I was always too focused on work to have time to even think about starting a family. Yet here I am, a doting mother.' She shrugged, smiling. 'These things happen. It's impossible to explain, but it changes everything.' Before she had Tom, she would never have believed what a difference one small life could make to her.

While Geraldine was talking, Ariadne focused quietly on her food. Glancing at her, Geraldine wondered whether she was talking about Tom too much and quickly changed the subject. Back to talking about holidays again, they were discussing the benefits of going away for a weekend as opposed to a longer break, when they were summoned to a briefing. They all exchanged a grave look. Unless they were mistaken, this might mean there had been a murder. Gulping down a final mouthful of coffee, Naomi jumped to her feet.

'Come on,' she said eagerly, before she turned and hurried away.

Ariadne stood up as well, as Geraldine downed the dregs of her coffee and clambered to her feet.

'Let's go and see what's in store for us,' she said, her usual burst of adrenaline at the prospect of starting a new investigation clouded by a faint sense of foreboding.

Detective Chief Inspector Binita Hewitt was waiting in the major incident room, impatiently tapping one gleaming shoe on the floor. Like Geraldine and Ariadne, the DCI had dark hair and bright black eyes. With her slender figure, trim bob and penetrating stare, her neat jacket seemed to reflect the precision she demonstrated in her work. Geraldine, Ariadne and Naomi were the last to arrive, and Binita began straight away by announcing that a woman's body had been discovered in the street, not far from the police station. Seeing an image of the victim appear on the screen behind Binita, Geraldine bit her lip to stifle a cry.

'Her name is Alice James,' Binita said.

The name confirmed what Geraldine already knew. The murder victim's aunt had asked her for help only the previous day and she had refused. All her adult life had been dedicated to seeking justice for the dead, but on this occasion she had failed to save the living.

'She was discovered just after eight this morning, stabbed in the heart,' Binita went on. 'It looks as though she was killed at the site where her body was found. She was on her way out or on her way back home, as the body was found at the entrance to an alley only a hundred yards from where she lived.'

Geraldine felt she could no longer conceal her knowledge of the dead woman. Briefly she told her colleagues about the concerns shared with her by the victim's aunt only the previous day.

'I advised her aunt to tell Alice to come here and report her situation,' she concluded. 'I did what I could to persuade her to encourage her niece to come forward, but it seems I didn't do enough.'

'What more could you have done?' Ariadne asked.

Geraldine shrugged. 'I could have spoken to Alice myself.'

'If her aunt couldn't persuade the girl to report her boyfriend, she was hardly likely to listen to you,' Ariadne replied.

'She might have taken exception to learning that her aunt had made these allegations to you,' Binita pointed out. 'And, in any case, I doubt your intervention would have made any difference.'

'If I'd acted sooner, she might not have been killed,' Geraldine muttered wretchedly.

Binita assured her that she had done nothing wrong. No individual officer could be expected to follow up every complaint and accusation immediately, especially not when it appeared to be a domestic problem. If they did, they would never have time to investigate serious crimes.

'I didn't think it was worth mentioning,' Geraldine explained to Ariadne as they were driving to the crime scene. 'But I should have taken action more quickly, done more to help her.'

'You need to stop thinking like that. You can't blame yourself,' Ariadne insisted. 'You didn't know what was going on, and you could have had no idea what was going to happen. How many women argue with their boyfriends, and how often does it end in a fatality? Haven't you ever argued with Ian? In any case, even if you were planning to speak to her later on, it would probably have been too late. There's nothing you could have done to save her.' She paused. 'I think it's going to rain,' she added, in a transparent attempt to change the subject.

Ariadne's attempt to draw attention to the weather was pointless as they had already arrived in Wenlock Terrace, where the body had been found. They were only round the corner from the police station.

'It would have been just as quick to walk here,' Ariadne grumbled.

Geraldine didn't answer. She was wondering if Lisa had heard the devastating news yet and, if not, who would be tasked with telling her Alice was dead.

3

Binita had hesitated to put Geraldine on the investigation team, since she knew the victim's aunt and had discussed the victim's situation with her. Geraldine had argued quite forcefully that she had met Alice only once, and then just for a matter of a few seconds, so she couldn't claim to have any real connection with her. As for Lisa, Geraldine pointed out that she was the victim's aunt, and so not even immediate family. After some persuasion, Binita had finally agreed to allow Geraldine to be part of the team investigating Alice's murder. Geraldine was pleased. For once her reasoning wasn't entirely rational, but she felt she somehow owed it to Lisa and to the dead girl to track down this killer and make sure he faced the full force of the law.

Alice had lived in one of a row of old terraced cottages in Wenlock Terrace. The properties had been split into apartments which appeared to be well maintained on the outside. The brickwork was in need of repointing on some of the house fronts, but the paintwork generally looked reasonably fresh, at least from a distance. There were several magnificent trees on the opposite side of a street which would have looked like any other pleasant residential area, were it not for the white forensic tent casting a shadow over its immediate surroundings.

A light rain had begun to fall by the time they arrived at the crime scene, which was located at the entrance to a narrow lane running between Wenlock Terrace and the next parallel street, Ordnance Lane. The far end of the alley was closed, and the pavement and road on either side of the tent were cordoned off. Uniformed officers were on duty at either end of the alley, preventing members of the public from entering the lane. Pulling on a protective suit and shoe covers, Geraldine entered the tent where officers were busy collecting evidence. Markers had been placed by several dark patches on the ground. Closer examination revealed them to be blood stains presumably left when the victim had staggered, or had been dragged, into the alley. A scene of crime scene officer greeted her and explained that the forensic tent had been erected before a light rain had started, so fortunately the ground around the crime scene was still more or less dry.

'A stroke of luck for us, eh?' he added cheerily.

Geraldine nodded without answering. Whatever good luck there was at the scene had not extended to the victim. Having looked around, she asked if they had established when the attack had taken place.

A second scene of crime officer shook her head, her eyes wrinkled in a cautious smile of greeting. 'The doctor placed the time of death at between three and seven this morning. It's lucky she was reported in time for us to get here before the rain,' she added. 'That could have complicated matters.'

Geraldine frowned on hearing a second officer refer to the good luck the forensic team were enjoying at the crime scene. Wondering whether Alice's death had been the result of a targeted attack, with a tremor of guilt she remembered how Lisa had begged for her help. If only Geraldine had acted on Lisa's concerns, perhaps Alice would still be alive. But Ariadne was right. There was no point tormenting herself with speculation about what might have been. Whatever had happened to lead to this tragedy, the fact remained that Alice was dead. All Geraldine could do now was concentrate all her efforts on finding the killer. Nothing could be allowed to distract her from that objective, certainly not any emotional response to the murder.

Reluctantly, Geraldine turned her attention to the body. As a rule, she was curious to see a victim whose unlawful death she was investigating, but she found it disturbing to see the face of a woman whom she had recently seen alive, however briefly. Alice was lying on her back. A scene of crime officer confirmed that was the position in which she had been found, just at the Wenlock Terrace end of the short alleyway. She lay sprawled on a bed of dirty weeds and litter that had been dropped in the alley, or had blown in from the street. It was a depressing scene. Everything looked empty: a discarded beer can, a crumpled cigarette packet, a small plastic water bottle, a dead woman's eyes. Other than the team of officers in their protective clothing, a few straggly weeds provided the only signs of life.

Drawing closer, Geraldine gazed down at the dead woman's ghastly white face. Her eyes appeared to be staring fixedly at anyone who leaned over to look at her. She had no obvious injury, other than the one blazoned by a large blood stain showing almost black against the pale fabric of her shirt. The front of her jacket was streaked and blood had dripped down her jeans, suggesting that she had been upright when she was stabbed.

'No defence wounds,' the scene of crime officer said grimly, as though the victim's failure to resist her assailant was somehow more shameful than the attack itself. 'She didn't even try to fight back.'

'It probably happened unexpectedly and too quickly for her to react,' Geraldine replied, feeling compelled to defend the victim. At the same time, she made a mental note that Alice appeared to have made no attempt to fight off her attacker. 'Hopefully she managed to scratch her killer and we'll be able to find something under her fingernails,' she added. 'There's always a chance.'

'If we're lucky,' the scene of crime officer agreed.

Geraldine stiffened on hearing the word 'lucky' again. Tempted to yell that nothing could be considered 'lucky' at a time like this, she looked away and kept quiet. There was nothing to be gained by carping at the use of an inappropriate word. It wasn't as though Alice could hear them talking and take offence at any disregard for her feelings.

'I hope so anyway,' her colleague went on. 'I really hope so. Poor woman. What a way to go. Let's hope you catch the brute who did this soon, and we can all go home and die peacefully in our beds.'

'I'm not sure I'm ready to go home and die quite yet,' Geraldine said, attempting to speak lightly. 'And before I do, I want to know I've helped put the monster who did this behind bars,' she added, with sudden intensity.

'Amen to that,' her colleague replied fervently. 'Prison's too good for some people, if you want my opinion.'

'How did she die?' Geraldine asked. 'It looks like a chest wound?'

Her colleague confirmed that Alice had been fatally stabbed in the chest. 'By person or persons unknown.'

Geraldine nodded. A stabbing was certainly what the state of the victim's clothes suggested. She stared down at the dead woman, but there was nothing more to be gained from standing there, so she went to question the man who had reported finding the body to see if he had anything to add to what she had already learned.

'I was on my way to work,' a bespectacled young man told her, wiping the back of his hand across his brow. 'I cycle to school along the lane. It's a short cut. I'm a maths teacher,' he added apologetically, as though his job was somehow embarrassing. 'Well, as I told your constable, I was cycling along this morning, minding my own business, as usual, when I saw her lying in the alley. I nearly went straight past. To be honest, I thought she was drunk or on drugs or something. My wife's not happy about my cycling in the alley but you don't expect to run into trouble in the daytime, do you?'

Geraldine thanked him for stopping and reporting the body.

'That's quite all right. It's what anyone would do. I told them I'd get to school as soon as possible, so I wonder if you still need me here? I mean, I'm more than willing to stay if you think I can be of any further assistance. To be honest, if I had to choose between finding a dead body and facing Year Nine first thing in the morning, it would be a hard decision.' He broke off, shaking his head. 'I'm sorry. That must have sounded very flippant. I didn't mean any disrespect to the poor woman. It's just that behaviour seems to be at an all-time low at the moment and we're all struggling to keep control in the classroom. And they think *Lord of the Flies* is fiction. Well, good luck in your job when these kids are let loose on the streets with nothing to do all day, that's all I can say.'

The witness had given his contact details to one of Geraldine's colleagues and he had nothing to add to what they already knew. Thanking him again, she let him go and he cycled off with an air of desperate determination.

4

ALICE HAD BEEN LIVING with her boyfriend, Rob, who was a builder, decorator and all-round handyman. He was at work that day, so Geraldine had Ariadne drive her to the site where he was currently employed as a plasterer. The stocky foreman of the building site looked faintly puzzled when Geraldine asked to speak to Robert Stiller.

'Robert Stiller?' he repeated, literally scratching his large bald head. Geraldine was about to explain, when his bewildered expression cleared. 'You mean Rob? Rob Stiller. Yes, of course, Rob Stiller. Well, I'm sorry, but he's busy. Plastering is skilful work and time-consuming, and on a job like this time is money.' He winked, before continuing earnestly, 'I don't suppose you realise this, but if I were to call him away from what he's doing and let you hold him up, the mixture would start to set and that could be an expensive blunder for us. Listen, Miss, why don't you come back about ten to five? He knocks off at five so you can catch him then.' He turned away.

'I'm afraid this can't wait,' Geraldine replied, holding up her warrant card. 'I need to speak to him right away.'

The foreman stared at her. 'What's this all about? Is he being arrested? What's going on?'

'He isn't being arrested,' she reassured the foreman. She didn't add 'for now', instead saying, 'We'd just like to ask him a few questions. It won't take long. But we do need him to come with us right now, plaster or no plaster.'

'Plastering is skilful work,' the foreman bleated. 'He can't just abandon a wall halfway through. He has to finish the section he's working on or it will end up all uneven.'

'I'm sure you can manage,' she replied firmly. 'I'm sorry, but we do need to speak to him right now. If the work can't wait, you'll have to ask someone else on your team to take over from him. There's a patrol car parked just outside your fence and another officer waiting at the back of the site, so you can tell him there's no point in him trying to avoid us. It really will be much easier all round if he comes with us quietly.'

Cursing, the foreman went to find Rob. He returned with a tall man at his heels. Rob was wearing a black baseball cap and his blue dungarees were speckled with white paint and flecks of plaster. He smiled at Geraldine as he asked what she wanted with him. She asked him to confirm his name without returning his smile. His relaxed manner made it seem almost unbelievable that he could have stabbed his girlfriend that morning before coming to work, but she reserved her judgement. No two murderers were alike, and it was impossible to tell whether the man facing her was completely innocent or a violent killer. She couldn't even tell whether his insouciance was genuine. He could be adroit at concealing his feelings, or he might be a psychopath, able to kill without a shred of remorse. It was even feasible that he had some kind of dissociative personality disorder that rendered him capable of killing without understanding or even remembering exactly what he had done.

'We'd like to talk to you at the police station,' she said quietly.

Watching him closely, she saw him display irritation but no fear. He removed his cap, revealing close-cropped fair hair, and gazed at her with long-lashed blue eyes. His response made him appear innocent, but once more she was aware that his reaction might be misleading.

'The police station? Whatever for?' he asked, sounding surprised rather than defensive.

'This way, please,' she replied.

Whatever her impression of him, he was the main suspect in a murder enquiry, and it did not harm to let him wait and wonder what evidence had been gathered so far. Not until they reached an interview room did Geraldine explain the reason for questioning him.

'I'm sorry to tell you that your girlfriend's body was discovered in an alley near your lodgings at eight o'clock this morning,' she said quietly.

'Alice?' he blurted out, his air of bewilderment turning to shock. 'Alice's body found in an alley? My Alice? I don't believe it. You must be mistaken. There was nothing wrong with her. You're making a mistake.' He shook his head in apparent disbelief.

'I'm afraid there's no doubt about it,' Geraldine replied, keen to give away as little as possible.

If Rob let slip anything that confirmed he knew how she had died, it would be tantamount to a confession.

'What makes you think it's her?' he asked, his shock turning to perplexity. 'It can't be Alice. I don't believe it. Found in an alley? What was she doing in an alley?'

His reaction was exactly how an innocent man might respond, but also how a careful killer might behave if he was covering up his guilt. Noting how he seemed to remain in control of himself, Geraldine wasn't convinced either way.

'I'm really very sorry,' she said gently. 'I'm afraid there's no doubt the victim is Alice James. We have evidence confirming the identification.'

Geraldine didn't add that she herself had recognised the dead woman. Meanwhile, Rob had turned pale. He kept shaking his head, as though trying to throw off what he had heard.

'What's happening?' he asked in a voice that was suddenly hoarse. 'What are you talking about? Is she ill or was there an accident? Is she going to be all right? Where is she?'

'I'm sorry to tell you Alice is dead.'

'I don't understand. What's happened to her?'

'What were you doing between three o'clock and seven o'clock this morning?' Geraldine asked him.

Rob stared at her with a stunned expression. 'Are you saying she was murdered?'

Geraldine repeated her question.

'Are you seriously asking me for an alibi?'

Geraldine wondered if he was playing for time while he decided what to say. His next words were even less helpful.

'Do I need a lawyer? I think I need a lawyer, don't I? I'm entitled to a phone call and a lawyer.'

Unable to continue with the interview until the duty brief arrived, Geraldine went to speak to Naomi, who had been looking into Rob's history. Ariadne came over to join their conversation, and they went to the canteen for a quick coffee while they discussed what Naomi had discovered.

'I think he would have been more demonstrative if he was guilty,' Geraldine told Ariadne and Naomi. 'If anything, I think he was in a state of shock and struggling to believe what he was hearing.'

'Shocked that his girlfriend was dead, or shocked that he had been picked up so quickly?' Ariadne asked.

'Perhaps he just hadn't had time to work out his defence,' Naomi agreed.

'That's what we're going to have to find out,' Geraldine replied. She turned to Naomi. 'In the meantime, what have you come up with?'

'He was charged with assault seven years ago, but that was a fight with another man, not a domestic. He was on probation for a year after that and doing community service. Apparently he was influenced by an older lad who ended up in prison. It was Rob's first offence and he was still a teenager, so the court were lenient. There's been nothing since. Either he's a reformed character, or he's been more careful not to get caught.'

'So he's capable of violence,' Ariadne said thoughtfully.

'Everyone is capable of violence,' Naomi pointed out acidly, before dropping her gaze and reaching for her coffee.

Geraldine wondered whether to report what Lisa had told her, but decided not to mention that Alice's aunt had suspected Rob of abusing her. Without any supporting evidence, such speculation might only cause unnecessary confusion.

'Could this incident have been a mugging that went wrong?' Geraldine murmured, studying the report on Rob's earlier assault. 'It took place outside on the street. Perhaps it was a mugging that went wrong, and he panicked. There was presumably no evidence of premeditation.'

'And it was a few years ago,' Ariadne chimed in. 'But even if he tried to rob someone on impulse, the fact is he broke his victim's nose and it looks like he wasn't going to leave it there. If a couple of lads hadn't seen what was happening and intervened, the victim could have been seriously injured.'

'We don't deal with speculation about what might have happened,' Geraldine said. 'It was a first offence that could have been an opportunist mugging that went wrong. He was a teenager when it happened.'

'That was his defence,' Naomi said sourly. 'They argued at the time that his victim put temptation in his way and he was too hard up to resist. If you ask me, the courts are far too lenient with casual street crime. It was only by chance he didn't seriously hurt his victim.'

'Innocent until proven guilty,' Ariadne said.

'But he wasn't innocent!' Naomi protested. 'He was caught, red-handed, in the act of mugging someone. If he'd been dealt with severely enough at that point, while he was still young, who knows what future violent crimes might have been prevented?'

Geraldine sighed. She had been through that argument with

Naomi before. Her young colleague was adamant that light sentences for minor infringements encouraged offenders to go on to commit more serious crimes.

'You could be right,' Geraldine conceded, partly to draw the argument to a close before it had really started, 'but we're not responsible for the courts' decisions, and who can say whether their ruling was misguided? Anyway,' she went on rapidly, seeing Naomi opening her mouth to protest, 'in the meantime, we've got a job to do. Let's hope the pathologist's report will give us something definite to go on. If there's any evidence Rob was present at the time of the murder, we'll have this wrapped up in no time, with or without any history of mugging.'

But she had an uneasy feeling the case might not be resolved so easily.

5

HOPING ROB WOULD BE more willing to talk after a night in a cell, Geraldine left the police station. A few of her colleagues were setting off for the nearby pub for a quick pint before going home, but she declined Naomi's invitation to join them. Before Tom was born, she used to enjoy the opportunity to unwind with colleagues at the end of a day's work, but today it was her turn to pick Tom up from the childminder. For once, she wasn't looking forward to collecting him, but she couldn't avoid Lisa indefinitely. Even if Ian agreed to swap with her and collect their son that afternoon, Geraldine would still have to face the childminder the next day. She was afraid Lisa would say she could no longer look after Tom. It was difficult finding someone suitable to take care of him and, having found someone they liked and trusted, it would be devastating to have to move Tom now he was settled and happy with her.

Rehearsing what she might say when she arrived, Geraldine drove slowly to the small house in Maple Grove where Lisa lived. All along the street, the front yards were narrow, with space for little more than large rubbish bins in front of the windows, but they all looked neat and well kept. A few had large flower pots displaying shrubs and flowers placed near the step up to the front door. There was no pot on the ground in the yard outside Lisa's house, but a basket of bright red geraniums and trailing blue lobelia hung beside the door, brightening up the appearance of the house. Usually Geraldine paused for a second to admire the display, but today she had no interest in Lisa's flowers with their blood-red petals.

When Lisa came to the door, it was obvious she had been crying.

'I'm so sorry about Alice,' Geraldine blurted out clumsily. 'Would you like me to come in? If you want to talk?'

Tears slid down Lisa's cheeks as she nodded. 'Thank you. Daisy's not here today, so it's just me and Tom.'

She led Geraldine into the living room and they both sat down.

'Now,' Lisa said, pausing to blow her nose, 'I want to know what happened. She was my niece, but she was more like a daughter to me. When she was growing up she spent more time in my house than her own. My sister works and I used to help out, picking Alice up from school when she was small and bringing her back here for tea.' A ghost of a smile crossed her face. 'She still used to come to me for advice, even—' She broke off again to look at Geraldine, her face pale and taut. 'I know I shouldn't have asked you for help, but I was desperate. When your colleague came and told me… I couldn't really take it in. I just wish I'd been more assertive. I should have made you understand the danger she was in.'

'Please,' Geraldine interrupted her firmly. 'Don't go on. You have nothing to apologise for. You did everything you could to help her. And you certainly don't need to apologise to me. It was perfectly understandable that you would want to reach out for any help you could find. I'm just sorry I couldn't do anything to help.'

Tom gurgled happily and nuzzled Geraldine's neck as Lisa murmured that she had been told Alice's body had been found near where she lived.

'They told me she was murdered,' Lisa added. 'Is that true?'

'We're investigating the circumstances of her death,' Geraldine replied carefully.

'They said she was stabbed,' Lisa said. 'Tell me, please, is that what happened?'

Geraldine nodded. A press release would soon be going out, with a request for any witnesses to come forward. There was no point in keeping anything from Lisa that would be reported on the local news channel before long. 'We suspect she was killed in the early hours of this morning by one stab wound to her chest. It would have been over very quickly,' she added helplessly, aware of how futile any attempt at comfort was in such a situation.

'How quickly?' Lisa asked woodenly. Her expression had become fixed, as though she had been turned to stone. Only her eyes betrayed her anguish as she struggled to process what she was hearing.

'She wouldn't have suffered,' Geraldine assured her, although they both knew there was no way of knowing whether that was true or not.

'She wouldn't have suffered,' Lisa repeated flatly.

'There was just one stab wound that pierced her heart.'

All at once, Lisa lost control and burst into noisy sobs. 'Her heart,' she wailed. 'Her poor heart. Oh, Alice, Alice. She was such a good-hearted girl. She would always do anything for anyone.'

Tom stopped wriggling on Geraldine's lap and turned to blink sleepily at the childminder.

'I'm sorry,' Lisa mumbled, still sobbing. 'It's such a lot to take in. I can't believe she's dead. She was always so healthy. So fit. She went for a run every morning and joined a gym. She should have lived a long life. I know she was worried, but I never really took her concern seriously.'

You took it seriously enough to ask me for help, Geraldine thought, but she kept that to herself, instead asking whether Lisa had a friend who could keep her company until her husband came home.

Lisa turned a stricken face to Geraldine. 'I'll be all right, but what about my sister? Do I have to be the one to tell her?'

'A family liaison officer will be with Alice's mother now,' Geraldine replied.

As she spoke, the phone rang.

'That's probably her now,' Lisa said. 'I should answer it.'

Geraldine nodded and hesitated before offering to arrange for her to be driven to her sister's house.

'Let me speak to her first, see if she needs me,' Lisa replied, latching on to an impulse to support Alice's mother as a distraction from her own loss.

As Lisa listened on the phone, Geraldine wondered whether she would want to look after Tom the next day. If necessary, Ian could stay at home for a few days, while Geraldine focused on the investigation into the murder.

'I know,' she heard Lisa say. 'I can't believe it. How are you?' There was a pause while she listened to her sister on the other end of the line. 'No, Andy's not back yet. There's a police officer here.' Another pause. 'Yes, the one whose baby I look after.' She listened again. 'I know, I know. Look, would you like me to come over now and be with you?' There was another pause before she added pitifully, 'I just thought you might want me there.' She listened for a moment. 'All right, all right. That's fine. It's absolutely fine. You know where I am. You can call me at any time, you know that. Any time at all. I'm here for you.' After another pause, she said goodbye and hung up.

'She doesn't want me to go there,' she told Geraldine, tearfully. 'Alice's father's there and she said there's a policewoman with them, and she doesn't want anyone else fussing around. She said she wishes everyone would leave her alone.' She sniffed. 'That's typical of my sister. She never thinks about how anyone else might be feeling. Oh well, on we go, I suppose. You don't have to stay here, really. My husband will be home soon. I'll just tidy up here and get going making the supper. I guess you want to get Tom home.'

Understanding that, rather like her sister, Lisa wanted to be left alone, Geraldine took her leave. Before she went, she checked that she could drop Tom off in the morning.

'We'd understand if you wanted to take a day off to deal with this,' she added, half hoping Lisa would refuse the offer.

'That's very kind of you but, really, what difference does a day make? She's gone, and she's not coming back. Never. No, I mustn't start thinking like that. It's better to carry on. Tom will give me something to focus on other than poor Alice. Please, bring him tomorrow as usual. I'll be expecting you, yes I will,' she added, smiling tearfully at Tom.

Geraldine wasn't sure whether to apologise for having ignored Alice's plea for help. Deciding that Lisa was probably feeling guilty about failing to support her niece, Geraldine decided to say nothing. She drove home, still not sure whether she had made the right decision to leave before Lisa's husband came home.

'I felt terrible,' she admitted later to Ian as they were sitting down to a plate of pasta. 'I was thinking more about needing to keep Lisa as a childminder than about what she must be going through right now. Does that make me a bad person?'

Ian lifted a forkful of pasta and smiled gently at her. 'If you're looking for reassurance that you're a good person, you've come to the right place.'

'Meaning anyone else would judge me more harshly?'

Ian gazed at her, ignoring the pasta slithering off his fork back on to his plate. 'No one in the world could judge you as harshly as you judge yourself. If you're genuinely asking what I think, my advice would be to stop beating yourself up about this and focus on finding whoever it was killed the poor girl. There was nothing you could have done to save her, but you can try to put her killer behind bars. Because if anyone can do that, it's you. Now, let's eat before it gets cold.

With that, he turned his attention to his supper, leaving Geraldine hoping his confidence in her would not prove misplaced. It was true she had an excellent record in solving murder cases, but each investigation was unique and positive results in the past were no guarantee of future success. All she knew was that a murderer was walking freely on the streets – and they might already be planning their next attack.

6

THE NEXT MORNING, GERALDINE dropped Tom off at Lisa's house as usual. She had determined to say nothing about Alice, but Lisa brought up the subject as Geraldine was handing the baby over on the doorstep.

'Will you be involved in the case?' she asked, peering anxiously over Tom's head.

There was no point in pretending she didn't understand exactly what Lisa meant, so Geraldine nodded without speaking.

'I know this might not be appropriate,' Lisa went on quickly, before Geraldine could turn away, 'but will you let me know if you find anything? We're all convinced it was Alice's boyfriend. I mean, we *know* it was him. Who else could it have been? My sister's already told the policewoman who's been sent to support them. She said the policewoman's very nice, but I'd really appreciate it if you could speak to whoever's in charge of the investigation. They need to know. My sister's certain he did it, and so am I.' She gazed at Geraldine earnestly.

'I've read the reports and seen your sister's statement,' Geraldine assured her. 'Investigations like this are a major undertaking, and there's a whole team of people working hard to establish what happened. It takes time, so you're going to have to be patient.'

'We know what happened,' Lisa insisted, almost tearfully. 'It was him. We all know it was him. Why won't anyone listen to us?'

'You can rest assured your views will be taken into account,' Geraldine said, resorting once again to her professional voice. Seeing Lisa looking dashed, on impulse she added, 'We have Alice's boyfriend at the police station at the moment, and we're questioning him as a possible suspect. But that's really all I can tell you right now. It's as much as we know. And I shouldn't really have told you that much. Please, trust me that we're doing everything we can, and be patient. As soon as there's anything I can tell you, I will.'

Lisa nodded and thanked her. 'I'm glad to know you've caught him. Thank you for telling me. I knew you would want to help.'

'It's the least I can do,' Geraldine replied and then wished she hadn't said anything. 'I will pursue this investigation with the same rigour and distance as I would do any other case,' she added, and then regretted her formality.

Leaving, she wondered whether she ought to recuse herself from the investigation, since her childminder was the victim's aunt. It wasn't too late to step down. But Lisa had come to her for help. Irrational though it seemed, it would feel like a dereliction of everything she believed in if she were to walk away leaving the job to someone else to complete. All the same, she resolved to be more careful in future and hold back from telling Lisa anything more about the progress of the investigation. And she certainly didn't tell Lisa that she was leaving her to find out what the post mortem on Alice's corpse could reveal about her death.

Deep in thought, she drove to the hospital and found a parking space without too much difficulty. It was drizzling when she arrived, and she scurried to the back entrance of the hospital, where the blonde anatomical technology assistant at the mortuary greeted her with a friendly smile. Avril seemed less ebullient than usual, leading Geraldine to wonder whether her recent marriage was not living up to her expectations. Once she started talking, Avril tended to go on and on. Keen to crack on, Geraldine attempted to hurry past her without pausing to chat, but Avril detained her.

'How's your little lad?' she asked.

Geraldine hesitated, but she couldn't ignore the question without appearing rude. Having assured Avril that both Tom and Ian were well, she felt obliged to ask how Avril was.

'I never showed you all the pictures from the honeymoon, did I?' Avril replied, her eyes brightening with excitement. 'Honestly, divine doesn't even come close. I wish I was there now. The only bodies we saw were sunbathing on the beach,' she added, laughing.

Making her excuses, Geraldine said she would love to see the pictures when she wasn't so busy and hurried off.

'We must catch up some time,' Avril called after her as she strode away along the corridor.

Geraldine felt a twinge of contrition at not stopping to spend time with Avril, but she wasn't her friend or confidante. They only met occasionally at work and they both had a job to do. Geraldine was busy, even if Avril had time for a natter. So she hurried on, focused on her task. The pathologist waved a bloody glove in the air as she entered. They had worked together on many cases, and greetings were no longer really necessary. Even so, Jonah liked to indulge in a little frivolous banter before getting down to the grisly business of discussing the physical details of a murder. But for once, he seemed serious.

'How's your little boy?' he asked.

Geraldine smiled. Jonah had forgotten Tom's name, but at least he remembered she had a son.

'Tom's fine,' she replied. 'How about your family?'

'Don't even ask,' Jonah replied, with a theatrical sigh. 'Give me a corpse over a living teenager any day.'

'You shouldn't say such things,' she scolded him. 'Although if you have any advice about dealing with sons when they're growing up, I would like to hear it.'

'You're right,' he agreed, opening his hands in a gesture of capitulation. 'I consider myself duly chastised. Slap on the wrist. Although if you had to put up with the noise my son subjects us to when he forgets to put on his headphones, you might feel very differently. Now, let's see what we've got here.' He indicated the body lying on the cold slab. 'And no more talk of teenagers and the racket they call music these days.' He gave a theatrical shudder.

Having had time to process what had happened, Geraldine felt more comfortable seeing Alice's body for a second time. Paradoxically, her nakedness made her seem less human. The shocking blood stains on her clothes were no longer in view and in any case it was somehow easier to observe her in the familiar setting of the mortuary. No longer the body of a woman who had come to her for help, Alice was now a murder victim requiring all of Geraldine's attention in her professional capacity as a detective. With a sigh, she recognised that she was in her comfort zone.

'Do you think we're unnatural?' she blurted out.

She had worked with Jonah for long enough for her to feel she could speak freely to him. Their conversations were witnessed only by the dead.

'I doubt very much if you are, but I almost certainly am,' he replied, shaking his head. 'Is it natural for a father to find refuge in talking to cadavers rather than attempt to engage in civilised discussion with his own son?'

'That's what I mean.' Geraldine sighed. 'This obsession with the dead, does it mean we're unnatural?'

Jonah just shrugged and launched into a litany of complaints about his son's wayward behaviour. According to Jonah the youngster was, among other things, lazy, disrespectful and sullen.

'He's on his computer half the night and then he wants to lie around in bed all morning.'

'Well, that sounds perfectly natural to me.' Geraldine laughed. 'If not wanting to get out of bed in the morning is so terrible, it's an affliction that seems to affect us all. But I'll bear everything you've said in mind and make sure Tom has a strict routine when he's older. Bed at seven and lights out at eight.'

'Good luck with that,' Jonah said.

He still seemed less cheerful than usual, but they didn't have time to dwell on the domestic problems which seemed to be bothering him. After a few moments, they turned their attention to the body lying between them. Alice was lying on her back, the wound in her chest exposed.

'This seems to be a straightforward case,' Jonah said briskly. His earlier dejection had vanished. 'Here we have a healthy young woman of around twenty, slim but not undernourished. She was probably watching her figure and good muscle tone suggests she worked out or at least exercised regularly in some way.'

He paused, contemplating the body, his expression dejected once more.

'And the cause of death?' Geraldine prompted him.

He nodded, briskly professional again. 'I'd say you're looking for a long blade, some sort of kitchen knife, perhaps. Razor sharp. The blade penetrated a thin cotton jacket and a cotton blouse. The blow must have been fast and quite powerful, but we can't really deduce much about the killer from that. The angle of the entry wound suggests the killer was taller than the victim, but again that's not necessarily the case, as he might have struck from a position where his arm was raised, perhaps brandishing the knife in the air.' He stretched out his arm and suddenly raised his hand above his shoulder, as though to illustrate the point.

Lowering his arm again, he shook his head. 'It's difficult to understand why she failed to resist, so she was probably attacked in the dark. What is interesting, from your perspective, is that there was only the one blow, and it would have been enough to fell her instantly. The blade penetrated right through the heart. She didn't stand a chance. Don't quote me on this, but either it was a lucky strike that killed her more or less instantly, or her assailant knew exactly what he was doing.'

Geraldine knew that the victim's boyfriend was reputedly abusive, but somehow this methodical targeted stabbing still didn't seem like the kind of injury a violent partner might inflict.

'The medic placed the time of the attack as between three and seven on Tuesday morning,' Jonah said thoughtfully. 'I wonder what our young lady here was doing out and about so early?' He turned the girl over and indicated some scratches. 'Dirt and post mortem abrasions to the back of the head and bruising to the upper arms indicate the body was probably gripped under the armpits and dragged along the ground after the attack. That's about all I can say for now. We'll have to wait and see if the tox report comes up with anything else.'

He broke off, hesitated, and then resumed. 'There is something else that might interest you. This bruising occurred post mortem.' He pointed to Alice's armpits. 'But there's evidence of further bruising that was inflicted before she was killed, on several occasions, possibly days before she died. There might have been other injuries from earlier assaults that have now faded.' He pointed out faint grey smudges on the victim's shoulder, arm and side. 'She could have knocked herself, but this looks suspiciously like marks left by fingers. And there's evidence of further bruising like this one on her stomach that was inflicted before she was killed, on several occasions, possibly days before she died.'

Geraldine studied three small grey blotches on Alice's arm and then studied the large contusion.

'That is interesting,' she muttered, remembering what Lisa had told her. 'Her aunt seemed to think Alice was being physically abused before she died and possibly in some danger.'

Jonah raised his eyebrows questioningly, but said nothing, and Geraldine didn't elaborate.

She thanked him before she left. 'This has all been really helpful,' she fibbed.

Looking for a weapon that could possibly be a large kitchen knife and a killer who might be taller than Alice didn't give them much to go on.

7

ALICE HAD NEVER BEEN one to hang around with a bad crowd. On the contrary, she had always been sensible, even as a child. Lisa had never had to remind her to do her homework. The truth was, Alice had never been any trouble at all until Rob had turned up. She had done well at school and from an early age had set her sights on becoming a nurse, a valuable member of society helping to alleviate pain and save lives. And now her life had been brutally snatched away. Lisa struggled to hold back her tears. She had responsibilities and couldn't allow herself to succumb to the dark thoughts that hovered at the edge of her mind. It didn't help that one of the mothers whose child she was looking after was a detective investigating Alice's murder. She managed to control herself when the mothers dropped off her charges and collected them again, but during the day she broke down periodically. Tom babbled contentedly, but at two Daisy was more aware of her environment and gazed at Lisa who had to force herself to keep smiling.

Now that her worst fears had been realised, Lisa was more convinced than ever that Rob had been physically abusing Alice for a while. With hindsight, killing her had been the inevitable conclusion to his violent behaviour. She had no way of proving his guilt, but she knew she was right. Lisa had never been happy about Alice seeing him. She had suspected all along that he was dangerous, but Alice had been infatuated with him. Lisa had only met him once, but that single encounter had been enough for her. He was much taller than Alice, with very short blond hair and blue eyes, and Lisa could understand why Alice found him attractive. But good looks were no guarantee of good character. She had tried to warn Alice, but her niece had refused to listen to a word of criticism of her boyfriend.

'I'm not saying anything against him,' Lisa had fibbed, in an attempt to persuade Alice to be more careful. 'It's just that you don't know much about him. How long have you known him?'

Alice mumbled crossly that how long she had known Rob made no difference to her feelings.

'But what do you really know about him?' Lisa had persisted.

'What does anyone know about anyone else?' Alice had countered, not unreasonably. 'I don't get what you've got against him. He's a respectable man with a steady job.'

'He's a builder.' Lisa had regretted the words as soon as she spoke, but Alice had heard her.

Alice had let out a disbelieving laugh. 'I never realised you were such a snob, Aunty. So what if he's a builder? What's wrong with that? At least he's got a real job and plastering is skilled work.' She didn't add that her boyfriend didn't sit around at home looking after other people's babies, but she might just as well have said as much. 'Or is being an expert craftsman not good enough for your high standards?'

'You know perfectly well that's not what I meant.'

'Oh, really? What did you mean, then?' Alice had tapped one foot impatiently on the floor, her pretty face twisted in a scowl. 'Well? What did you mean, exactly?'

'Just that you could find someone else,' Lisa had murmured. 'That boy might be good looking, but how is he going to protect you, keep you safe? He hasn't got a permanent job. How will he look after you?'

She had known at once that had been another gaffe. It seemed that lately she hadn't been able to do anything right where her niece was concerned.

'I can take care of myself, thank you very much,' Alice had retorted, spitting out the words and glaring at Lisa as she spoke. 'Ever since I got a job at the hospital you've been waiting for me to meet a doctor, haven't you? Come on, admit it, you want me to see me married to a consultant so I can live in a big detached house and drive an expensive car, and go on exotic holidays. Well, that may be your dream, but it's not mine. Why don't *you* go and marry a doctor if you're so stuck on the idea? I'm with Rob and you might as well get used to it. I'm not leaving him. I'm not going to hook a doctor. I'm happy with my common-as-muck, working-class builder, thank you very much.'

It seemed there was nothing more to say. At first Lisa had been too shocked to respond when Alice had told her Rob was moving in with her, but she had realised it was pointless to remonstrate. Once Alice made up her mind, there was no budging her, and Lisa could see she was determined to stay with Rob. She suspected Alice knew she was making a mistake and that was why she was so set on refusing to back down. Reluctant to fall out with her niece, all Lisa could do was make sure that Alice knew she would be there to comfort her when her relationship with Rob failed. Convinced they wouldn't stay together, Lisa had resolved to be patient, but when she had begun to suspect Rob was abusing her niece, she could no longer remain silent. The trouble was, she had no evidence to support her conviction.

Thanks to her aunt's scepticism about Rob, Alice had become wary of her. Where once she had popped in to see Lisa almost every day, her visits became infrequent, and she kept Rob away from everyone else in the family as well. Lisa hated the way her relationship with her niece had deteriorated. They had once been so close. She wasn't naïve. She had always known Alice would meet a man and that would inevitably affect her relationship with her aunt. But Lisa had never wanted them to end up feeling estranged. She wished Alice would bring Rob to see her again, so that she could at least make a show of welcoming him into her home, although she suspected Alice would see through any duplicity. In any case, it would be difficult for Lisa to pretend she was pleased to see Rob.

On the one occasion when she had met him, something about him had alarmed her. Perhaps because of her experience around children, Lisa seemed to have developed a sixth sense that alerted her whenever people were expecting to be hit. Nothing had happened, but at one point Rob had raised his arm to brush his hand through his hair. If Lisa had blinked, she would have missed Alice's reaction. The girl had flinched, displaying an involuntary flash of fear. The moment had passed and Lisa had never mentioned what she had observed, but she had stewed on the memory. Sure something was wrong, she had been increasingly concerned.

The impression that Rob was intimidating Alice hadn't faded when she had spoken to her niece afterwards. She had finally decided to tackle her, but before she could pluck up the courage to mention her misgivings, Alice had raised the subject herself.

'What have you got against Rob, anyway?' she had asked. Her unexpected belligerence had only confirmed Lisa's conviction that her niece knew something was amiss.

'What are you talking about?' Lisa had blustered.

Alice had shaken her head at the dissemblance. 'You think he's not good enough for me, but you're in no position to judge him. You don't know him at all.'

Lisa had decided to speak plainly. 'The problem is, I don't think you know him.'

'So you keep saying. But you're wrong. I do know him. How much better could I know him? I live with him.'

And that, Lisa had thought, was what she found so worrying, but she hadn't said anything more at the time. Now she regretted having held back. If she had only been able to persuade Alice to be more careful, she might still be alive. The thought tormented her. She would have done anything for Alice, but in the end she had failed her in the worst way possible, because she had seen what was coming and had not prevented it. And now it was too late to put matters right.

8

Rob glared at Geraldine across the table, his blue eyes red-rimmed and bloodshot. At her side, she heard Ariadne stifle a cough.

'Tell us about your relationship with Alice,' Geraldine began, keeping her eyes fixed on the suspect.

He shrugged and shook his head. He leaned back in his chair, his posture relaxed, but his eyes burned and his voice betrayed suppressed anger. 'I don't know what you want me to say. I didn't kill her, if that's what you think. Are you accusing me of killing her? Is that why I'm here?'

'Let's start at the beginning,' Geraldine said quietly. 'Tell us how you met Alice.'

When Rob didn't answer, Geraldine repeated her request. With a sigh, he told them that he had known Alice for six months. They had met while he was on a decorating job at the hospital. He had moved in with her almost immediately. Prior to that he had been sleeping on a friend's couch. Geraldine kept her opinion to herself, but she felt a flicker of sympathy for Lisa's reservations about her niece's relationship with Rob.

'Have you never had a home of your own?' Ariadne asked him.

If the question had been intended to undermine his confidence, the insinuation clearly passed him by, as he answered breezily that he had never needed to.

'Isn't it a bit precarious, relying on the goodwill of friends? Wouldn't you prefer to have some security in your life?' Ariadne pressed him.

He gave a careless shrug. 'Something always turns up. I've got plenty of mates.'

He folded his arms with an air of complacency that Geraldine found slightly offensive, given that his girlfriend had just been killed.

'Did Alice decide it was time for you to leave?' Geraldine asked.

Rob gazed at her with a blank expression.

'She wanted you to leave and that made you angry,' Geraldine continued. 'Anyone might lose their temper faced with the prospect of being thrown out like that. What happened next? Tell us about it.'

Rob shook his head. 'I don't know what you're talking about, but if you think you can trick me into saying whatever it is you want me to say, you couldn't be more wrong. Do your worst. I've got nothing to hide.'

'Were you in the habit of assaulting Alice?' Geraldine went on, speaking almost casually.

Rob started as though he was surprised by the question and sat up abruptly. 'What the hell are you talking about? I never touched her! Who told you that? It's a lie!' He turned to the lawyer, a red-faced young man who had a faint sheen of perspiration on his forehead. 'They can't go around spreading lies about me. Can't you do something? You're supposed to be defending me. It's slander. Say something, will you?'

The young lawyer spoke in a curiously high-pitched voice. 'My client refutes the allegation that he assaulted anyone at any time.'

'At any time?' Ariadne repeated. She opened a file on her iPad. 'We have a report here about an assault perpetrated by your client.' She read out the main details.

'For Christ's sake, where did you dig that up from? It was nearly ten years ago,' Rob burst out. 'I was just a kid. A mixed-up adolescent.'

'You were sixteen,' Geraldine pointed out.

Rob turned to his lawyer in exasperation. 'They can't bring that up now, can they? And in any case,' he added, turning back to scowl at Geraldine, 'it was a fight outside a pub, not an assault. I was acting in self-defence. Read the report. It's all there. I might have finished it by knocking him out, but I wasn't the one who started it.'

'My client has already answered your questions,' the lawyer said curtly. 'He has nothing further to add.'

After a break for a brief consultation with his lawyer, Rob stuck to responding 'No comment' to all further questions. The interview was effectively over. With no evidence to place him at the crime scene, they had to let him go. Geraldine knew Ariadne well enough to sense how reluctant her colleague was to terminate the interview, but they had no choice. Rob remonstrated feebly when Ariadne warned him not to leave York, as they might want to speak to him again. After that, he left, with the lawyer trailing behind him.

Ariadne was convinced Rob was guilty, but Geraldine reserved her judgement.

'I know, I know,' Ariadne said, sounding irked. 'We can't draw any conclusions until we have proof.' Her black eyes were inscrutable, but her voice betrayed her impatience.

'We have to keep an open mind,' Geraldine replied calmly.

At work, she had no difficulty in controlling her feelings. Outside of work, she struggled to maintain the same composure. Collecting Tom at the end of the day, she steeled herself to face Lisa's questions.

'I know I shouldn't keep asking, but have you caught anyone yet?' Lisa asked as soon as she opened the door.

'The investigation is ongoing. I'm really sorry but I can't say more than that,' Geraldine replied, doing her best to hide her discomfort.

'I saw in the news that a man is "helping you with your enquiries". Does that mean you've arrested Rob? There isn't anyone else, is there?'

Geraldine gazed stonily at Lisa. 'I'm sorry, really I am, but I can't tell you anything. I understand you are convinced of his guilt, but unless you have further information to share about Alice's boyfriend, then there's nothing more to say.'

'I get it. You can't tell me anything but you expect me to tell you everything I know.'

'Like I said, I'm sorry, but I really can't tell you anything. It's not down to me. I'm part of a team investigating a murder and we can't make exceptions for anyone.'

Geraldine followed Lisa into the living room, where Tom was lying on a play mat, kicking his feet and waving his hands in the air.

'I know you've spoken to Rob,' Lisa said. 'He was doing some work at the hospital last year. That's how he met Alice.' She fell silent.

Geraldine picked Tom up and played with his tiny fingers. He smiled and poked a finger up her nose. She pulled his hand away, smiling down at him, and bent forward to kiss the top of his head. Listening to what the childminder had to say, Geraldine wondered if Lisa was genuinely convinced Rob was guilty, or if she was simply desperate to see someone punished for what had happened to Alice. It was also possible that she might feel, quite irrationally, that she was partly to blame for failing to protect her niece. People close to murder victims often tormented themselves wondering if they could have done more to prevent the tragedy.

'You know you're not in any way responsible for what happened to Alice,' Geraldine said gently.

'It's not that,' Lisa replied miserably. 'I just know he did it. I think he started hitting her before he killed her and it escalated. I tried to warn her,' she added. She pulled a tissue from her sleeve and wiped her eyes.

Geraldine sighed. 'I can't say you're not right, but we just don't know. We're looking for proof he was involved. Your comments will be taken into account but there's nothing more you can do. You need to leave this with us,' Geraldine said, standing up. 'I've already said far more than I ought to have done. Please keep anything I've told you between us. I shouldn't have said anything. I think it's best if we don't discuss this again.'

Lisa nodded, looking anxious. Geraldine wished she could console her, but beyond trotting out the usual platitudes, there was nothing she could say.

'Please don't worry,' she blurted out as she was leaving. 'We'll find whoever did this. We'll find him and make sure he's convicted and locked up.'

'And throw away the key,' Lisa muttered, loudly enough for Geraldine to hear.

9

THE WEATHER HAD FINALLY turned warm, and there was a breath of summer in the air. As she turned away from the house, the sun came out and Geraldine was bowled over by a jumble of childhood memories that seemed to intertwine in a complex tapestry of sensations: hot sand burning her bare feet, the icy, sugary taste of ice cream on her tongue, and the chilly shock on her legs as she splashed into the sea. In her arms, Tom let out a squeal of joy as a dragonfly fluttered past. Glancing down at him, Geraldine wondered what future childhood memories he would store up to revisit in later years. She hoped they would be unequivocally happy ones. The idea of him becoming an adult made her feel edgy. She knew she couldn't stop him growing up, but at the same time, it seemed almost inconceivable that he would ever be anything other than a happily gurgling, fist-waving infant. The prospect of one day having a conversation with him excited her more than anything else she could imagine, although she also found it strangely terrifying.

'I can't wait for Tom to start talking,' she said to Ian when she arrived home and put Tom down in his cot. 'It's frustrating not knowing what he's thinking.'

'Is he really so different to us? Do you know what I'm thinking right now?'

'No, of course not, but the point is, you can tell me. We communicate with each other in words.'

'Not only words,' he replied, pulling her towards him and kissing her.

It occurred to her that Ian was right and that people could communicate without words as well. She thought about Lisa's disquiet and wondered if there was something the childminder wasn't telling her about Alice. Thinking back over what Lisa had said about Rob, she could remember nothing specific that might help them to build a case against him. All Lisa had been able to confide was that she was convinced he had been abusing Alice, but that wasn't enough. She was sure that Lisa would have given her details if there was any substance to her accusation. Yet the fact that she could offer no substantive proof did not mean her feelings were groundless. It was hard to imagine how frustrated Lisa must be feeling, but her impression of Rob could be wrong. Geraldine felt as though she was going round in circles trying to decide how seriously she ought to take Lisa's vague allegations.

'You're very thoughtful this evening,' Ian said.

'Sorry, I was just thinking about the case.'

'You're full of surprises,' he teased her, and she laughed, her melancholy train of thought broken.

With the days getting longer, they decided to have supper on their balcony overlooking the river. The outside space was one of the attractions of the flat and one reason why Geraldine was reluctant to move. She pointed out that they had all the advantages of a garden for next to no effort. Ian had placed a few large pots of flowers on the balcony. The daffodils were finished, and the geraniums were in flower, their scarlet petals displaying a brilliant flash of colour. As she laid the table, Geraldine watched a boat gliding along the river, almost too far away for her to be disturbed by its engine. A faint hum was all she could hear. Another boat approached from the opposite direction. The river was rarely completely empty of boats: working barges, small leisure craft, yachts and rowing dinghies. She finished laying the table and sat down to wait. Just as Ian brought out a tray of food, they heard Tom cry.

'Typical,' Ian grinned. 'Oh well, don't worry, I'll go.'

'No,' Geraldine said, standing up. 'You made the supper. I'll go. It's my turn.'

'Hurry back, then,' Ian called after her. 'Don't let your pasta get cold.'

They sat eating and watching the boats go past, as the sun slowly sank over the horizon. Tom was in his high chair, swinging his legs and burbling cheerfully. Geraldine gave him a plastic spoon and he amused himself happily banging it on his little tray.

'As long as he's with us, he's happy,' Ian said, reaching across the table and placing his hand on Geraldine's. His skin felt warm against hers and she smiled involuntarily. 'There's nothing to worry about,' he assured her, holding her gaze. 'Tom's going to be fine.'

She stared into Ian's blue eyes, crinkled at the edges with laughter lines, registering the lines on his forehead and the white streaks in his hair, and didn't admit that she had been thinking about Alice. They both glanced across at Tom, who was studying his hand and wriggling his fingers. Suddenly he made a grab for Geraldine and gripped her finger.

'Look at that,' Ian said. 'He's making the connection between your fingers and his own. Look how he's focusing. You can see how hard he's thinking. I told you he's clever.'

Geraldine smiled, gently retrieved her hand and waggled her fingers at Tom who squealed with pleasure.

'He just wanted something to put in his mouth,' she replied, but she wondered if Ian was right.

Reliant on her powers of observation in her job, she had hardly noticed how fast Tom was developing, right in front of her. She wondered what else she might be overlooking. Although she was doing her best to consider the murder from every possible angle, she couldn't shake off an uncomfortable feeling that she was missing some key aspect of the case. Her reservations were hazy, but she couldn't imagine Rob stabbing Alice with such skill. He stood to gain nothing by her death, and her murder did not seem like a crime of passion. Either there was something about Rob that they had yet to discover, or he was not responsible for Alice's death.

10

Geraldine hoped Lisa would not start talking about Alice when she dropped Tom off the next morning. She felt slightly uncomfortable about seeing the childminder again, but, as it turned out, neither of them said much and the encounter was brief, if slightly awkward. Lisa avoided meeting Geraldine's eye as she took Tom from her.

'See you later,' Geraldine muttered hurriedly as she turned away.

She was afraid Lisa would have second thoughts and call out seeking to detain her, but instead she heard the front door close behind her. Relieved, she walked away quickly. With luck, Lisa had recognised that it was inappropriate for her to ask questions about the case while it was still ongoing, and hopefully once it had been concluded as well.

The weather continued bright under a clear blue sky and Geraldine was feeling more cheerful. Despite not yet having made much headway with the investigation, for no particular reason she was beginning to feel more positive about it. The most frustrating stage in any investigation was when they reached an impasse, but for now they had plenty to do. They had a suspect in mind and several avenues yet to explore in an attempt to establish whether or not he was guilty.

Her first task that morning was to track down Rob's ex-girlfriend and question her. Searching through Rob's social media accounts, Naomi had traced a Spanish girl called Maria, who appeared to have been in a relationship with Rob for about six months before he met Alice. Maria had posted photos of him on Instagram, some with her posing beside him, by the sea, on the London Eye, and seated outside various pubs in York. She worked as an au pair for a family in the nearby small town of Haxby. It was not far away, and Geraldine drove herself there and drew up in a pleasant street of red brick houses, sizeable and well maintained, with small manicured front gardens. She rang the bell and almost at once the door was opened by a black-haired girl who smiled uncertainly at her.

'Are you Maria?' Geraldine asked.

The girl nodded, her smile less confident. When Geraldine introduced herself, the girl's smile faded altogether and a flicker of fear crossed her face before she lowered her enormous black eyes, fringed with what appeared to be naturally long lashes. Geraldine knew better than to read much into someone appearing nervous once she disclosed her identity. There was more than one reason why Maria might be scared of speaking to the police, only one of which was that she was guilty of murder. All the same, Geraldine noted the girl's reaction.

'Shall we go inside?' Geraldine asked.

The girl hesitated. 'Missus is not here.'

'That doesn't matter. You're the one I want to talk to. Is it convenient for me to come in or would you prefer to accompany me to the police station to answer a few questions there?'

The girl hesitated before stepping aside to allow Geraldine to enter. She led her into a spacious kitchen where they sat down on wicker chairs set around a white table. The room had large windows on two sides, giving the kitchen plenty of natural light, and the window at the back overlooked a well-stocked garden.

Thinking that Maria's English was probably limited, Geraldine decided not to waste time on subtleties. 'Tell me about Rob,' she said bluntly.

Maria's large eyes narrowed in suspicion. 'Why do you want

to know?' She spoke with a pronounced accent, but her English was fluent enough to be easily understood.

Squirming uncomfortably on her chair, she insisted that she had nothing to say about Rob, adding that she hadn't seen him for a few months. Clearly Maria wasn't keen to talk about her relationship with Rob, so Geraldine decided to be more specific with her questions.

'Were you his girlfriend?'

Maria nodded anxiously.

'How long were you together?'

'Not long. It wasn't good. Please, I don't want to talk of this. He is not my boyfriend now.'

'Why did you and Rob split up?'

Maria shrugged. 'I told you, it was no good.' She frowned, struggling for the word she wanted. 'We weren't suitable.'

Geraldine wanted to ask whether Rob had ever been violent towards her, but she hesitated to put any leading questions. 'Was there anything particular about his company that you didn't enjoy?' she asked.

Maria shook her head. 'He is nice man – a nice man,' she corrected herself. 'I like him, but we both know it is not good for us.'

'Can you tell me why?'

Maria sighed. 'Rob is very nice but he is the very serious person. I want to go out.' She waved her hands in the air. 'Where I live, in Spain, is a small village. Here is the chance to go out.'

'What do you mean?'

'I like to dance. Rob, he likes to sit at home, watch the TV. This I can do in my parents' house in Spain.'

'So you would have stayed with him if he wanted to go out more?'

'Maybe. Other girls I meet, the other au pairs, they go out a lot,' Maria said plaintively. 'Rob tells me, why you want to go out all the time?'

Geraldine spoke gently, hoping to goad Maria into saying more. 'It must have been difficult for you when he started seeing someone else.'

'I don't know if he has the new girlfriend,' Maria replied. 'He is not my business now. I don't see him for months.'

'Did you end the relationship?'

Maria nodded.

'Did he ever hurt you, Maria? I mean physically. Did he ever hit you?'

The girl shook her head nervously. 'No,' she whispered. 'No, he never do that.'

'I want you to think very carefully,' Geraldine said solemnly. 'Rob's girlfriend has been murdered.'

Maria gasped and her eyes opened really wide.

'Why did you leave him, Maria?'

'I told you. I don't want to waste more time in the relationship that isn't good for me.' She hesitated. 'I want to go out.'

'So you want a boyfriend who will take you out to nice places?'

'Yes. That's what I want. In Spain in my village, there is no money, no jobs, no nice men.' Her hands fluttered excitedly as she spoke. 'Here I get the job, I learn English and I meet men.'

'And have you?' Geraldine asked. 'Have you met other men?'

Maria scowled. 'It is difficult. English men, they are only wanting sex.'

'I wish you luck,' Geraldine replied.

She took down a few more details about when Maria had first met Rob, when exactly they had parted company, and how much longer she would be staying with her current family. Then she thanked the girl and took her leave to Maria's evident relief. Driving away, Geraldine struggled to make up her mind what she thought about Maria.

'Her English was really good, but it's not her first language,' she explained to Ariadne when she was back at the police station. 'So it's possible I missed something, some nuance, in what she was saying. She was certainly pleased to see the back of me, that much was clear. That could have been because she just didn't want her employer to suspect she was in any trouble with the police. But—'

'But equally it might suggest she was keen to hide something from you?' Ariadne finished the thought.

Geraldine nodded pensively. In some ways, Maria had been very open with her, but Geraldine couldn't help suspecting there was more to the Spanish au pair than she had managed to discover.

'I think we might need to bring her here to answer a few more questions,' she said.

'No stone unturned,' Ariadne said, and Geraldine smiled.

'No stone unturned,' she repeated quietly.

11

SLOWLY THE KILLER OPENED the cutlery drawer and smiled grimly before reverently taking out the razor-sharp chef's knife. The blade was spotless, shining with a glint that seemed to emanate power. Having served its purpose, it now posed the threat of discovery. Despite being scrupulously careful, cleaning the weapon and putting it through the dishwasher several times, it had been difficult to get rid of the smell of bleach which had lingered for days however many times The Knife, and the worktops, were scrubbed. Still, even after cutting steak with the murder weapon in an attempt to mask any vestiges of human blood, there remained the possibility that traces of the victim's DNA might be discernible on the smooth blade or the hard handle.

Fear of discovery was ever present. The police were not only clever, they had a terrifying number of resources at their disposal, meaning they could do almost anything. But negative thoughts like that were dangerous. It had to be possible to escape detection. The challenge was not insurmountable. For now, it was time to brew a cafetière of coffee and settle down to consider the various options. So far, so good; there was nothing to point the police to the truth and that was how it needed to stay. The upshot of a further hour's deliberations was that it would soon be necessary to get rid of The Knife. Whatever else happened, after one more use it would be too risky to hold on to it any longer. Once the time came, it would take careful planning to dispose of it safely and speedily. The Knife had done its job well and it would be a wrench to dispose of it, but there was no point in becoming sentimental. Such feelings had been many a killer's undoing. Not this one.

The cherished knife had now become a focus of fear. Only if it was smashed to smithereens would they be truly free, but a steel blade with a hard wooden handle was indestructible. The only safe course of action would be to discard it somewhere it could never be found. The bottom of the river might work or perhaps a garbage disposal truck, if it could be dumped in either of those without anyone noticing. That was the biggest risk. Leaving it in a disused car sent to a scrapyard to be compressed might be a better option. Crushed in a rusty old car, The Knife would be irretrievably lost and it might be relatively easy to hide it in a car.

There remained the problem of how to find a car that was about to be demolished. Above all, no one must suspect what was happening. So far, The Knife had escaped attention, but how long could that continue? If the police came sniffing around, they must find nothing incriminating. The cafetière was rinsed and the grounds thrown away, the worktop wiped and The Knife slipped into a plastic carrier bag before the worktop was cleaned again with bleach. The smell was horrible, but it had to be done. With the clean-up completed and a new pair of rubber gloves and an unused pair of woollen gloves placed ready on top of the bag, everything was in place.

Googling how to find a site where cars were routinely crushed revealed a number of scrapyards. None of them served the purpose. The Knife could quite easily be discovered by someone stripping a car for parts, which might arouse suspicion. The police routinely crushed uninsured vehicles, but it was important to avoid having anything to do with them. Besides, it would be an ignominious end for so valuable a weapon, to be crushed beyond recognition. It would be better, after all, to dispose of it at a deserted spot, away from prying eyes.

The chances of it being found at the bottom of the river were remote. All things considered, the river seemed the safest bet, since anything to do with scrapyards or discarded cars would involve other people who might see what was happening and possibly report it to the police. Not only that, but the river was an appropriate resting place for The Knife which had served its purpose so well. It would remain out of sight on the river bed, like King Arthur's Excalibur lying underwater in the lake at Avalon. The Knife deserved to be treated with honour after its years of service.

Resolved to slip down to a remote stretch of river at night and drop The Knife in the water, it was only necessary to wait for the sun to set. With no one else around to watch, The Knife would sink by itself but, just to be sure, it could also be carefully attached to a heavy tool, like a mallet or a hammer. That ought to do it. As long as no one saw it fall in the river, all would end well. It should be simple to accomplish discreetly.

But before The Knife could finally be disposed of, it was going to be used one more time.

12

It was difficult trying to work out what he wanted, every minute of the day. She could only really relax when he went out, but even then she never knew when he might return. She watched him from beneath lowered eyelids, trying to hide her fear. If he interpreted her silence as defiance, he was bound to take it as a provocation. On the other hand, if he realised how frightened she was, he would be annoyed with her for making him feel like an ogre. Then again, if she dared to utter a word and he objected to what she said, she would be equally at risk. Whatever she did, she was never completely safe, however careful she was, but she had learned to recognise when he was about to lose his temper. These days, she was learning to avoid incurring his anger, at least most of the time. Life could be worse.

To be fair, everything was usually fine and he was rarely angry with her. But since his recent battering, he had definitely been more irascible than normal. She clasped her hands in her lap so he couldn't see them shaking and kept her eyes fixed on the floor, noting a threadbare patch and several black spots where Danny's cigarettes had burned holes in the carpet. Without moving a muscle, she stared fixedly at one of the scorch marks, hoping he would go out and leave her alone.

He didn't say a word, but the silence in the room crackled with menace. She struggled to breathe without making any sound, afraid of what was coming. If she could remain completely silent, he might forget she was there. Perhaps she could creep out of the room without him noticing. She risked glancing up and winced as their eyes met. He was staring sullenly at her with his one undamaged eye. From the swollen side of his face, the slit of his other eye peered at her, while his battered lips curled in a sneer. But even his scowl and his hideous injuries could not blight his good looks. After a few moments, his face relaxed in a smile and she felt a surge of relief. She was his and she would never leave him.

They had been together for nearly a year. For the first few months, their life together had been idyllic. He had given her a roof over her head and supplied her with as much booze and cigarettes as she wanted, promising her she would never want for anything. It had been a relief to escape from the women's shelter where she had been staying. But then, one day, he had lost his temper. He had promised her it would never happen again, but it had. Again and again. Once, she had run away. He never found out. The duty manager at the shelter had urged her to leave him, but she knew she could not live without him. In spite of the abuse, she loved him, and love was stronger than anything. The manager hadn't understood. No one did. She just had to be patient and wait for him to recover from whatever was troubling him and his violent phase would pass. Then they would return to their idyllic life and everything would be fine. They had been happy once, so it stood to reason they could be happy again.

'I know he loves me,' she had assured the manager at the shelter. 'He can't help it. He's suffering. He only hits me out of frustration and it never lasts long. He's always very apologetic afterwards.'

'But then he does it again,' the manager had said, shaking her head. 'You can't believe he's genuinely sorry as long as he continues physically abusing you.'

'You don't understand. He doesn't mean to hurt me. He doesn't know what he's doing when he's had a few drinks.'

'You must know that's not true,' the manager had replied.

'No man strikes a woman he loves. Remember that the next time he hits you. Do you want to discuss leaving him, before he causes you a serious injury?'

'He's not going to hurt me. It's not as bad as you think. I shouldn't have come here. It's all a mistake.'

'Why are you so keen to protect him when he mistreats you like that? Next time he might kill you.'

She had laughingly brushed the warning aside. The manager was obviously jealous because Lauren had a boyfriend. Not only that, but her boyfriend was Danny. That sad, lonely woman from the shelter claimed she only wanted to help, but her advice was pointless because Lauren saw through her resentment straight away. The truth was that Lauren loved Danny and she knew he loved her. No attempt to sabotage her happiness could ever change that.

'You know where we are if you need us,' the manager had told her as Lauren took her leave. 'In the meantime, be careful and think about what steps you are going to take to keep yourself safe.'

Dismissing the memory of the manager's words, Lauren watched Danny flick his cigarette butt on the floor. It lay smouldering on the patchy carpet while a thin trail of smoke rose towards the ceiling in an untidy spiral.

'What happened?' she asked him, unable to control her curiosity. 'How did you hurt yourself?'

'It was only a scrap. Stop fussing, will you?'

He sprang to his feet, prompting her to let out an involuntary cry of alarm. Seeing her fear, his face lit up with a flash of elation, the kind of expression she saw on his face only when he was screwing her or beating her. It seemed to make no difference to him, as long as he was dominating her physically. She held her breath and lowered her head as he crossed the room in two strides until he was standing right in front of her. He raised his hand.

'Why are you questioning me?' he demanded. 'You don't question me!'

She turned away and his hand slapped the side of her head, missing her face by a second.

'Look up,' he snarled. 'Look at me!'

She shook her head. 'What are you going to do?' she mumbled. 'Are you going to hit me? Don't do it. Please don't do it. Please leave me alone. Please.' She was on her knees now, crying as she mumbled, pleading with him.

'Stop snivelling,' he snapped. 'Look at me.'

Not daring to breathe, she tore her eyes away from the floor and looked up at a face so twisted with rage she hardly recognised him.

'On your feet!' he roared. 'On your feet! Stand up!'

'I was worried about you,' she cried out. 'I care about you. I love you.'

Lunging forward, he grabbed her arm and yanked her to her feet.

'You're lying!' he shouted. 'You're a stupid, selfish cow and I don't want you prying into my affairs. It was just a fight in the pub, that's all.'

He spun her round, and she squealed in protest, staring giddily as the room whirled around her. Suddenly released, she staggered dizzily and fell to the floor, hitting her shin painfully on the table on the way. She drew her knees to her chest, shielding her head between her arms to protect her face. It wasn't merely vanity. She didn't want anyone to see her injuries. It was not her face alone that she was protecting.

When she awoke, she thought she was on her own. Usually he went out after assaulting her. Hearing a noise, she turned her head with difficulty and saw him slumped in a chair, fast asleep and snoring gently. Cautiously she hauled herself to her feet. Her chest and head felt as though they had been violently pummelled, and her leg throbbed from where she had banged into the table as she fell over. Keen to avoid waking him, she moved as quietly as she could. It wasn't easy. Her leg really hurt, but at least she could move it, which must mean it wasn't broken. She leaned sideways against the wall and dragged herself along.

It seemed to take her hours to reach the kitchen, but she finally made it and poured herself a glass of water. Her hand shook as she raised it to her lips. She didn't know what to do. The manager of the shelter had said she could return, but she didn't want to go crawling back there, begging for help. She could imagine the women there whispering behind her back.

'I told you we'd be seeing her again.'

'Well, d'uh. We could all see how that was going to end.'

'…should never have gone back with him.'

'…too stupid to see that man's no good.'

She didn't hear him approach. His voice surprised her and she dropped the glass, which smashed on the floor with a loud crash, sending water and splinters of glass flying everywhere.

'It's all my fault,' he cried out. 'I shouldn't have startled you like that. I'm sorry. I'm so sorry. I didn't mean to hurt you. It won't happen again. I'll never hurt you again, I promise.'

She smiled through her tears because, finally, everything was going to be all right and they would be happy again.

13

Over an early lunch, Geraldine, Ariadne and Naomi discussed the findings from the post mortem. Reluctant to stay away from their desks for long, they homed in on a few points that intrigued them. Naomi had been talking to some of Alice's colleagues. No one the victim had worked with had been aware that she was being abused, although one of the other ICU nurses had reported noticing a few minor bruises on Alice's arm. The other nurse hadn't thought anything of it at the time and hadn't even asked Alice how she had acquired the injuries.

'That's interesting,' Geraldine said. 'How long ago was that?'

Naomi shook her head. 'I did ask, but she was vague.'

'I wonder if we could follow that up? I'm concerned about the evidence of further bruising that was inflicted before she was killed, on several occasions, possibly days before she died,' Geraldine said. 'And for all we know, there could have been other injuries from earlier assaults that have now faded.' She flipped open her phone and read aloud from the post mortem report. 'Small bruises on her shoulder, arm and side that looked like they were made by fingers. And there was a large bruise on her stomach.' She looked up. 'The pathologist thought she'd been physically abused before she died which suggests Rob was violent and—'

'It doesn't suggest that at all,' Naomi interrupted brusquely. 'Now who's jumping to conclusions?'

She spoke so sharply that Geraldine turned to look at her. It was not like Naomi to be sceptical about women having abusive partners. Controlling her surprise, Geraldine asked Naomi what she meant.

'Just that bruising doesn't necessarily mean she was physically abused,' Naomi replied. 'It doesn't actually tell us anything at all, if you think about it. We have to be careful not to misinterpret some detail that turns out to be misleading. What something appears to mean and what it actually means aren't always the same. We all know that.'

'The evidence tells us she was hurt,' Geraldine pointed out. 'There's nothing misleading about that. And Lisa suspected Alice was being physically abused before she ended up dead. We can't ignore that.'

'That was just idle speculation by her aunt. Her bruises don't tell us anything about how she sustained those injuries. It's quite possible she hurt herself in a perfectly innocent way.' Geraldine and Ariadne exchanged a puzzled glance as Naomi continued. 'We're always so quick to find a negative explanation for anything that happens, anything at all. That bruise on her stomach, for example, could easily have been caused by her falling over or knocking into something. Perhaps she was drunk and bumped into the furniture.'

'What about the finger marks on her arm?' Ariadne asked. 'Do you think there's some innocuous reason for those?'

Seemingly oblivious to Ariadne's dismissive tone, Naomi answered the question seriously. 'That would tie in with the idea that she was drunk,' she said. 'If she was unsteady on her feet, don't you think someone would have grabbed her to stop her falling over, in which case they could have accidentally bruised her arm when they tried to hold her up.'

Geraldine nodded. 'You could be right,' she conceded thoughtfully. 'It's certainly plausible.'

Despite appearing to agree with Naomi, Geraldine was troubled by her young colleague's agitation, which she had clearly been struggling to conceal. Geraldine mentioned her concerns to Ariadne, who said she had not noticed anything unusual in Naomi's behaviour. Ariadne's indifference failed to reassure Geraldine, and she decided to tackle Naomi about her concerns. Her young colleague was studying a report and did not notice her approach. Absorbed in reading, Naomi raised a hand to brush her hair off her face. The movement caused her sleeve to fall back, and Geraldine caught a glimpse of a bruise on her arm. She might not have paid any attention to it had Naomi not hurriedly pulled her sleeve down to conceal the mark, glancing around with a mortified expression.

'Is everything all right?' Geraldine enquired, drawing close.

'We're investigating a murder and we have no clue about the identity of the killer, so I wouldn't say everything was all right, exactly.' Naomi dismissed her with an impatient scowl, keeping her eyes fixed on her screen.

Geraldine glanced around to make sure no one else was within earshot, but it was still lunchtime and the nearby desks were all empty. Aware that other colleagues would soon be back, Geraldine spoke quickly.

'I wasn't talking about the case.'

Naomi frowned. 'I don't know what else you could be talking about.'

Geraldine sighed. 'Naomi, are you sure there's nothing wrong? You know you can talk to me as a friend, not just as a colleague. If there's anything on your mind, anything at all, you can share it with me. I'm always here to help you in any way I can.'

'Everything's fine,' Naomi replied curtly. 'There's nothing to worry about.'

There was nothing more to be said. Dissatisfied, and not a little perplexed, Geraldine walked away.

That evening, Tom was asleep in the nursery and Geraldine and Ian were in the kitchen eating supper and relaxing after their working day. It was Friday and Ian had opened a bottle of wine.

'We can always finish it tomorrow if we don't drink it all tonight,' he said.

Geraldine laughed. 'I don't think there's much danger of that.'

They chatted about their day, and Geraldine remembered Naomi's comments about Alice's injuries. She mentioned the exchange to Ian who thought Naomi had a point. The victim's injuries were no proof of abuse and could have been accidental.

'It wasn't so much what she said, but how she said it,' Geraldine explained. 'She seemed to be personally involved in the discussion, as though she was somehow part of it.'

'I'm not sure what you mean.'

'To be honest, I'm not actually sure myself. I just felt that Naomi seemed upset by the idea that the victim had been physically abused before she died.'

'Why wouldn't she be upset? It's an upsetting situation.'

'Of course, but it's hardly the first time we've dealt with victims of abuse. She's never reacted like that before. Something's bothering her and I don't know what.' She hesitated before adding, 'I saw a bruise on her arm.'

'I dare say Naomi can look after herself. Don't go overboard looking for signs of abuse where there aren't any. You did nothing wrong in not acting on Lisa's concerns. That's all they were. Unsubstantiated concerns raised by a third party.'

'They weren't unsubstantiated.'

'You couldn't possibly have known that when Lisa spoke to you,' Ian said. 'You can't blame yourself for not being omniscient.'

'What about Naomi's bruise?'

'I dare say she'll get over it.'

Geraldine nodded. But if something was disturbing one of her team, she wanted to find out what it was. They finished their supper. Ian poured the rest of the wine into their glasses and they took them into the living room. As they settled down to watch the next episode in an entertaining series they were following sporadically, Tom let out a yell.

Geraldine laughed. 'He always sounds so indignant when he wakes up,' she said. 'I'd better go and get him before he climbs out of his cot again.'

'We're going to need to think about him sleeping in a bed soon,' Ian said when Geraldine returned holding Tom in her arms.

'But he's still a baby,' she protested.

'A baby who can climb out of his cot,' Ian replied.

'If he can climb out of a cot, what's to stop him falling out of bed?'

'Can't we put a mattress on the floor?'

'We need to find out how other people manage.' She sighed, accepting the inevitable.

'Well, let's not wait until he hurts himself falling out of his cot,' Ian said.

'I know, you're right. I'll ask Lisa tomorrow. She was a bit surprised when I told her he climbed out of his cot, but she said it's not that unusual at his age.' Geraldine heaved another sigh. 'A year old and he's already climbing out of his cot. He seems to be in such a hurry to grow up.' She leaned down and kissed the top of Tom's head, savouring the warm scent of baby shampoo and talcum powder. 'I'm going to miss this,' she whispered.

'He's still a baby,' Ian said, draining his glass. 'Sleeping in a bed doesn't mean he's about to leave home any time soon.'

14

MARIA MIGHT AS WELL not have bothered attending her English class that morning because she couldn't focus on any of the exercises. She wasn't sure why she was unable to concentrate. It wasn't as if that morning's exercises had been particularly challenging. They had started with a listening task, where two women were arguing over a dog. She had scarcely followed a single word of it. After that, the class had been asked to work in pairs to devise their own conversations in which two people were having a row.

'You might be a customer arguing with a manager in a shop, or you could be two motorists who have had an accident,' the tutor suggested. 'You can use one of those suggestions or you can think up a scene of your own where two people are having a row. See what you can come up with. Use your imagination.'

When they had finished preparing their presentations, they were going to read out their scenes in front of the class.

'Arguments but no fights,' the tutor told them with a grin. 'So no physical contact, please. We don't want anyone complaining about being given a black eye or reporting me to the police for encouraging violent behaviour.' She laughed, and Maria shuddered at the mention of violence coupled with the police. 'So remember, use your language to express your feelings. Use the vocabulary list on page twenty-seven and, when you're reading aloud, don't forget to think about your intonation.'

Usually Maria enjoyed this kind of exercise. It was more fun than doing repetitive grammar exercises. She was sitting next to a serious-minded Chinese girl who was scribbling furiously, her forehead furrowed in concentration. She had nearly covered a page in her spiky illegible handwriting.

'You're supposed to be creating a scene together,' the tutor told them, as she paused in her walk around the room, checking work and helping students who were stuck. 'It looks like your partner's doing all the work, Maria.' The tutor smiled to show she wasn't angry.

The students were mostly girls, and almost all of them were earnest about their studies. Usually Maria was as keen as any of them to work hard and improve her grasp of English. But today she was distracted. She tried to ignore her memories of Rob. There was no doubt he had a temper. He had actually raised his hand against her on more than one occasion, but that had only happened when he had been drinking and he had never really hurt her. Not only that, he had always been very apologetic afterwards. She didn't believe he could ever have hurt her enough to cause any real injury, although she had been a little afraid of him at times. In the end, his temper was the real reason she had left him, although she hadn't admitted that to the police. She hated the thought of being responsible for landing him in trouble. Even though she hadn't exactly lied about him, she felt uncomfortable at having concealed his violent streak from the detective. But she couldn't believe Rob was capable of killing someone. Not the Rob she had known.

She hurried off as soon as the class finished, so she could get home in time to tidy up the house before collecting Jason from school. On her way home she tussled with her conscience, aware that a few words from her might land Rob in a lot of trouble, possibly even see him facing a murder charge. She had no wish to be instrumental in bringing that about. Having decided to walk away from the situation and forget about Rob and his troubles, she felt a sense of relief. She collected Jason from school, took him home, and had just settled him down with cartoons on his tablet when the doorbell rang. Maria struggled to hide her dismay on seeing the dark-haired detective standing on her doorstep.

'The missus is at work.' She started to close the door, but the detective stepped forward.

'That's fine. It's you I've come to see,' she said. 'Shall we talk inside?'

Maria wondered how the police officer would react if she used some of the vocabulary she had been practising that day. Her Chinese partner had come up with some colourful epithets. She recalled the structures they had been using.

A question: 'What are you doing here?'

An imperative: 'Go away and leave me alone.'

A conditional: 'If you don't stop I will call the police.'

Only, of course, the detective who wanted to question her *was* the police.

'If it's more convenient, I can come back later,' the detective went on, 'when your employer is home.'

Whatever else happened, Maria didn't want her employer to find out she was being questioned by the police, even if she had not been accused of any wrongdoing. Swallowing her alarm, she invited the detective in for a second time.

'What you want to know?' she asked, when they were both seated at the kitchen table again.

'Is there anything else you want to tell me about your ex-boyfriend? Think carefully, Maria. This is important.'

Maria shook her head. The detective was only doing her job, but she was the police and she seemed to be going after Rob. Even though she was no longer in a relationship with him, Maria felt a sudden resurgence of affection for him. They had been happy together for a while. She had once even considered how she might answer if he proposed, although he had never given her any indication that he wanted to marry her. She didn't want to give the detective the wrong impression of him and see him ending up in trouble because of something she said.

'I told you, I haven't seen him for many months. He is good man. I don't think you should be questioning me. I don't understand what is happening but it's not how it should be.'

The meeting seemed to go on endlessly, but at last the detective left, and shortly after that her employer, Julia, returned home. Delayed by her uninvited visitor, Maria had not yet made supper for her young charge who was happily glued to his tablet. Her employer was annoyed.

'You haven't even cleared up in the kitchen and why hasn't Jason had his supper? I can't believe you haven't given him anything to eat. What on earth have you been doing?' Julia broke off, suddenly concerned. 'Is something wrong? Maria, what is it?'

All at once, the stress of her recent encounters with the police overwhelmed Maria and she broke down in tears. 'I'm sorry,' she mumbled, 'I have headache. I have headache. Is nothing wrong. All is good.'

Julia sat down next to Maria. 'Why don't I put the kettle on and then you can tell me about it?' she said kindly. 'I'm sure it can't be as bad as all that,' she said a few moments later, as she put a mug of tea down in front of Maria. 'What is it? Boyfriend trouble?'

Maria burst into tears again.

15

ON SUNDAY, GERALDINE AND Ian both had a day off. They spent the morning together, doing housework and going shopping, and playing with Tom in between chores. Geraldine did her best to put the investigation out of her mind, but her meeting with Maria on Thursday had proved unsatisfactory, and she couldn't stop thinking about Alice and her injuries.

'You'll sort it out,' Ian said, smiling at her as they finished their lunch.

'Sort what out?' she asked.

'You were thinking about your case.'

'No, I wasn't. I was listening to you.'

'What was I saying then?'

Even before she hesitated, they both knew she was lying. She gave an apologetic grin. 'We're just stumped at the moment.'

'At the moment,' Ian repeated. 'Tomorrow might be a different story. There's nothing you can do about it right now, so why not just forget about it for one afternoon? That way you'll be able to start with a clear mind tomorrow.'

Reminding herself of what Ian had said, she went into work the next day determined to make progress. She was concerned when Naomi appeared dismissive when she went to speak to her.

'Is this important?' Naomi asked, looking agitated. 'Only I've got a lot to get through this morning.'

'It will only take a moment. I just want to know that everything's all right.'

'Later,' Naomi replied. 'I really do need to get on.'

Ariadne looked round, hearing Naomi's voice slightly raised, and Geraldine returned to her own desk. She searched for Naomi at lunchtime but couldn't find her at her desk or in the canteen. That afternoon, Geraldine approached Naomi at her desk and invited her young colleague her to join her for a coffee. Naomi refused.

'Are you sure you're okay?' Geraldine asked her, pulling a chair over to sit down beside her.

'Yes, yes. I'm okay. Why wouldn't I be? Why do you keep asking me?'

Geraldine shrugged. 'You just don't seem yourself. It's probably me.' She tried to laugh off her question, but Naomi turned away from her with an irritated expression.

With a sigh, Geraldine stood up. If Naomi refused to tell her what was bothering her, there was nothing she could do about it. And as long as Naomi was doing her job, there was really no justification for prying. But Geraldine couldn't help feeling concerned. She decided it was time to ask around and see what else she could find out. Reluctantly, she decided to speak to Ariadne who was close to Naomi, since it was possible she had noticed something unusual about their young colleague.

'Can I speak to you?' she murmured to Ariadne.

Ariadne looked up from her screen and smiled. 'Of course. What is it?'

'Let's go outside,' Geraldine said. 'I want to speak to you in confidence.'

Looking intrigued, if not worried, Ariadne nodded, logged off and stood up straight away. Geraldine led the way to the car park. When she was sure no one could overhear them, she turned to Ariadne.

'Have you noticed anything different about Naomi recently?'

Ariadne looked puzzled. 'Different in what way?'

'I don't know. It's just that – does she seem like her normal self these days?'

'Her normal self?'

'I don't want to put ideas in your head.'

'What is this? I'm not a witness, am I? Or a suspect?' She laughed. 'What are you talking about?'

Geraldine shrugged. 'I don't know. She doesn't seem like her usual self, that's all. I hope there's nothing wrong. It's just a feeling I have.'

Geraldine hesitated to say anything else. There wasn't much more to say anyway, only the possibly irrelevant detail of the bruising Geraldine had seen on Naomi's arm. She was reluctant to mention that as Naomi hadn't willingly shared it with her and, in any case, she had no idea what had caused it. But she remembered how defensive Naomi had seemed about it and how aggressively she had insisted that Alice's injuries might have been caused accidentally.

'Well…' Ariadne hesitated. 'She has been looking a bit peaky lately and I suppose she has been a bit snappy. But I don't think there's anything to worry about. We're all feeling frustrated about the case. Why? Has she said something?'

'No, and I'm sure you're right. It's nothing. Forget I mentioned it,' Geraldine said. 'Come on then, let's get back. We've got work to do.'

They called Rob in for questioning one more time. They knew that unless they could persuade him to confess, in the absence of any evidence linking him to his girlfriend's death they would have to stop pursuing him. Geraldine and Ariadne exchanged a worried glance as he was brought into the interview room, accompanied by his lawyer.

'I've got nothing more to say to you,' he mumbled as soon as he sat down. He turned to his lawyer. 'How much longer can they keep doing this? You said they'd leave me alone. This is an outrage,' he added, but he sounded beaten, as though he had no energy left to argue with them.

His blue eyes glared dully at them and his shoulders

slumped forwards. If he hadn't been a suspect in a murder enquiry, Geraldine might have felt sorry for him, he seemed so woebegone. He looked as though he hadn't slept for days and was in need of a good meal. She wondered if he was feeling tormented by grief or guilt.

'You need to let my client go,' the lawyer spoke up in his oddly high-pitched voice. 'You haven't charged him with any crime, because you have no evidence against him. You can't hold him here for no reason, not unless you exceed your authority and are prepared to break the law.' He gave a sneaky smile and Geraldine saw Ariadne's expression harden.

'Rob,' Geraldine tried one last time. 'Tell us about Alice.'

He shook his head. 'I don't want to talk about Alice, not with you or anyone. I want to go home. All this is doing my head in. I lost my girl and you lot are doing nothing about it and now, on top of everything else, you're hounding me.'

'Are you going to let my client leave now, or are we going to have to lodge a complaint for police harassment?' the lawyer asked. He sounded confident, as though he could sense Geraldine's resolve weakening.

'There's no need for threats,' Geraldine said calmly. She turned to Rob. 'You're free to go, for now.'

Rob shrugged and rose to his feet. 'I'm out of here,' he said. 'And you lot had better start doing your job properly.' His face darkened. 'Find out who did for my girl and then let me have him. Give me five minutes alone with him and I'll make him sorry he was ever born. I'll snap his legs like twigs and make sure he never walks again.'

The lawyer stood up. 'My client is upset,' he said. 'He's grieving for his girlfriend. He is not a violent man.'

16

ALL THROUGH MONDAY MORNING, Geraldine kept an eye on Naomi, and was relieved to see she appeared to be focused on her work. She was leading a team looking into the victim's background. If Alice had been in contact with anyone else who had a history of violence, they were determined to discover it. Even though it was a time-consuming and tedious task, Naomi appeared to be enjoying herself as she ferreted around searching for information to add to what they already knew about the victim.

'How's it going? Have you come across anything useful?' Geraldine asked her, perching on Naomi's desk halfway through the morning.

'Nothing so far,' Naomi replied, looking up with a rueful smile. 'But we haven't finished yet.'

'If there's anything there, even a hint of a hint, I'm sure you'll find it.'

'All we've uncovered so far is that Alice used to share a flat with a girl called Hayley who now works in a restaurant in Foss Lane.'

Geraldine smiled. 'Well done for ferreting that out. We'll see if she has anything useful to tell us.'

Normally Naomi would have smiled at such praise from Geraldine, but she merely turned her attention back to her screen. Soon after she left Naomi, Geraldine was informed that a member of the public had contacted the police station to say they had come across something suspicious and wanted to speak to someone involved in the investigation into the murder of Alice James. It was irritatingly vague and likely to be a waste of time, but nothing was too insignificant to ignore. Sometimes the most ostensibly trivial lead could end up cracking a case wide open. Hoping this would prove to be a useful lead, Geraldine went down to see what it was about.

The elderly woman who had asked to see her was wearing a thick beige coat, even though it was quite warm outside. Her face was covered in a veneer of powder and her skin looked pale against her garish red lipstick. Sitting down, Geraldine introduced herself and asked what the woman wanted to tell her.

'Are you in charge of the investigation into that poor girl's murder?' the woman asked her. 'I want to speak to someone in charge.'

Reassured that Geraldine was leading the investigation, the woman rubbed a veiny hand across her lips.

'I found it in the front garden,' she murmured, gazing earnestly at Geraldine.

Geraldine nodded and tried to look encouraging, although she was not surprised. From time to time people came forward with bones they had dug up, agog at the possibility that a murder had been committed. The bones invariably turned out to be from sheep or some other domesticated animal.

'What did you find, Mrs Fallon?'

'Call me Irene, Inspector.'

Controlling her impatience, Geraldine repeated her question. 'Irene, what exactly did you find in your front garden?'

Irene drew in a deep breath. 'Oh sorry, I'm sorry, I never explained.' She grinned nervously. 'I saw on the news that you haven't found a murder weapon for that young woman who was stabbed. So I thought you must still be looking for it. You see, I think I may have found it.' Her eyes were shining with excitement now, but she still seemed hesitant.

Geraldine waited.

'I found a knife and I think it might be the one you're looking for.'

Geraldine waited again, but Irene didn't say anything else.

'What makes you think the knife you found is a murder weapon?' Geraldine asked at last.

'It's not so much the knife itself,' Irene said. 'It's more about where I found it, if you follow me.'

Geraldine nodded, wondering how long this was going to take and whether she had made a mistake in not leaving this to a constable to follow up. 'Go on.'

Irene explained that she was used to paying attention to detail, having worked in a local bank until she retired. Geraldine listened patiently as the woman talked, waiting for her to reach the discovery of the knife. In the end she prompted her.

'Yes, yes, the knife,' Irene replied. 'I'm sorry. I do tend to ramble. Now, where was I? Oh yes, the knife. The thing is, I live in Wenlock Terrace, just two doors down from the alley where the body was found. It looked as though it had been hidden there, in the hedge in my front garden, which seemed a bit suspicious.' She frowned. 'That's what I thought anyway. So I thought I should say something, in case it is the one you're looking for.'

'Where is the knife now?'

'I didn't want to touch it more than I had to, so I put it straight in a plastic bag. That's what you're supposed to do, isn't it?'

Irene had found the knife almost a week after Alice was stabbed. Geraldine thought quickly. If the knife had been discarded straight after the stabbing, that meant it had been lying in Irene's garden for days before it was found, but with luck it could still give them enough information to track down the killer, assuming it was the murder weapon.

Geraldine sent for Sam to take Irene home to fetch the knife. 'Do you need me to come back here to answer any more questions afterwards?' Irene asked.

'No, that's fine. You've already been very helpful.'

'Very well. If you're sure,' Irene said. She hesitated. 'You will tell me if the knife was used to kill that woman? Only I took it indoors in my bag. If I carried a murder weapon in my bag, I won't be allowed to keep it, will I?'

'That's all right. You can keep your bag,' Geraldine assured her. 'It's the knife we're interested in.'

'But I can't use a bag that had a murder weapon in it! Won't you need to take my bag away for examination?' Irene insisted plaintively. 'If I have to hand it in, you'll replace it, won't you? I have to have a bag, don't I, and I won't be able to use that one.'

Having made a note of exactly where the knife had been found, Geraldine returned to her desk from where a team was immediately dispatched to search Irene's front garden and the area around it. A week had elapsed since the murder and no one was confident they would find anything else useful there, but Geraldine knew her colleagues would do a thorough job. She wished she could be there with them herself, ferreting through the undergrowth, searching for clues, but she had to leave it to the search team. In the meantime, she had her own work to do. The knife would be sent off for urgent forensic examination, and all they could do then was wait and hope they would glean something helpful from it.

17

Maria continued to worry. Once again, she struggled to focus in her language class. The Chinese girl who had worked with her the previous week had partnered up with another girl without even greeting Maria. Clearly the Chinese student wanted a more responsive partner. By the evening, Maria was worn out from struggling to maintain her self-control as she collected Jason from school and gave him his dinner of fish fingers and oven chips. He seemed even more demanding than usual, complaining that some of his chips were burnt when they were only brown at the edges, and she was aware that she was more than usually impatient with him. As soon as she had put him to bed, half an hour earlier than usual, she went to her room and closed the door with a sigh of relief before throwing herself down on her bed and bursting into tears. About an hour later there was a knock at her door. With an effort, she pulled herself together.

'Yes?' she called out, sitting up on the bed and blowing her nose. 'What is it?'

'Can I come in?' Julia asked, pushing the door open without waiting for a reply.

Maria wiped her eyes and tried to smile brightly, but she couldn't hide her tears. 'Something's the matter, isn't it?' Julia asked, gazing at her with a worried frown. 'Tell me what's wrong, Maria. I don't like to think you're keeping something – anything – from me. While you're living here with us, I want you to think of us as your family.'

Maria hesitated, but she could hardly pretend there was nothing wrong when she had obviously been crying. She wished she was back at home with her family. Her sisters would have sympathised with her and that would have been some comfort, at least temporarily, and her mother would have known what to do. Maria could imagine what she would say.

'Stop snivelling, Maria,' her mother would say, completely misunderstanding why Maria was upset. 'He's not worth it.' Her brusqueness would snap Maria out of her dejection. 'He's just one man. There are plenty more men in the world but you won't find a husband by crying and making yourself look hideous, and you won't meet anyone by staying in your room feeling sorry for yourself. Get up, wash your face and go out. Life's a battle, and when things don't go your way, you have to get out there and fight for what you want.'

But her mother wasn't there, and meanwhile, her employer was being sympathetic, which made Maria break down in tears again. She didn't want to blame her distress on homesickness in case Julia decided to contact the agency and say she was no longer happy to stay in England. Julia pulled a chair closer to the bed and sat down.

'Are you feeling unwell, Maria? If you are, you need to let me know.' Julia paused. 'We won't mind. We want you to be happy here with us.' She spoke stiffly, as though she was embarrassed by Maria's emotional outburst, but her words were kindly meant.

Maria shook her head vigorously and blew her nose. 'No, no. I'm not sick. I'm fine. There's nothing wrong.' She sniffed, and a phrase she had learned that morning popped into her head. 'As it happens,' she added.

'Is it your boyfriend who's making you miserable, then?'

Julia hadn't even realised that Maria was no longer with Rob. Seizing on this opportunity to account for her behaviour, Maria nodded and burst into tears again. Still sobbing, she explained that she and Rob had broken up. That, at least, was true. She didn't add that she hadn't seen him for months.

'It's his loss,' Julia said. 'I'm sure you'll find someone else. You're a beautiful girl, Maria. You need to move on from this. It happens to us all. Some men find it impossible to commit to a relationship. It's no reflection on you. It's better you found out what he's like sooner rather than later. Some women waste years waiting for a man to decide to settle down, only to be disappointed at the end of it.'

Julia was being so kind, suddenly Maria didn't want to lie to her any more. 'It's not that,' she said. 'It's not that.'

She was crying too hard to speak. She had made up her mind never to mention her encounter with the police, but somehow it slipped out. Her employer had been leaning forwards, almost close enough to touch Maria. Now she sat bolt upright, looking startled.

'The police?' Julia repeated. 'What are you talking about? Did you say the police came here? Are you telling me the police came here, to this house?'

Maria was so taken aback by her employer's shocked reaction, she stopped crying at once. With a sinking feeling, she suspected she might have talked herself out of a job. She had come across other au pairs who had to take care of two or three obnoxious children and knew she was lucky with her own family. Jason could be annoying, it was true, but he was only one child and although he was spoilt, he was never spiteful. On the contrary, he was quite affectionate towards her. She didn't want to leave the household. Anxiously she hurried to reassure her employer that far from being in trouble with the police, she had been helping them. And she was certain they weren't coming back.

'I tell them I don't see my boyfriend again,' she assured Julia earnestly. 'They want only to know everything I know about him. I tell them everything and that is all. They will not speak with me again.'

Instead of leaving her alone, Julia continued to question her, curious to know when she and Rob had parted company and why the police were interested in him. Maria shrugged and said she didn't know, but Julia was not easily put off. Her eyes were bright with curiosity, and Maria began to wish she had never mentioned the police.

'Well, what exactly did they want to know?' Julia insisted.

Maria hesitated, but Julia was kind and well meaning. All at once, the temptation to unburden herself overwhelmed her, and she told Julia exactly what the police had asked her.

'And was he? Violent, I mean?' Julia pressed her, looking horrified.

Maria had no reason to remain loyal to Rob and Julia was easy to talk to. She heard herself admit that Rob had hit her a few times. As soon as she told Julia what had happened, she regretted having blurted out the truth.

'It wasn't all his fault,' she went on, in a clumsy attempt to justify herself for having tolerated the abuse.

'No,' Julia retorted sharply, standing up indignantly. 'Don't you dare take responsibility for someone else's abusive behaviour. We all make mistakes, but if that man hit you then you should have left him at once and reported him to the police straight away. Now they've come here asking about him, you have to tell them everything.'

'But he never hurt me, not really he hurts me. Most of time we are together he is nice. He only is angry when he is drinking,' Maria said, aware that her English was becoming garbled in her agitation.

'Maybe he didn't hurt you badly, but his next girlfriend might not be so lucky,' Julia said grimly. 'And if she's not badly injured, maybe it could the one after her. In the meantime, the police want to question you about him, which suggests he may already have been abusing someone else who has come forward to accuse him. So if you ask me, you have a duty to tell them what he's capable of. You can't just look away and pretend it never happened. Do you understand what I'm saying, Maria? If this man is allowed to get away with assaulting women, one day he might end up hurting someone really seriously. Maria, you have to tell the police the truth. You have to tell them he was physically abusive. They need to know he's violent towards women.'

'No, no,' Maria wept. 'He is not a bad man. He is not a bad man.'

Julia scowled, her eyes glittering with suppressed anger. 'I'm calling the police right now and you're going to tell them what you just told me.'

Maria blew her nose and said she would go to the police station and speak to the inspector who had questioned her earlier.

'I speak to the police lady myself. I do this. I promise you.'

'Just make sure you do,' Julia replied. She gazed anxiously at Maria, who trembled.

'I do what you tell me. I do not want to lose my job,' she said, speaking very carefully to make sure Julia understood.

'You must do this because it's the right thing to do,' Julia said. 'Not for any selfish considerations. And you must do it today.'

Maria wondered what her mother would say if she knew. She had decided not to mention any of this to her family. If they found out what had been happening, her parents were bound to insist on her returning to Spain at once. In some ways that would be a relief, but she didn't want to go home yet. Apart from anything else, she would have to give a reason for her early return, and her friends and acquaintances were bound to gossip about her if they heard she had been seeing a suspect in a murder enquiry. Even if it turned out he was innocent, the fact that his next girlfriend had been killed was enough to set tongues wagging.

'I go to the police,' she told Julia. 'I go and I tell the police lady everything.'

18

It was disappointing to see absolutely nothing in the news about the discovery of a knife hidden in the bushes of a garden near the alley where the most recent body had been found. The knife had not been very well hidden, with the handle sticking out of a leafy shrub. Whoever lived in that house should have noticed it by now, but after two days, there had been no reports of the knife being discovered. At this rate, it might not be spotted until the bush shed its leaves in the autumn and possibly not even then. That front garden had seemed like an obvious place to conceal a replica murder weapon, being so close to the site where the latest victim had been killed. It also looked well kept, which was important because it suggested someone spent time tending the garden. It was possible the knife had been found and the householders had decided to keep it for themselves. That seemed unlikely and slightly ghoulish, given the fuss in the media about the police looking for a murder weapon. Perhaps the residents weren't interested in the garden after all, and it looked better cared for than it really was. Appearances could be so deceptive. As a rule, that wasn't a bad thing.

Concerned that the police might be getting close to the truth by now, it had been a shrewd move to throw a misleading knife into the mix; any tactic to confuse them had to be worth pursuing, especially when it was so simple to implement. A knife paid for in cash in a large department store in Leeds left no trace of the purchaser. A hood to mask their face had been an easy way to avoid any risk of identification on security cameras. If the householders failed to notice the replica knife, a passerby was bound to spot it and report their discovery to the police, who would proceed to waste time harassing the householders in whose garden it had been planted. By the time the police were done with the false trail, The Knife would be lying at the bottom of the river and the elusive killer would have left the area, striding away into another life and freedom.

It was a good idea that should have worked. The problem lay in the timing because, before an opportunity presented itself to hide the duplicate knife in the bushes, it seemed the police had given up searching the area. A few days earlier and they might have found it, but with a police presence it would have been reckless to risk being spotted leaving it there. So the tactic to misdirect the police appeared to have failed. It was a minor irritation. What mattered were the killings, which were proceeding exactly as planned. In fact, things couldn't be going better. The second knife had only ever been intended to serve as a distraction to send the police off on the wrong tack. There had never been any intention of putting it to any serious purpose.

Meanwhile The Knife, the one true faithful blade, would continue to serve its purpose. Like King Arthur's Excalibur, it played a mystical role, verging on the sacred. No replica knife could ever assume that mantle; The Knife's history set it apart. And now, The Knife had one last job to perform before it was laid to rest at the bottom of the river, submerged like Excalibur in the Lake at Avalon. There would be no unexpected setbacks because this was The Knife's ordained task. As when Sir Bedivere hurled the once and future king's sword into the lake, The Knife would whirl through the air, causing glorious flashes of lightning in the moonlight, until it sank out of sight beneath the dark surface of the water.

19

THE FORENSIC REPORT ON the knife found in Irene's garden was both surprising and, at the same time, disappointing. The dimensions of the blade matched the one that had been used to kill Alice exactly, but an initial impression that they had found the murder weapon was dispelled once it appeared that the blade Irene had come across had never been used. Geraldine called the officer who had conducted the study of the knife to check she fully understood his report. He was terse in his responses, and she hastened to reassure him that her enquiry was no reflection of his thoroughness. It was rather an admission of her own ignorance.

'What if the knife had been thoroughly cleaned and even sharpened before it was hidden?' she asked him, desperate for some positive evidence that they had found the murder weapon. 'Surely that could make it look as if it was new?'

'No. It's never been cleaned.' The forensic scientist described the join where the blade met the handle. 'We found traces of the polymer wrapper it was sold in. It looks as if whoever bought it removed the packaging in a hurry and hid it in the neighbour's garden without letting the blade come in contact with anything once it was unwrapped. The blade has no markings on it at all. It's as flawless and uncontaminated as the day it left the factory in its PVC blister packaging, and the handle appears to be untouched. Whoever unwrapped it was careful to leave virtually no trace. There's just one speck that could have been left by a rubber glove, but even that's not clear and could have been left there in the factory when it was packaged. It looks as though all the wrapping was removed right there in the garden and the knife dropped with minimal contact from whoever left it there. It's very unusual to come across something so clean. I'm sorry we can't give you any more information, but that's all we have for you.'

They both agreed it was odd.

'What can you tell me about the knife itself?' Geraldine asked.

The officer paused to consult his report. 'We're talking about a twenty-five-centimetre sharp kitchen knife with a stainless steel blade, rust-resistant and wear-resistant. The blade is two millimetres thick with a sharp V-shaped double-beveled edge for precise cutting tasks. The handle is pakkawood.'

'What's that?' Geraldine asked.

'Pakkawood is a wood and resin composite designed to be hard wearing and durable.'

'So could the pakkawood handle help to narrow down where it was purchased?' Geraldine asked.

Her flicker of hope was extinguished as her colleague told her that wasn't possible.

'Pakkawood is a very popular material used for knife handles,' he said. 'They can be purchased online as well as in any supermarket or kitchenware store. I dare say you've got a knife with a pakkawood handle in your own kitchen.'

Not only was the knife blade clean, but the handle gave them no information either. All they knew for certain was that someone had bought a knife that matched the murder weapon and had concealed it in Irene's garden.

'It wasn't well hidden, so whoever left it there must have expected it would be found at some point. They must have known the area might be searched.'

'I don't know how the search team missed it,' Ariadne said.

'It must have been left there after the team finished,' Geraldine replied. 'Anyway, it makes no difference, because we know it wasn't the murder weapon and whoever planted it there made sure they left no clue to their identity. All we can say is that it's likely it was put there by the killer, because whoever left it must have known the exact blade used in the attack. Assuming it was put there after the search team had finished, we have a window of roughly two days between the search being called off on Friday and Irene finding the knife. We need to check any eye witnesses or security cameras from the immediate area over the course of that weekend, from Friday evening until Irene found the knife. We're looking for a sighting of whoever deposited it in Irene's garden. I'll leave it to you to set up a door-to-door team looking for eye witnesses and CVTV footage.'

Ariadne nodded briskly. 'Do you think Irene hid it in her own garden?' she asked. 'Did she just tell us she found it there?'

'At this stage, anything's possible,' Geraldine replied. 'But why would she go to all the trouble of concealing her identity if she was going to bring the knife to us herself? And it seems too much of a coincidence for someone who hadn't committed the murder to have hit on the exact same blade as the one used to stab Alice. How would anyone else have known the width of the blade? It seems to me that whoever hid that knife in Irene's garden knew exactly what knife had been used in the murder and decided to hide a replica nearby. Was this an attempt to throw us off the scent, do you think? Or are they taunting us in some weird way?'

Ariadne frowned. 'You don't think Irene could be the killer?'

'What possible motive could she have for coming to us with a replica knife? We had no reason to suspect her, and we've found nothing to link her to Alice.'

'Could she have hidden the knife herself for the attention?' Ariadne suggested.

It wasn't unheard of for cranks to come forward with fabricated evidence and false confessions.

'How would she have known the exact knife to use? No, it would be too much of a coincidence,' Geraldine insisted.

'There must be standard-sized knife blades,' Ariadne pointed out. 'It wouldn't be that much of a coincidence, would it?'

'In any case, she insists she found it,' Geraldine replied, 'and I'm inclined to believe her.'

Geraldine was called away from the discussion because Maria had turned up at the police station asking to speak to her. When Geraldine joined Maria in an interview room, she could see straight away that the girl had been crying. She waited for a moment, but Maria sat silently twisting a damp tissue in her hands.

At last Geraldine cleared her throat and began to question the girl. 'Have you remembered something that you forgot to mention when we spoke on Thursday?' she asked gently.

Maria shook her head and her black hair flicked around her pale face.

Geraldine tried again. 'Is there something you want to tell me? I'm listening,' she said. She was tempted to add that she was very busy and couldn't afford to see time-wasters. 'Is this about Rob?'

Maria nodded and stared at the floor.

Geraldine thought she knew what Maria had been holding back from her. She had suspected as much the first time she had seen the girl. 'What is it you want to tell us about him? Maria, it's important you don't hide anything that could help us in our investigation.' When her urging failed to achieve a result, Geraldine decided to take a different tack. 'Maria,' she said severely, 'this is a murder enquiry and you could end up in very serious trouble if you conceal evidence from the police. You must tell us everything you know about your ex-boyfriend and you must tell me right now.'

Maria nodded and looked up. 'You are right. I do not tell you everything when you come to the house. I am too surprised,' she whispered. 'It is not true Rob is a nice man. I told you he is a good man, but he is not. Not all the time. Not when he is drinking.' She was trembling with fear. Recalling how young the au pair was, Geraldine hastened to reassure her.

'Don't be frightened, Maria. You're quite safe here. No one here is going to hurt you and we won't let Rob hurt you either. All you need to do is answer my questions honestly and you'll be fine. Now, it's time for you to tell me the truth. Did Rob ever hit you?'

Maria nodded and suddenly began talking very fast. Geraldine listened closely.

'It's a pity she didn't tell us all about her charming ex the first time I questioned her,' Geraldine said bitterly, when Maria had gone. 'It's my fault. I should have pressed her then.'

'You can't blame yourself for that,' Ariadne said quickly. 'If someone refuses to help us, there's not much we can do about it.'

'Maybe, but I had a feeling at the time that the girl was keeping something back. I should have tried harder to persuade her to talk.'

Ariadne reassured her that it would have made very little difference, but Geraldine knew that Maria's admission would have enabled them to put pressure on Rob. If only Maria had been honest from the start, they might have been able to force a confession from him. As it was, they had now given him and his lawyer plenty of time to prepare his defence. But Rob and his lawyer didn't know that Maria had come forward to tell them how he had mistreated her.

20

UNLIKE THE PREVIOUS OCCASION when he had been brought to the police station for questioning, Rob seemed relaxed. No longer even vaguely annoyed, he grinned cheerily across the interview table as he removed his baseball cap and ran his fingers through his hair. His smile was almost flirtatious as he made eye contact with Geraldine, and she could appreciate how women might find him attractive.

'Here we are again,' he said jovially. 'Look, I appreciate you're just doing your job and I suppose an apology is in order. The thing is, I was—' he paused, as though searching for an appropriate way to describe his feelings. 'I was upset, you know.' His face twisted in a brief spasm of misery before his expression cleared again. 'I'd only just heard about Alice and before I had time to even begin to process what had happened, you were bombarding me with questions and I lost it. But I told you the honest truth. It wasn't me. I would never have hurt her. I loved her.' His voice broke suddenly and he stopped.

Without missing a beat, Geraldine asked him how often he had assaulted Maria. Rob's façade of bonhomie vanished at her words and he gaped at her, fleetingly speechless. Geraldine waited.

'What the hell's this?' he blurted out at last. 'Aren't we done with all these questions? You've got no right to harass me like this.'

'Your girlfriend was murdered,' Geraldine replied evenly.

'We want to ask you a few questions. I hardly think that's unreasonable.'

Rob was clearly rattled. 'I want my lawyer here if you're going to start on at me again.'

They took a break while they waited for the lawyer to arrive. Before long, Rob and his red-faced brief were ready. As before, the lawyer looked slightly sweaty, as if he was nervous. Geraldine wondered how experienced he was. He looked very young, and this was possibly the first time he had been called on to represent a suspect in a murder enquiry. Compared to his lawyer, Rob looked relaxed, even though he was the one under scrutiny. Geraldine opened the interview by repeating her earlier question which had prompted Rob to demand his lawyer be present. Rob looked surprised and opened his hands in a gesture of helplessness.

'My client has already denied being physically abusive,' the lawyer objected in his curiously high-pitched voice. 'If there's nothing else, I suggest you desist and let him go. You've questioned him before.'

'That was before Maria spoke to us this morning,' Geraldine said. She turned to Rob. 'Your ex-girlfriend came here to tell us about how you used to abuse her physically. There's no point in denying it,' she added as Rob began to protest that there must have been a misunderstanding.

'She's Spanish,' he added to the lawyer, as though that explained everything.

Ariadne read out Maria's statement, accusing Rob of hitting her more than once when he had been drinking.

'She's lying!' Rob cried out.

The lawyer raised a restraining hand, but Rob refused to be silenced.

'That girl's a liar,' he exclaimed. 'Can't you see? She's just trying to make trouble for me because I dumped her and found someone else. She's a lying, jealous bitch.'

'Why don't you tell us about your problem with alcohol?' Geraldine continued, disregarding his outburst. 'Take your time and please don't leave anything out.'

To begin with, Rob denied having an issue with alcohol. Eventually, he conceded that he had lost his temper with his ex-girlfriend a few times after he had drunk too much. That, he explained, was why he had stopped drinking so much. But he insisted he had never hit her and she was to blame for their disagreements.

'She was like a child,' he said. 'She used to drive me nuts. Not that that's any excuse for getting angry,' he added, 'but she was always on at me. Sometimes I just couldn't bear it and – well, I admit I lost my temper with her. It was never a happy relationship. We wanted different things. I think I pushed her away a couple of times, when she went for me. But I didn't hit her. If anything, it was the other way round. I had to physically restrain her more than once from grabbing hold of me. That's why I had to end it.'

'So you were the one who ended the relationship?'

'I guess it was mutual. It wasn't doing either of us any good. Like I said, we were never happy together.'

Without warning, Geraldine changed the subject. 'Tell me again where you were on Monday night.'

Rob looked at her in surprise but he didn't answer.

'Weren't you disturbed when Alice went out very early on Tuesday morning?' Geraldine pressed him. 'Weren't you curious about where she was going?'

'No.'

'What do you mean? Didn't you see her every morning before you went to work?'

'No.'

'How early did she go out?'

He shook his head. 'It's difficult to say as I was usually asleep when she went out. But I sometimes woke up at six and she'd already gone out. But in any case,' he added, his expression clearing, 'I wasn't at home on Monday night.'

It was Geraldine's turn to feel surprised, although she hid her reaction. 'Where were you?'

Rob replied that he had been out with some workmates. They were going to be out late so he had stayed overnight with one of them.

'That's a coincidence,' Ariadne said sharply.

'Not really. We get together every few weeks, usually on a Monday evening, and I stay over and we go to work together in the morning.'

'You just told us you don't drink,' Ariadne pointed out.

Rob looked confused. 'Not like I used to. I might have a pint or two, but I'm careful not to get drunk.'

Geraldine wasn't sure she believed him, but she waited to hear what else he was going to say.

Before Rob could speak, his lawyer interrupted.

'My client has told you where he was. He has nothing more to say.'

Geraldine took down details of the friends Rob claimed to have spent Monday night with.

'Why didn't you mention this the last time you spoke to us?' Geraldine asked.

'I've told you now,' he replied irritably.

'You didn't mention this the first time we spoke to you,' Geraldine repeated.

He shrugged. 'I was in a state. I wasn't thinking. Can I go now?'

'Isn't it a bit unusual to go out on a Monday evening?'

'Not for us. It's a night when we're all free so it works for us. So I wasn't even at home when it all happened.'

Geraldine terminated the interview for the time being while she organised a team to check out his alibi. Once again Rob was going to be left to kick his heels in a cell. He was led away, grumbling irritably that he would lose his job if this carried on for much longer, and muttering about compensation.

The lawyer interrupted his client's muttering. 'Unless you have any evidence to justify detaining my client, you need to release him now.'

'It still seems a bit of a coincidence,' Ariadne said when Rob had been taken back into custody, with the lawyer accompanying him, still protesting. 'Rob's girlfriend having been killed on the one night of the week when he was frequently away from home. Could he have slipped away and deliberately killed her on the Tuesday morning, knowing he had a ready-made alibi?'

'Or perhaps someone else chose to kill her early on a Tuesday, knowing she would be alone,' Geraldine added thoughtfully. 'Rob said he often went out on Monday nights. I wonder who else might have known about that arrangement?'

'But how did the killer know Alice would be out of house that early on that particular morning? Doesn't that suggest it was someone she knew?' Ariadne asked.

'Yes. They could have been there waiting for her on more than one Tuesday morning, before she finally turned up. But Rob said she regularly went out for a run early in the morning, so she might just as feasibly have met her killer by chance while she was out running.'

'Which means it wasn't necessarily someone she knew,' Ariadne said gloomily. 'It could have been a completely random attack and we're back where we started.'

Geraldine shrugged. 'Come on, let's check out this alibi of Rob's.'

21

Just over a week had passed since Alice was murdered, and they were still no closer to finding out who had killed her. Even though Binita was confident they had the right suspect, Rob's alibi might yet be corroborated, so they couldn't afford to overlook other potential culprits while they were checking his story.

It was possible Alice had been killed by a stranger who had come across her by chance on her early morning run and had mugged her, as the media persisted in claiming. Sensational headlines like 'Killer Stalks the Streets' ran in local papers and online news channels, along with the journalists' favourite complaint that the police weren't doing anything. One described police inaction as 'deplorable', while another posed rhetorical questions asking for details of what the police were doing, insisting they were obliged to give taxpayers a full and public account of their actions.

'Sure, why don't we just tell the killer what we're doing?' Sam muttered crossly.

No one took the nonsense in the media seriously, least of all the police who were under instruction to ignore such provocation, however histrionic it might be. Even so, sometimes Geraldine's less experienced colleagues found it galling.

'They should try doing our job,' Sam grumbled. 'Day in day out, following up leads that go nowhere, picking ourselves up and carrying on, while all they do is sit around on their backsides and spin yarns to whip up hysteria. I'd like to see those parasites do some real work for a change.'

Binita was keen that nothing be said that might contradict the story reporters had concocted. It was important the police were careful not to reveal their suspicions. If Alice had indeed been killed by someone she knew, the less the killer knew about the progress of the investigation, the better. As it happened, there were some glaring holes in the popular notion that Alice had been the victim of a random assault. To start with, she had not been robbed, which was enough to make the team question the theory that she had been mugged. It was possible a mugger had been frightened off by a passerby during the attack but, if that was the case, a witness ought to have come forward by now. It was feasible that whoever had disturbed the attacker had not realised what had been happening, or had left the area and forgotten about it, but both of those possibilities seemed unlikely.

In addition to not being robbed, the dead girl had no obvious defence wounds, which suggested she must have either been taken completely by surprise, or else recognised her killer. The investigating officers were split on which theory to believe. But however strongly they argued their case, whether or not the victim had known her killer was a matter of speculation, because so far they had found no evidence to confirm either view. There were a number of possible explanations for the attack. What was lacking was proof to support any of them. The media had for the most part jumped straight to the most sensational assumption they could dream up and run with it, as they usually did. In this instance, they might have drawn the correct conclusion, but they might not have done. All that was certain was that they had come up with a story that was not only plausible but dramatic as well. The public's imagination had been caught, at least for a few days, by the brutal stabbing of an attractive young nurse.

While a team was tasked with questioning local thieves and checking CCTV in the vicinity of the crime scene, Geraldine decided to take a closer look at Alice's history and find out whether there was anyone in her past who might have harboured a grudge against her. That afternoon she set off to question the girl who had been Alice's flatmate before she met Rob to find out whether she could share any useful information about the dead girl. Hayley was renting a room above an antique shop in Fossgate, where she worked as a pastry chef in an upmarket restaurant. Geraldine drove to a car park in the centre of town and walked down to the restaurant. She timed her arrival between lunch and teatime, hoping the restaurant would be fairly empty, but the place was surprisingly busy, even on a weekday in May before the tourist season had started in earnest.

'Have you booked?' a smartly dressed girl on the front desk asked, displaying a smile that looked natural. 'Is it a table for one and are you here for lunch?'

'No, I'm not looking for a table.'

Seeing the girl looking nonplussed, Geraldine explained that she wasn't there as a customer. Showing her identity card, she explained she needed to speak to the pastry chef, Hayley.

'Is she here?'

'I'll go and see.'

A moment later the table hostess returned, accompanied by a girl in a long white apron. Hayley had short auburn hair and a full figure, and she looked about the same age as Alice. She smiled at Geraldine, looking a trifle nervous as members of the public so often did when a police officer turned up asking to speak to them. Geraldine was so used to this reaction she was sometimes slightly suspicious if anyone appeared completely comfortable when speaking to her. More often than not, that was an act put on by people who had something to hide. Geraldine was sufficiently experienced to know how misleading first impressions could be. While there was nothing about Hayley's demeanour to alert suspicion, Geraldine studied her carefully.

'What's this about?' Hayley asked, sounding slightly defensive. 'What's wrong? Has something happened? Shouldn't you be talking to the manager? I just work in the kitchen.'

Geraldine gave a sympathetic smile. 'No, it's you I want to see. I'm here to ask you a few questions about your former flatmate.'

Hayley's expression darkened. 'This is about Alice, isn't it?'

'Is there somewhere we can talk?' Geraldine asked.

The girl hesitated. 'I'm supposed to be working. I can't just leave the ovens. I'm a pastry chef,' she added with a flicker of pride.

'This won't take long,' Geraldine assured her. 'I only need a few minutes of your time, that's all.'

With a quick nod, Hayley spoke to one of the waitresses before leading Geraldine into a small office and carefully wiping her floury fingers on her apron before sitting down.

'I'll tell you what I know, but I don't suppose it will be much help,' she said, with an anxious frown. 'I can't believe what happened to her.' Her voice grew taut with suppressed anger. 'I've been following it on the local news channels. She was mugged, wasn't she? It's on all the local news bulletins and there's a lot about it online, but no one seems to know much. I mean, they're all saying different things. Why haven't you caught him? Some vicious thug stabbed her to death and he's allowed to run around, a free man, and she's dead.' Her voice cracked suddenly and she dropped her face in her hands. 'I'm sorry, I'm sorry,' she said, pulling herself together after sobbing softly for a few seconds. 'Alice was – she was the nicest person you could ever hope to meet. We were friends for a long time. Good friends. And now, thanks to some maniac, she's dead. For no reason. Just some crazy.' She hiccuped. 'You know she was only twenty-one? Twenty-one! She didn't deserve to die like that.' She leaned forward in her chair. 'Did she know what was happening? Did she – did she suffer much? I keep reading about what happened, but there are so many different reports it's difficult to know what to believe. And he's still out there. What's to stop him doing it again?'

Geraldine reassured Hayley as well as she could that her friend's death appeared to have been relatively painless. 'It would have been over very quickly,' she said and Hayley sighed, shuddering. 'I don't think she would have known much about it.'

'I don't understand. Why would anyone do that? To Alice of all people.'

'That's what we intend to find out, and we're hoping you might be able to help us. Think carefully. Can you think of anyone who might have wanted to hurt Alice?'

'Hurt Alice? No, no one. Why would anyone want to do that?'

'What about boyfriends?'

Alice nodded slowly. 'She does have a boyfriend – I should say, she had a boyfriend.' She let out a sob. 'He's called Rob.' She scowled. 'I could be wrong but – no, it doesn't matter.'

'Go on. What were you going to say?'

'It's just that I don't think he was very nice to her.'

Geraldine waited.

'I could be wrong,' Hayley repeated nervously. 'I never even met him.'

'I appreciate you can't be certain, but what impression did Alice give you of him?' Geraldine urged her gently.

'It's just that I think – I think he used to hit her. But why do you want to know about her boyfriend? Wasn't she killed by a mugger? That's what all the papers are saying.'

Geraldine nodded. 'Yes, that certainly seems to be what happened. All the same, we're pursuing every avenue, trying to build up a picture of Alice and her life, while we're working out the sequence of events that led to her death.'

Hayley nodded uncertainly and Geraldine thanked her and left, feeling slightly more optimistic than she had been when she arrived. With any luck, Rob's alibi would fall through, in which case Alice's former flatmate's evidence could prove extremely helpful. On her way back to the police station, Geraldine called Naomi's phone but there was no reply. Disappointed, she headed straight back to the police station. But she couldn't shake off the uneasy feeling that Naomi was concealing something from her.

22

SEVERAL OFFICERS WERE SENT to question the friends Rob claimed to have been with on the Monday evening. Geraldine herself decided to see the man at whose flat Rob had allegedly spent the night. Carl worked at the same building firm as Rob, so she went to look for him at the construction site where he was working. Not much progress was in evidence, despite the signs at the entrance warning visitors of the activity going on behind the fencing. She could hear banging and shouting, and the air was thick with brick dust. As she walked through the gates, the foreman came forward to greet her, waving at her with an irritated frown of recognition.

'Sorry, Ma'am,' he said, striding over to intercept her before she could accost one of his team who was stacking bricks nearby. 'Rob's not here today. I thought he was with you, helping you with your enquiries.' He sounded disgruntled.

Geraldine nodded. 'Yes, you're right, he is, but it's not Rob I've come to see. I'd like to have a few words with Carl Robinson. Is he here today?'

With a sigh of resignation the foreman said he would find Carl and send him over to speak to her. 'You're not going to want to cart him away as well, are you? Only we've got a job to do here and, thanks to you, we're already a man down this morning.'

'I just want a few words with him. It shouldn't take long.'

'You can wait in the office,' the foreman said, scowling at a group of men who had gathered nearby and appeared to be listening. 'What are you lot looking at? What are you being paid for if you haven't got any work to do?'

Geraldine followed the foreman into a prefabricated hut where she took a seat on a rickety chair. A few moments later, a bulky black man entered and introduced himself as Carl.

'How can I help you?' he asked in a deep voice, perching on a chair which creaked under his weight.

'How well do you know Rob Stiller?' Geraldine asked.

Carl told her he had known the suspect for about five years. They worked closely together and socialised as well.

'Did you know Rob's girlfriend?'

'Alice?'

'Yes.'

'I can't say I exactly knew her. I met her once or twice, but only in passing. I was sorry to hear what happened to her.'

'What have you heard?'

Carl looked down and scuffed the dust on the floor with his boot. 'I heard that she was killed by a mugger,' he muttered. 'We were all shocked.'

'Tell me about your Monday evenings.'

'Monday evenings? Oh, you mean the poker game?' His puzzled expression cleared. 'Yeah, the guys come over to my place some Mondays and we play cards. Nothing serious, mind. There are four of us regulars. I mean, it's not like it's big money, nothing like that, just enough to pinch a little, you know. To give the game a bit of an edge.' He gave a faint lopsided smile. 'It's just a few friends getting together every few weeks on an evening when nothing much else is going on. Sometimes only three of us are free,' he added, 'but mostly we're all there. It's just a bit of fun. We're not gambling,' he added, looking faintly perturbed, 'not serious gambling.'

Carl confirmed that he and three friends, including Rob, had played poker the previous Monday evening at his apartment.

One of the four friends, who lived within walking distance, had left around midnight.

'Did he walk home?'

'No, his girlfriend picked him up. She usually does.' He shrugged. 'He likes to go home and it makes no difference to the rest of us. We usually pack up around midnight anyway and I haven't really got space to put everyone up, not without someone sleeping downstairs.'

Rob and the other friend had stayed all night. Carl was adamant Rob had stayed for the night and he and Carl had gone off to work together the following morning, the morning of the murder. Geraldine asked Carl several times if he had been with Rob all the time after midnight until eight on Tuesday morning.

'Yes, like I said. We played cards all evening, went to bed, had breakfast and went in to work together. We were together the whole time. And that's all I can tell you.'

'And you're quite sure Rob didn't go off on his own at any point before you went to work on Tuesday morning?'

Carl was positive. 'Unless he jumped out of a window or was in two places at once.' He gave an uneasy laugh. 'What's this all about? I don't understand. What's he supposed to have done? You can't think—' He broke off, looking perturbed and slightly angry. 'Tell me you don't think he had anything to do with what happened to Alice. You can't be serious. Not Rob. He's a decent bloke. He would never attack a woman.'

There was nothing more to say. Whether or not Rob would attack a woman, his alibi checked out. Not only Carl, but Rob's other two friends also corroborated his alibi. The ring camera on Carl's apartment block confirmed that Rob had not sneaked out of the property while his friends were asleep. Geraldine was convinced Carl was telling her the truth. Even if Rob was deceiving them about the way he behaved towards Alice, it was hard to believe three of his associates would lie to the police to protect him against a charge of murder. While Alice was being killed, Rob had been asleep in Carl's spare room, seven miles away. Disappointed, Geraldine went back to the police station where she found Rob in a cell, seated on the bunk, his fists clenched, his head lowered. He didn't look up when she entered.

'We've spoken to your friends,' she said.

Rob merely grunted, his gaze fixed on the floor.

'They have all corroborated your story,' she said. 'You're free to go. But before you leave, is there anything you can think of that might help us in our investigation into Alice's death?'

Rob looked up with a jolt on hearing his girlfriend's name. 'Alice?' he repeated dully. 'What about her? She's dead, isn't she?'

For an instant, Geraldine wondered whether he was going to break down in tears, but he remained immobile, staring straight ahead with a blank expression.

'We're investigating what happened to her. Rob, listen, this could be important. Can you think of anyone who might have wanted to harm Alice?'

'Harm Alice?' Rob repeated. 'Why would anyone want to harm her?'

'That is what we are hoping to find out,' Geraldine replied grimly.

Their only suspect's innocence was beyond doubt and they had no other leads. Even though she was preoccupied with her frustration about Rob, Geraldine couldn't help noticing that Naomi seemed more than usually distracted. She was used to her young colleague becoming despondent and even irritable when a likely suspect proved to be a dead end. Yet this time, Naomi seemed to be actively avoiding Geraldine, who had the feeling that there was more to her behaviour than understandable exasperation over the case. She kept a close eye on Naomi, surreptitiously, but spotted nothing specifically amiss with her work that she could discuss with her.

At lunchtime, Geraldine invited her young colleague to join her, but Naomi said she wanted to finish a task she was working on. Geraldine and Ariadne went to the canteen together. Ariadne thought Naomi was just feeling fed up with how slowly the investigation was progressing.

'She's experienced enough to cope with setbacks in an investigation,' Geraldine pointed out. 'It's not as if she hasn't worked on murder cases before. Progress is often slow and this isn't the first time we've seemed to be going round in circles getting nowhere.'

'That's true enough,' Ariadne agreed, with a rueful smile.

Naomi left the police station first at the end of the day and, on a whim, Geraldine decided to pay her colleague a surprise visit on her way home. She didn't intend to stay long. She just had a feeling something was wrong and wanted to reassure herself that her colleague was all right. Naomi lived in an apartment in a modern red brick block in Monkgate near Monk Bar in Micklegate. Geraldine had never visited her there before. Leaving her car in a car park across the road from where Naomi lived, she walked a few doors along to her apartment block and rang the bell. To her surprise, a man answered the entry phone. In spite of his gruff voice, she thought he sounded young.

'I've come to see Naomi,' she said, wondering if she could have come to the wrong address, even though the name 'N. Arnold' was clearly printed by the bell. 'Am I in the right place?'

The line crackled and a few seconds later the man hung up without speaking. Suspecting there was a fault with the system, Geraldine rang the bell again. This time, she was pleased to recognise Naomi's voice asking who was there.

'Naomi, it's Geraldine,' she replied. 'Can I come in?'

There was a slight pause as though Naomi was considering the request. 'What do you want?' she asked at last.

She spoke brusquely and Geraldine realised that Naomi must have a boyfriend with her. There was no reason why she shouldn't keep her personal life private, and Geraldine felt embarrassed at having turned up on her doorstep uninvited.

'I was just passing,' she muttered, feeling awkward, 'and I thought I'd call by. It's nothing that can't wait till tomorrow,' she added, in an attempt to make out she had come to talk about work, rather than to pry into Naomi's situation at home.

'You could have phoned,' Naomi snapped. 'I'm sorry, but I'm busy right now,' she added, before she hung up.

There was nothing more to be done, so Geraldine walked slowly back to her car and drove home, puzzled by Naomi's unexpected hostility. Even Tom's obvious exuberance on seeing her failed to lift her spirits. She did her best to hide her dejection but Ian picked up on it almost at once. When he pressed her, she admitted her concerns to him and he listened in silence, until she told him about the man who had answered the bell at Naomi's home. Then Ian whistled.

'So you agree there's something wrong?'

'What's wrong about this is that you've been poking your nose in where it's not wanted,' he replied sternly. 'What Naomi gets up to, and who she chooses to see in her own time and in her own home, is not your business.'

'It is if it's affecting her work,' she protested, although she knew he was right.

'And is it affecting her work?'

'Well, no,' she admitted. 'Not as such. That is, I don't know if it is or not. But she hasn't been herself lately.'

'What's happened? There's something you're not telling me.'

Geraldine shrugged unhappily. 'Nothing's happened, but there's something wrong. I know it. And I don't know what to do.'

'Do you really want my advice?'

She nodded.

'I think you need to stop prying into Naomi's private affairs, if you don't want to fall out with her. Her personal life is not your concern.'

23

MARIA HAD JUST COME home from her morning class and was about to make a start on the never-ending laundry. She could hardly believe how many garments Julia wore in the course of one week, and even the little boy sometimes got through more than two outfits in a day. She changed him out of his uniform into what his mother called his 'play clothes' as soon as they came home from school and then, as often as not, he would go and make himself dirty in the garden or the park and she would have to change him into a clean outfit before his mother came home. She thought it quite ridiculous the way she had to make him look pristine for his parents at his age. But when Maria tried to explain that he liked digging in the earth for worms, Julia wrinkled her nose in disgust and complained that Maria was inculcating bad habits in her young charge. In the end, it was easier to change Jason's clothes and clean his fingernails before his mother came home than try to persuade her employer that it was a normal and healthy pastime for a small child to play in the mud. If she ever had a son, she would take him to the beach and let him run wild on the sand.

As she was carrying a laundry basket down the stairs, the doorbell rang. It was still two hours before she was due to leave to collect Jason from school. Dropping the basket in the hall, she went to the door where she was taken aback to see Rob standing on the doorstep, looking red-faced and sweaty.

'What did you say to the police?' he demanded angrily, without bothering to greet her.

'What do you mean?' she stammered, backing away. 'I not know what you mean.'

'Don't lie to me. You've been talking about me, haven't you? To the police.' He took a step towards her, glaring at her threateningly. 'I don't appreciate being talked about behind my back. If you've got something to say about me, you say it to my face. Got it?'

She nodded, too scared to speak as he pushed his way into the hall.

'I'm going to ask you again. What did you say to the police?'

She wondered whether to risk denying having spoken to the police, but if he knew she was lying, that would only make him angrier. It was possible the police had mentioned they had questioned her. Rob might even have seen her going into the police station.

She shook her head, taking the time to breathe deeply and calm down. 'They ask me about you,' she replied, choosing her words carefully. 'But I tell them I do not see you now. Not any longer.' She spoke boldly, doing her best to hide her fear. 'I don't know what you want with me. I don't know why the police want to speak to me. But I say nothing to them. I say you were my boyfriend but no longer. What you want?' she asked. She dropped her eyes, hoping he would not sense her fear. 'I am busy. I have work I must do before I pick Jason up from school.' Tempted to add that she wanted him to leave, she held back, afraid of provoking his temper. 'I need to do laundry.'

All at once, Rob's shoulders slumped and he leaned against the wall as though he lacked the energy to hold himself upright. He looked curiously deflated. 'Ever since you left me, my life has been a mess,' he admitted. His voice trembled and she thought she saw his eyes glisten with unshed tears.

Forgetting for a moment how aggressive he could be, she felt a surge of pity for him. At one time, she had wanted nothing more than to be his girlfriend and she wondered fleetingly whether she had made a mistake. Perhaps she had been hasty in ending their relationship. Since they had split up, she hadn't managed to find another boyfriend. Now Rob was standing here, close to enough for her to reach out and touch, and he was hinting that he regretted their break-up. They had been happy together once and it seemed to be impossible to find someone else. Her fellow students in her English class were almost all girls. The few men who attended didn't interest her: a Chinese man of indeterminate age who never spoke, a gawky Greek boy who looked as though he still ought to be in school, and a tubby bald Egyptian man who was shorter than her and probably twice her age.

'You should make friends with some of the other girls in your class,' her sister had told her. 'Go out with them and you're bound to meet someone. You need to make an effort. Men won't just fall into your lap.'

But Maria was wary of trusting another stranger. Picking up a man in a bar was how she had met Rob and that hadn't turned out well. The next man she met could be even worse. She had heard terrible stories from some of the other girls in her class. Listening to them, it was easy to believe that all English men were liars and cheats. Several of the girls had been taken in by men who turned out to be married, while other men were only looking for a fling or a one-night stand. Local men seemed to believe that foreign girls were little better than whores.

'You just have to be careful,' her sister had said breezily. But it was easy for her. She had married her childhood sweetheart, a boy she had met at school. Their families were friends. Everything had been so simple for them. When Maria had first met Rob, she had been bowled over by him and convinced that her life would be simple too. Surely it wasn't unrealistic to hope she could find a man who would love her. She gazed at his beautiful eyes with their thick black lashes and had to force herself to remember how he used to hit her. And now his new girlfriend had been murdered violently. It was no good. Just the fact that she had entertained the possibility he might be responsible for another girl's death was enough to persuade her she would never be able to trust him again. Besides, when they had been seeing each other, he had been no fun. All he ever wanted to do was watch television, eat and sleep.

'I will say nothing to the police,' she promised him, uncomfortably aware that she had already told them more than enough to arouse their suspicions. 'Now I must wash the clothes, as it happens.'

She half hoped he would sweep her into his arms and tell her to forget about the washing, promising he would rescue her from her life of drudgery. She could almost hear him telling her she was too precious to be a servant for another woman. At the same time, she was uncomfortably aware that he was in the house and she was potentially at risk. Instead of making a conciliatory gesture, he leaned forward with an ugly expression on his face. Afraid he was going to hit her, she drew back, wishing he hadn't come into the house.

'Shut up about me, you understand? Not another word to anyone, especially not the police.'

She wanted to ask him why he was so afraid of the police. It could only mean he was guilty of something.

'I will be silent,' she promised, aware that he had possibly murdered his girlfriend and she could be next.

Muttering a curse, he turned and strode out of the house. Relieved, she stood in the doorway watching him lope off down the path. She stared at him until he was out of sight, before closing the door. Leaning down, she picked up the laundry basket, ignoring the tears blurring her vision.

'I'm sorry, I'm sorry,' she whispered. She wasn't sure if she was apologising to Rob or to herself. It was over between them and there was no going back. And, she reminded herself, it was possible he had killed his girlfriend. The police seemed to suspect him, and she knew he could be violent. She was definitely better off without him.

She could imagine her mother talking sternly to her. 'He's no good,' she would say. 'You must forget about him and find another man. Come back and meet a man here, at home where Papa and I can meet the family. It will be better for you.'

Miserably she went to put the washing on, before cleaning the kitchen. Tonight, she would go out dancing with some of the girls from her class and forget about Rob.

24

Lauren nodded dumbly, aware that anything she said might be misconstrued. She sometimes thought he deliberately misunderstood her, storing up her words to deploy against her. He would brood on them, launching them at her like missiles at an unspecified future date.

'You said you don't mind if I go out without you,' he reminded her. 'What did you mean by that?' His voice became dangerously quiet. 'What are you thinking of doing while I'm not around?' '

She had been trying to be nice and unselfish, not like some clingy girls who never wanted to let their boyfriends out of their sight. He was always complaining about how their girlfriends and wives kept his mates in chains.

'It's coercive control, that's what it is,' he would fume when one of his friends was unable to go out for a drink. 'He's not been his own man since he shacked up with that sour-faced bitch. The man needs to grow some balls.'

'Well?' he pressed her now, his eyes glittering dangerously. 'You like it when I go out, do you?'

'Of course not,' she muttered. 'That's not what I meant.'

'Why say it then?'

'I never said I like it when you go out,' she protested feebly. 'You know I don't like it when you leave me alone for too long.'

He seemed to amuse himself by turning her own words against her, however unjustly. There wasn't much she could do about it. There was certainly no point in trying to argue with him. He could easily overpower her and the more she tried to resist, the angrier he was likely to become. If she wasn't careful, a trivial disagreement could easily escalate into violence. He didn't often shout at her, and when he did he always apologised and promised her he would never do it again. She believed him because she didn't want to lose him. Despite his impatience with her, she knew she was lucky to be with him. He gave her somewhere safe to live and took her out to eat in nice restaurants. No other man had ever treated her so well. His occasional fit of temper wasn't hard to tolerate, because she knew he never meant to hurt her. Admittedly he completely lost his temper with her sometimes, but only when he felt provoked. He sometimes told her it was her fault for aggravating him and she knew he had a point. It couldn't be easy for him, having to put up with her.

Keeping quiet, she leaned against the wall, feeling its hardness through her thin jumper. The ache of the wall pressing against her back was nothing compared to the pain in her arm. Sliding to the floor, she drew her knees up to her chest and wrapped her arms around them, watching his face redden and preparing herself for the next onslaught.

The girlfriend she used to see had nagged her to leave him, but she couldn't.

'You don't understand,' she had replied.

'Explain it to me then.'

'He can't help it,' Lauren said. 'He has anger issues. He's going to get help.'

'Look at you,' her friend had scoffed. 'Your arm's covered in cigarette burns. He did that to you. How can you put up with the way he treats you?'

But her friend hadn't understood. No one understood what was really going on. She and Danny loved each other with a love so strong nothing could ever come between them. It was a pity about his temper, but apart from his fits of anger, he was as near ideal as a man could be. And anyway, no one was perfect. She certainly wasn't. She was as flawed as it was possible to be. So, far from wanting to leave him, she was devoted to him. Her greatest fear was that he would tire of her. She didn't expect her friend to understand.

'He loves me,' she had insisted, and her friend shook her head and gazed at her sadly.

'If he loved you, he wouldn't hurt you,' she had said.

As she stared at him now, raising his fist and shaking it in her face, she whimpered and remembered what her friend had said. 'If he loved you, he wouldn't hurt you.'

'Well?' he demanded. 'I asked you what you meant by it.'

She shook her head. 'Nothing,' she mumbled. 'I told you, it didn't mean anything. I was trying to be nice, that's all.' She wanted to explain that she had been thinking about his frustration with his mates and their needy girlfriends, and how she didn't want to be like them, but she couldn't find the words.

'Nice? What, like this?' He pointed at her arm before slapping her face.

Her head jolted back at the impact and hit the wall. She let out an involuntary groan.

'I've had it with your bullshit,' he shouted. 'Did you hear me? Stop that snivelling unless you want another slap.'

She scrambled to her feet and fled to the bedroom. Reaching the brittle sanctuary of bed, she crawled under the covers to muffle the sound of her crying and lay there in the semi-darkness, trembling and bracing herself for him to tear the cover off her and start berating her in earnest. But nothing happened. A few seconds later, she heard the door slam, but she didn't dare pull the covers back to see what was happening. In her imagination, she could see him standing beside the bed, hand raised, poised to hit her as soon as she looked out. Still nothing happened. It was hot under the covers and it smelled of sweat and spilt beer. Eventually she pulled the cover back, just a little, so she could peer out and take a gulp of cool air.

There was no sign of Danny. Her legs trembled as she crept into the hall. From the front room came the noise of the television blaring. It sounded like a football game, with a commentator yelling excitedly. She hated the way they shouted into their microphones, but at least Danny might not hear her moving around with all the racket coming from the television. Without thinking where she was going, she slipped on her shoes and went out, shutting the front door softly behind her. It would serve him right when he called her and discovered she wasn't there. She smiled, imagining his surprise. She hoped he would be worried. In her hurry, she had gone out without a coat and she swore under her breath when it began to rain.

Reaching the corner shop, she hesitated before walking past. Her purse was at home in her bag, along with her keys. If Danny were to go out, she would find herself locked out of the apartment. In any case, there was no point in continuing her walk. She had nowhere to go. With a shiver of fear, she remembered that a girl had recently been attacked and murdered on the street, not far away. She would be safer at home.

'Better the devil you know,' she thought grimly.

Looking round, she caught a glimpse of someone flitting into the shop, a raincoat flapping around his legs. It was probably just someone hurrying out of the rain, but she had a horrible feeling she was being followed. She couldn't have explained why she thought that. There was just something about the way the person had darted into the shop as soon as she turned round that had unnerved her. It was raining more heavily now. Shivering, she scurried towards home. Stopping to cross a side road, she glanced over her shoulder and noticed the same figure not far behind her. Before she could make anything out, the stranger spun round and strode rapidly away. Without pausing to see if any cars were coming, she darted over the road and raced back home. As she reached the front door, she glanced around. On the opposite pavement, a hooded figure was standing motionless in the rain.

Danny looked taken aback when he opened the front door to see her dripping and shivering on the doorstep. Hurriedly she explained that she had just gone out for a walk and had been caught in the rain. Danny gaped at her.

'A walk?' he repeated. 'Did you get me some fags?'

She shook her head, trembling now with fear not cold. 'I meant to,' she stammered through chattering teeth, 'but I left my purse at home.'

She was reassured to see that he had recovered from his fit of anger as, instead of yelling at her, he told her to get out of her wet clothes and dry her hair. She ran inside to get changed before going to the living room. As she sat down, the door opened and he entered, carrying a mug.

'Brought you some tea,' he mumbled.

It wasn't exactly an apology, but he was being understanding and she heaved a shaky sigh of relief. He was becoming more tolerant. Warily she took the mug of steaming tea. Her head was pounding where it had hit the wall and her arm was stinging, but other than that she was unhurt. It could have been worse.

'Thank you for the tea,' she said as brightly as she could. It would have been nice to have a biscuit with it, but she didn't want to push her luck. Instead, she repeated that it was a nice cup of tea.

'Tea, eh?' he said cheerily. 'You can't say I don't treat you well.' He laughed and she smiled, because suddenly everything was all right.

'You look after me,' she said softly. 'I don't know what I'd do without you.' She nearly added that she knew he would never hurt her again, but she thought better of mentioning what had happened. It was enough for her to know he loved her.

Gratefully she sipped her tea.

25

THE NEXT MORNING, GERALDINE went into work determined to find a clue to the identity of the killer who was so far proving irritatingly elusive. Her positive mood faltered when Naomi called in sick.

'I knew this wasn't going to be the end of it,' she muttered as she called Naomi's mobile. There was no answer.

'She's probably asleep,' Ariadne suggested, seeing how anxious Geraldine looked. 'That's why she's not answering her phone. Given that she's not well, I expect she's in bed. But there's nothing to worry about. She's obviously okay or she wouldn't have been able to call in to say she was sick.'

'She didn't call me or Binita,' Geraldine replied thoughtfully. 'Isn't that a bit odd?'

Ariadne shook her head. 'What are you talking about? You really don't trust anyone, do you? Not even your own colleagues.'

'It's not a question of trust,' Geraldine replied testily. 'I'm concerned about her, that's all.'

Ignoring Ariadne's protests, she decided to check with the sergeant on the desk, and went down to the entrance hall to speak to him in person. She was pleased to see that Cliff was on duty that morning. He was a cheery character, well suited to meeting and fending off members of the public. He certainly did a better job than some of their colleagues who Geraldine felt were more abrupt than was strictly necessary when dealing with the public. One or two of them seemed to go out of their way to send people away feeling disgruntled, despite their extensive training. The success of most police investigations depended on information from the public who were often more helpful than they realised. Without their support, many cases would probably never have been solved at all. It was counterproductive to alienate people who might help them.

'Top of the morning to you,' Cliff greeted her. 'How can I help you today?'

'I just wanted to ask you about a call you received this morning, from a colleague who called in sick.'

'Are we talking about young Naomi Arnold?'

Geraldine nodded and Cliff consulted his records to check the time the call had been made. He added that Naomi hadn't actually called in herself to say she wouldn't be coming in.

'Who was it then?' Geraldine asked with a touch of impatience and was concerned to learn that a man had phoned in with the message.

'Who was he?' she asked, more abruptly than she had intended.

Cliff shrugged, his smile momentarily slipping. 'Well, he didn't give his name and I didn't ask. He said he had a message from Detective Sergeant Naomi Arnold who was feeling off colour and wouldn't be coming in today. There was nothing unremarkable about it as far as I could tell. Am I missing something here?'

Geraldine frowned. 'No, no, not at all. Did he say what's wrong with her?'

'He just that she was feeling off colour. It didn't sound like anything serious,' he added lightly. 'From what he said, I expect she'll be back tomorrow.'

'Did the caller say that?'

'Well, not in so many words, but that was the impression he gave me. He said she's feeling off colour. Those were his words. "Off colour". That doesn't sound too serious, does it?'

Geraldine called Naomi's mobile again, but there was still no answer. By mid-morning she was feeling increasingly concerned so she took a break and drove to Monkgate, determined to speak to Naomi in person. It was raining as she left the police station and she regretted having left her jacket behind, but decided not to waste time going back for it. She didn't want to be away from her desk for longer than was necessary to put her mind at rest. Once that was done, she would be free to focus on her work without distraction.

She half expected no one to answer when she rang Naomi's bell, but the entry phone crackled almost at once and she heard Naomi's voice enquiring who was calling. With an irrational rush of relief, she announced herself.

'Geraldine? What are you doing here?'

'I just wanted to check that you're all right,' Geraldine said. 'How are you feeling?'

She heard her colleague sigh. 'I suppose you'd better come in, now you're here, but there's no need to worry. Honestly, I'm fine, really. It's good of you to care.'

'Don't be daft.'

'Give me a minute.'

Geraldine had to wait for about five minutes until Naomi buzzed her into the block. The door to the apartment was opened by a man of about twenty. A grey T-shirt hung loosely around his narrow frame. Fair hair hung to his shoulders and combined with his delicate features to make him resemble Naomi. He led Geraldine along a narrow hall with beige walls and brown carpet, and into a small neat living room. It was simply furnished with chairs that looked inexpensive but comfortable, a deep pile light blue carpet and matching curtains. Everything looked fairly new. Naomi was seated on an armchair and didn't look round when they entered the room. Not until she crossed the room to sit on another armchair did Geraldine see Naomi's face full on. Only partially masked by concealer, one of her eyes was bruised and swollen. Geraldine remembered the injuries she had spotted on Naomi's arm. There was no point in ignoring what she was seeing so she decided she might as well tackle it directly.

'What happened to your eye?' she asked bluntly.

Out of the corner of her eye she was aware of the young man staring at her. She glanced at him. Although his expression didn't alter, she registered the tension in his neck and shoulders. Something was definitely wrong. Naomi smiled uneasily at her and explained she had slipped over and hit her face awkwardly on a door jamb. Geraldine didn't query her colleague's story, although she didn't believe her for a second. She was sure Naomi knew she was sceptical but the young man let out a faint sigh of relief and seemed to relax. Geraldine turned her attention to him.

'Aren't you going to introduce me to your friend?' she asked.

Geraldine already suspected Naomi would introduce the man as her brother, Charlie.

'He's staying with me for a while,' Naomi explained. 'Geraldine is a colleague,' she added.

'Hello, Charlie. It's nice to meet you,' Geraldine said politely. She was tempted to add that she had heard a lot about him, but she held back out of concern for Naomi.

Charlie grunted in reply.

In front of Naomi's brother, Geraldine decided it would be sensible to keep quiet about what she was thinking, but there was only really one possible conclusion, given that Naomi's unexplained injuries coincided with the arrival of her brother in York.

'This kept me in bed for a day,' Naomi indicated her black eye, 'but I had it looked at and I'm fine. The headache's gone and my vision isn't affected at all, so I can still drive and I'll be back at work tomorrow.'

'As long as you don't fall over again,' Geraldine said.

Naomi's lips smiled brightly but her uninjured eye glared. 'I'll do my best.'

Geraldine smiled back at her. 'That's great. Meanwhile, I'd better get back right now.'

Clearly trying to hide her relief, Naomi thanked her for coming, but Geraldine could tell she wasn't sincere. It was obvious Geraldine wasn't welcome. She wanted a private word with Naomi, but it was difficult to see how she could manage that with Charlie hovering nearby. She wondered whether to ask if Naomi wanted to see her out, but was afraid that would appear too obvious. As though she had guessed what was in Geraldine's mind, Naomi preempted her by suggesting Charlie would see her out. He looked irritated but he stood up. Trying her best to sound sincere, Geraldine thanked him and reluctantly took her leave.

26

Doing her best not to dwell on her disturbing visit to her colleague, Geraldine's next trip was to the hospital where Alice had worked. After logging her decision and agreeing her day's tasks with the duty sergeant, she set off. It had started raining again, a steady grey drizzle that looked set in for the day. She passed few pedestrians, but the roads were busy, the slow-moving traffic delayed by road works which seemed to be everywhere. One side of the road was cordoned off by red barriers and traffic cones, although no workmen were in evidence. Just as she was beginning to think the temporary traffic lights were stuck, they changed and she moved off, eager to pass through before the lights changed again. She only just managed it. At last she reached the hospital where she had to drive around for a few minutes, searching for a parking space. Only when another car left was she able to park. It had been a frustrating morning so far, and she hadn't yet done anything useful. On the contrary, there was a chance her visit to Naomi might have caused trouble for her colleague. Resisting the impulse to call her, she climbed out of the car and hurried through the rain to the hospital.

She followed signs to the intensive care unit, where everyone in uniform appeared busy, and finally tracked down the senior nurse who ran the team Alice had worked on. The nurse was a broad-shouldered woman with short fair hair and a brisk manner.

'We were all shocked by what happened to Alice,' the nurse said, with a practised air of gravity. A woman accustomed to talking about death, her words were appropriate yet oddly formal given that she was talking about someone she had worked with. 'She was an asset to the team and we hoped she would stay on once she qualified.' She sighed and continued with what sounded like a rehearsed speech. 'Our work isn't always easy, as you can imagine, and it takes a certain kind of person to cope with the patients we see here. It's a tough job and not for everyone, but Alice was a natural. She had a good future ahead of her. It's tragic to lose her like that. Absolutely tragic.' After a few more glowing words about her dead colleague, she ended her eulogy and enquired how she could help the police.

Geraldine explained that she wanted to learn as much as possible about Alice. 'The more we know about her, the clearer a picture we'll be able to build of her. We are keen to learn as much as we can about her life before she died, both at work and beyond. Is there anything you can tell me about her? Did she seem worried at all recently?'

'I'm afraid I'm not really in a position to help you very much. I only encountered her in a work context and she didn't seem any different to usual, as far as I could see. She was working steadily and consistently right until the day she was killed. Like I said, it was a huge shock to us all. I'm sorry I can't be of more help. But you might want to talk to Tess,' she added. 'She and Alice were close. I had the impression they socialised outside work. I'll fetch her for you, if you like.'

Geraldine thanked her for the suggestion and said it would be extremely helpful to speak to Tess.

'Very well. But please, don't keep her long, will you? We're short-staffed enough at the best of times and losing Alice is going to stretch us almost beyond capacity.' She sighed again. 'It's the patients who suffer. It's always the patients who suffer.'

Geraldine assured the senior nurse that she only had a few questions for Alice's friend and would only need to speak to her for a few minutes. Asked to wait, Geraldine found a chair in the corridor and sat down. Nearly ten minutes passed and she was growing impatient. She was considering going to search for Tess, when a tall thin young nurse approached her.

'Are you the police officer who's looking for me?' she asked hurriedly, adding that her name was Tess.

Geraldine confirmed her identity.

'I was told you want to talk to me about something urgent?'

The young woman's drawn face softened when she smiled, but as soon as Geraldine mentioned Alice, her features grew taut and grim. She took a seat next to Geraldine, who asked her how well she had known her colleague.

'Why did it happen?' Tess asked, without answering Geraldine's question. She looked away and wiped her eyes on a tissue. 'You probably think I'm overreacting,' she added, glancing around and looking embarrassed. 'I mean, we work in intensive care here. It's not as if we're not used to losing people. It's an occupational hazard. Patients die all the time. I suppose it's the same for you, investigating fatalities. But it's different when it happens unexpectedly to someone you know, isn't it?'

Tess seemed inclined to talk, so Geraldine nodded and listened without interrupting her.

'Alice was a good person, you know? And she was fit and healthy. It shouldn't have happened to her, not like that. It's different if people are ill. That's tragic too, of course, especially when they're young, but it's just something that happens. It's no one's fault. But what happened to Alice seems so random. So pointless. Just some maniac out on the street and she's dead.' She blew her nose noisily. 'Who was it?' she enquired in a low voice. 'Who killed her? Not that it makes any difference to her, but I'd like to know.'

More than a week had passed since the murder, but the truth was the police had no idea who had killed Alice. They no longer even had a suspect in mind.

'Can you think of anyone who might have wanted to harm your friend?' Geraldine asked quietly.

Tess shook her head. 'No, I can't. I'm sorry. No one who knew Alice could have wanted to hurt her. She was a nurse.' She hesitated before adding miserably, 'So I'm guessing you don't know who did it?'

Geraldine murmured evasively that they were following several leads.

'Following several leads?' Tess shrugged. 'What you mean is, you don't have a clue who did it.' She turned to face Geraldine, her expression fraught. 'You won't let him get away with it, will you? You will find him and make sure he's convicted for murder, won't you? The news is all about how this was a mugging that went wrong, but he can't be allowed to get away with it. Just because it wasn't premeditated doesn't make it less of a murder, does it? He can't get away with manslaughter. Whatever his intention, it was a deliberate attack and he murdered her, even if he hadn't set out to kill her.' She broke off and pressed her tissue to her lips, unable to continue. Geraldine waited and, after a moment, Tess resumed. 'I'm sorry. You must think I'm being vindictive.'

'Not at all. Your friend was killed. It's understandable you'd be upset. It's only natural to want to see her attacker punished.'

'No punishment could ever be enough for a crime like this,' Tess said. 'Although it was probably some loser drugged up to his eyeballs, who didn't know what he was doing.' She shook her head. 'Some sad, dysfunctional, mentally damaged addict. He probably had no idea what was happening or what he was doing or why he was doing it. I don't know if that would make it worse, if there wasn't even any reason for it. I just can't imagine why anyone would do it knowingly.'

Geraldine sighed. The trouble was, the police had no idea why the attack had happened either.

'What can you tell me about Alice's boyfriend?' she asked.

'He's – he was called Rob and she liked him, I mean she really liked him.' She shrugged. 'That's all I know, really. I never met him. Alice kept saying we should go out on a double date, but I'm not seeing anyone, and anyway there never seemed to be time.'

'What about previous boyfriends? Did she ever mention anyone else?'

Tess shook her head. 'She was only interested in this,' she gestured at their surroundings, 'until Rob came along, that is. But she wasn't any less dedicated to our work here,' she added quickly, as though concerned that her comment might seem like a criticism of her dead friend. 'She was so – so... She was such a good person. You will find out what happened, won't you? And let me know?'

'We're doing everything we can,' Geraldine assured her.

'In my job, doing everything we can isn't always enough,' Tess replied in a low voice.

Geraldine didn't answer.

27

THE FOLLOWING MORNING, GERALDINE decided to speak to Alice's parents. A family liaison officer had been assigned to offer them support for a few days, giving her a chance to observe them and question them gently. She had now moved on and they were apparently coping without police support. Geraldine wanted to find out for herself what they thought of Rob. Alice's murder was still very recent, and she appreciated she would need to be gentle in her questioning. Since Tom had come into her life, she had found herself sympathising on a visceral level with bereaved parents. For a few months after his birth, she had found herself overwhelmed by nature programmes where young animals encountered danger. Unused to breaking down in tears for no good reason, she had sometimes been dumbfounded by her emotional state. Aware that hormones commonly had that effect on new mothers, she had never expected to become so sentimental herself. It seemed she had not known her own character as well as she had once thought. She had regained control of her emotions, but was nevertheless aware that she needed to guard against allowing feelings to colour her impressions.

Alice's father was out when Geraldine called and her mother came to the door. She looked like an angular version of Lisa, with her sister's brown eyes and pale complexion, but without the childminder's warmth and vivacity. Her hair was scraped back off her face, making her pointed features appear even sharper than they might otherwise have done.

To be fair to Alice's mother, Geraldine thought she probably seemed listless and careless about her appearance because she was grieving for her dead daughter.

'Do you have any news?' Mrs James enquired dully. 'Not that it's going to make any difference to her, but it would be good to know the monster who killed her is behind bars. They ought to lock him up and throw away the key.'

Geraldine recalled Lisa muttering the same sentiment. Once again, she couldn't disagree.

'I'm afraid there have been no definite developments as yet,' she replied cautiously, hoping Alice's mother would prove less demanding than her aunt. It wasn't really a fair comparison as Lisa knew Geraldine, whereas she was a complete stranger to Mrs James.

'Well, you'd better come in,' Mrs James said. 'Let's get this over with, whatever it is you've come here to say.'

She led Geraldine into a small comfortably furnished living room that was almost cosy. There was something a bit cold about it. Looking around, Geraldine realised there were no photographs, no plants and no ornaments on the mantelpiece. There was nothing personal about the room at all. Despite the comfortable armchairs, it felt like a waiting room. She wondered whether photographs of the family had been removed from the walls, along with knick-knacks and holiday souvenirs from Alice; in short, anything that might remind them of their daughter.

She asked about Rob and learned that Alice's parents had only met him once and they hadn't thought much of him.

'We're not judgemental people,' Mrs James added. 'We wouldn't say no one would be good enough for our daughter, but he wasn't the sort of person we would have wanted to see her with.'

She declined to elaborate, but she had made her feelings clear. It seemed no one in Alice's family had approved of

Rob. That was perhaps interesting, but it didn't mean he had killed her. Murmuring her condolences and concealing her disappointment, Geraldine took her leave.

That afternoon, Lisa called Geraldine to say that Tom was miserable and refused to settle. At first, Lisa said, she had thought it was just his teeth bothering him, but he felt hot and she now thought he had a slight fever. Instantly, Geraldine felt a thrill of alarm. She wanted to cry out that she didn't know what to do, but before she could speak, the childminder carried on.

'That happens quite often when they're teething, but I suggest you take him to the doctor just to have him checked. It's probably nothing serious, but you need to come and collect him. I'm keeping him away from Daisy, just in case he's going down with something, but you appreciate that he can't stay here if there's any question that he might be incubating anything infectious.'

Assuring Lisa that she would be with her very soon, Geraldine informed Binita of her movements and left straight away.

'I'd be more worried if he was lethargic,' Lisa reassured her, as they entered the living room where Tom was lying on the floor, fretting and grumbling and irritably hitting a rattle. As she was driving to the doctor's, her phone rang. She had left a brief message for Ian who was calling to ask what was wrong.

'It's probably just his teeth,' Geraldine said, repeating the reassurances Lisa had given her. 'But I'm taking him to the doctor just to check. He's got a slight fever and it could be the start of something.' She paused, momentarily afraid of breaking down in tears. 'If anything happens to him—' she began and was unable to continue.

They didn't have to wait long. The GP was sympathetic when Geraldine said apologetically that it was probably nothing and she was afraid she was wasting the doctor's time.

'It's always best to be cautious with little ones,' the doctor replied with a reassuring smile. 'We'd rather dismiss a needless concern than overlook a potentially serious issue. And you can't tell us what's wrong, can you?' she added, grinning at Tom who waved his hands and babbled happily.

'The GP thinks it's just his teeth,' she told Ian on the phone as she drove home with Tom in the back of the car. 'He seems fine now.' Geraldine glanced at Tom, who was sleeping peacefully. 'We're on our way home and he's fast asleep. See you later. I'll cook tonight, if you like.'

'Sounds good. What are you going to make?'

'You'll just have to wait and see.'

Her scare about Tom reminded her that Lisa had told her that Alice had been more like a daughter to her than a niece. When she was growing up, Alice had spent more time in Lisa's house than her own. Recalling Lisa's anguish, Geraldine felt more determined than ever to discover the truth about Alice's death.

28

GERALDINE SMILED AT TOM as he lay sleeping in his cot, his tiny lips intermittently puckering and relaxing, his little fingers clutching his blue fleecy coverlet.

'Good morning, little man,' she whispered. 'It's the weekend and we're going out for the day.'

Leaving Tom sleeping, she went to find Ian, who was lying flat on his back in bed with his eyes half open. She called his name softly, and he groaned and swore at her to go away and leave him alone. Surprised by his animosity, she perched on the edge of the bed and took his hand in hers. His skin felt hot. Touching his forehead confirmed that he had a fever.

'You're staying in bed today,' she said firmly.

'That's what I said,' he replied groggily. 'I'm staying in bed. Get up later.'

'There's no way you're getting out of bed today. You're not well.'

He shook his head slowly, grimacing at the effort. 'I'm fine. I just need to sleep. I'm tired. Go away and let me sleep.' He turned on his side, with his back to her. 'I'll get up soon.'

She didn't stop to argue with him. Ignoring Tom, who had woken up and started grizzling, she fetched a packet of paracetamol and a glass of water for Ian.

'Take these,' she said, holding out a couple of pills.

He rolled on to his back and shook his head. 'Nothing. Nothing.' He waved her away.

'It will bring your temperature down,' she insisted. 'Swallow them. Now.'

They had planned a day out together. After another hour in bed Ian felt a lot better and his temperature was back to normal, but he felt too weak to do much and they agreed he should stay at home for the weekend and rest.

'The paracetamol has brought your temperature down, but you're not fit for anything. I need to go and see to Tom and then I'll bring you some tea and porridge in bed. Don't go anywhere and don't try to get up.'

Ian laughed and muttered something about Florence Nightingale.

'As you're staying at home today,' Geraldine said later, after Ian had eaten a light lunch and they had finished their afternoon tea, 'do you mind if I leave Tom with you and pop into work this afternoon? There's something I really want to do today. It won't take long. It's just that Ariadne has the weekend off and this could be my opportunity to have a private word with Naomi.'

'Still harping on about Naomi?' he grumbled.

'I'm just worried that her brother might be abusing her.'

'Geraldine, listen to yourself. You can't suspect every scratch and bruise you see is a sign of physical abuse.'

'I just want to talk to her. What's wrong with that?'

Ian sighed. 'What's wrong is that you're feeling unjustifiably wracked with guilt because you didn't perform a miracle and save Alice, and now you're transferring that feeling of guilt on to other people, trying to save them when they aren't potential victims at all. It's a fantasy, Geraldine. If Naomi was feeling threatened, do you really suppose she wouldn't be able to deal with the situation herself? And wouldn't she come to you for help if she needed it?'

'He's her brother, Ian. Maybe she's protecting him. I'm only going to have a word with her. You can call me if you need me and I'll come straight back.'

Ian sighed. 'We'll be fine. Believe it or not, I can manage without you looking after me. And so can Naomi.'

Ignoring his last comment, Geraldine leaned down to give him a peck on the cheek. 'Keep your phone with you and call me at once if you take a turn for the worse.'

'Don't worry,' he assured her. 'I'm feeling much better.'

Geraldine fiddled about at her desk for a few minutes before inviting Naomi to join her for a drink at the end of the day. At first Naomi was reluctant to agree. As Geraldine was the senior officer, she hoped Naomi would feel obliged to comply when she insisted.

'There's something I want to talk to you about,' Geraldine added.

'Can't it wait? My brother's still here and I said I'd take him out for a Chinese this evening.'

'You can spare half an hour for a quick drink on the way home, surely? There's something I want to talk to you about,' Geraldine repeated. 'It's a bit delicate. I'd rather we discussed it when no one else is around.'

'By no one else you mean Ariadne?'

Geraldine didn't answer and after another moment's hesitation, Naomi finally agreed to accompany her to the pub. Geraldine felt a spasm of guilt as she and Naomi walked out of the police station together, but she didn't feel confident about putting her hands on her colleague while they were at the police station. It was a dodgy thing to do anyway, and she knew she would be overstepping the mark. Somehow she would have to try and make it seem like an accident. They walked the short distance to the pub in uneasy silence.

'So what's this about?' Naomi asked, when they were seated at a table in a corner of the pub. 'What's the big secret?'

'I just want to be sure you're all right,' Geraldine said awkwardly.

Naomi raised her eyebrows, making no attempt to conceal her irritation. 'I've told you I'm fine,' she snapped. 'Why do you keep going on about it? You're worse than my mother. Even she trusts I can look after myself.'

Geraldine shrugged. 'I thought you had something on your mind, that's all.' She hesitated before asking what the time was. As Naomi lifted her arm to look at her watch, Geraldine lunged across the table and seized her by her wrist. 'And then there's this,' she said. Before Naomi could stop her, Geraldine leaned over and pulled Naomi's sleeve back to reveal a row of small bruises on her arm. 'Do you want to tell me what this is all about?'

Naomi snatched her hand away. 'Get off me. What are you doing?' She gazed around the pub in consternation, but no one seemed to have noticed anything unusual in two women sitting together having a quiet drink.

'I'm just worried about you,' Geraldine said. 'That's all. Naomi, you can't keep pretending nothing's wrong.'

Without another word, Naomi gathered up her things and stalked off, her drink untouched. With a sigh, Geraldine followed her out of the pub. She could see Naomi striding swiftly off, already half way to her car. Geraldine would have to run to catch up with her. Although she walked quickly, she reached the police station only in time to see Naomi driving away. Geraldine's attempt to discuss Naomi's situation had failed miserably. Arriving home, she was pleased to find Ian on the floor of the living room, playing happily with Tom, seemingly fully recovered from his bug. He asked whether her trip to the police station had been successful, and whether she was feeling all right. He was worried in case she had caught his illness. She dismissed his questions with a sigh, assuring him she was feeling well, and had not gone back to work for anything important.

Ian looked at her sceptically. 'So you left Tom with me, knowing I wasn't well, for "nothing important" that you really needed to do today?'

With a shrug, she admitted that he was right to suspect she had concealed her true motive for going in. She had wanted to quiz Naomi discreetly away from the police station, when Ariadne wasn't around.

'I get it that you're concerned,' Ian said when she had finished her sorry tale, 'but Naomi's an adult. You shouldn't pry.'

'I'm not prying,' she protested, but she knew he was right.

That evening as they were finishing supper, Geraldine's sister, Celia, phoned for a chat.

'How are you all?'

'We're fine,' Geraldine replied. 'Ian had a bug but he's over it now. It was just a twenty-four hour thing. It was nothing, really.'

'How's Tom?'

'Tom's fine. I think he might have had the bug, or he could have been teething. It's difficult to tell, isn't it?'

'Did the doctor see him?'

'Yes, but by the time I got him there, he had recovered from whatever it was.' She laughed.

'We're really hoping you can come and see us again soon,' Celia said. 'Chloe's desperate to see Tom again.'

'We'll come, as soon as we can,' Geraldine assured her. 'It's a bit busy at work at the moment.'

'At the moment?' Celia echoed, laughing. 'When are you ever not busy at work?'

As Celia chattered, Geraldine recalled how her sister had once admitted feeling too humiliated to admit when her husband had been unfaithful. Wondering what might be going on that Naomi was embarrassed to talk about, she felt more determined than ever to discover the truth and help her young colleague. She had a responsibility to look after her team and if that required her to pry, that was exactly what she would do, whatever Ian said. She had failed to help one young woman who had been at risk from an abuser; she wasn't going to make the same mistake with Naomi.

29

THEY HAD FINISHED THEIR supper and were sitting in the living room. He was flicking through channels on the television, watching the screen, while she sat covertly watching him. As long as she could see only one side of his face, he appeared normal. No, much better than normal, he was perfect. She could never look at him without a flutter of excitement. He was so good-looking, she could sometimes hardly believe he wanted her, out of all the girls he could have as a girlfriend. Fishing through his pockets, Danny searched for a cigarette and swore on finding only an empty packet. He chucked it on the floor, and kicked it aside with a petulant grunt. Announcing his intention of going out to buy more, he heaved himself to his feet. His good eye smiled at her. He tossed his head to flick his fringe off his face and winced with pain at the sudden movement of his head.

'Have a cold beer waiting for me when I get back,' he called out as he went into the hall.

On the doorstep, he paused and swore because it had started raining. He slammed the door and moved back into the hall. Remembering that he had lost his jacket, she darted forward and snatched her raincoat up off the floor.

'I'll go and get your fags,' she offered eagerly, fiddling with the zip on her coat. 'There's no point in you getting drenched out there without a jacket, when I've got a raincoat.'

She didn't add that she thought he ought to sit still and conserve his energy for healing. It would probably only provoke him if she mentioned his black eye. He insisted it was nothing and didn't even hurt. 'You should have seen the other fellow,' he joked, but she didn't find it amusing.

'Let me go,' she repeated, putting on her shoes and smiling at him.

'Absolutely not,' he replied. 'I don't want you getting wet on my behalf.' But he made no move to pass her and reach the front door.

'That's so nice of you.'

'Why wouldn't I want to be nice to my girl?' he asked cheerfully.

'You're always nice to me,' she lied. 'Now, I'm going to get those fags for you, and that's all there is to it. I'd better go now as it's getting late. So you can just go back inside and sit down and put your feet up.' She nearly added that he could shut his eyes, but stopped herself just in time. He might take that the wrong way.

'You're the best,' he said. He reached out and stroked her cheek, and she felt her spirits lift with joy at his tender gesture.

Danny was being so kind to her, going out for his cigarettes was the least she could do, and it made a change for her to boss him around, even if it was only because she was doing what he wanted.

'I'm going, and that's all there is to it,' she repeated happily.

'All right then, if you insist. But don't be too long. I'll be waiting for you here, babes,' he said, leaning forward to kiss her.

She pulled up her hood and set off, smiling to herself. With patience, she was going to persuade Danny that she was the only woman he needed in his life. One woman was enough for any man. She hurried to the corner shop, pleased to run this small errand for him. It made her feel useful. It was dark out, and the rain was heavier now, but she didn't have far to go. Pulling her hood further over her face she scurried on, splashing through puddles, ignoring the cold touch of rain on the back of her neck where the seam in her coat let water in. Checking, she found she had enough cash for three packets of cigarettes. It meant she would be broke, but it would be worth it to see Danny's grateful smile.

The bespectacled little man behind the till barely glanced at her as he slapped three packets of cigarettes on the counter and collected her money with his stubby fingers. She stored the cigarettes carefully in her bag and left, walking home quickly along the dark street. A car swept by, its lights briefly illuminating the deserted street, the noise of its engine muffled by the swishing of its tyres on the wet tarmac. Someone sped past on a bicycle, crouching over the handlebars, a plastic cape flapping behind them. Then there was silence, apart from the distant hum of traffic and the gentle plashing of rain.

Ahead of her, the pavement was empty, but as she approached a broken street lamp she thought she heard footsteps behind her. It was difficult to be certain, with the noise of distant traffic and the sound of the rain all around her. Shivering as more rain found its way through the seam in her coat, she hurried on. Danny had asked her to be quick. Probably he was just impatient for a smoke, but she preferred to think he was eager to see her. She smiled, picturing his reaction when she handed over not one but three packets of cigarettes. He was going to be so pleased with her. She was glad she had found enough money in her purse for so many packets.

At the periphery of her vision, she caught a glimpse of an indistinct outline flitting through the shadows, and the sound of footsteps grew louder. She took no notice and hurried on her way. The footsteps drew closer, muffled by her hood and the hiss of softly falling rain. With a sudden feeling of unease, she quickened her pace. Without warning, strong fingers grasped her arm from behind, squeezing painfully. She barely had time to yelp in alarm before a hand was slapped across her mouth, silencing her cries. She tried to bite her attacker, but a hard leather glove pressed against her chin, clamping her jaws together. She struggled, desperate to hold on to her bag. If her assailant stole it, she would lose Danny's cigarettes and he would punish her failure, even though it was not her fault. She fought back frantically but she had been unprepared, and her attacker was too strong.

The pressure on her mouth was released suddenly.

'I haven't got any money,' she gasped, free of the vicelike grip. 'You can take my bag. Take it or I'll scream.'

Letting go of her arm, her assailant seized her by the throat, crushing her windpipe until she felt dizzy. She should have screamed while she had the chance. Groping blindly, behind her back her fingers encountered only a plastic coat.

The voice came softly. 'I don't want your bag. It's you I want. Don't make a fuss. I have to do this. You know that, don't you? You understand.'

She stiffened at the sound, recognising the voice. Shocked, she tried to plead with her attacker.

'You don't want to do this. You're strangling me. Please, stop.'

As she writhed, the grip on her throat tightened until she could no longer breathe. In the grey moonlight, she saw the flash of a blade. Only then did she truly understand what was happening. Panicking, she felt her legs buckle. Her hood fell back as she sank to the ground, and she was aware of rain pattering on her face, cool and gentle. The pressure on her throat became unbearable, relieved only when a raging pain shot across her chest. Spreading her hands out flat on the grainy pavement, she felt its wet surface scratch her skin as she scrabbled around for a weapon, anything with which to fight back, but her fingers encountered only paving stones and scrubby weeds. In desperation she pulled up a grassy weed and waved it feebly at her attacker.

With a fierce rending, pain sliced through her, setting her chest on fire. A moan gurgled wetly in her throat. She tried to reach out, to plead for help, but it was too late to fend off the darkness. All she wanted was for the agony to end.

30

On Monday morning, Geraldine and her team were summoned to the incident room where the detective chief inspector was waiting for them, looking more than usually solemn. Her hair was tousled, as though she had been running her fingers through it carelessly. Her eyes darted rapidly around the room, seeming to be searching for answers to an unspoken question. Her unusually restless demeanour made Geraldine uncomfortable, as she waited impatiently to hear what her senior officer had to say. Glancing around, Geraldine saw her own unease reflected in the faces of her assembled colleagues. One or two more stoical officers looked relatively cheerful, but most of the team seemed to be waiting anxiously for whatever Binita had to say.

'Are we about to get a bollocking for being so slow to identify Alice's killer?' Naomi muttered.

'It's hardly our fault. We couldn't be doing much more,' Sam Cullen replied in an equally low tone.

'It's only two weeks,' Geraldine added.

'Not even two weeks,' Ariadne said. 'Not until tomorrow.'

If Binita heard their murmuring, she ignored it. 'Early yesterday morning a young woman was found fatally stabbed in Low Ousegate,' she announced.

'Another one?' one of the constables said.

'Why has this come to us?' Geraldine asked, with a sick feeling in her stomach. 'We've already got our hands full with Alice, chasing leads that are going nowhere.'

Ignoring the question, Binita displayed an image of a young woman. 'This victim was stabbed.' She hesitated and looked around with a tense expression. 'It looks as though she may have been killed by the same person as Alice. That's why we've been asked to look into it.'

'*May* have been killed by the same person as Alice?' Naomi repeated irritably. 'What does that mean?'

'Presumably there's some fairly compelling evidence it was the same killer, if we're being asked to investigate both murders,' Geraldine said. 'There must be a reason this one is ours as well.' She wondered what reason Naomi had for sounding so agitated.

'She was stabbed once in the chest,' Binita continued, paying no attention to the interruptions. 'A long blade entered deeply enough to pierce her heart. It was sharp enough to penetrate with one forceful slash. The victim was murdered in the street, but at first sight the incident does not appear to be a mugging. Her bag was found lying on the pavement close to the body, with her purse and keys and three packets of cigarettes in it. The purse was empty. It looks as though she might have gone out to buy cigarettes as there were three packets in her bag, all unopened. She's been identified from her debit card as Lauren Stokes, residing with a boyfriend in Fetter Lane. Her injury looks very similar to Alice's. That's as much as we know so far. This is going to take a lot of work. On the bright side, if the two deaths are connected, it should give us more to look into,' Binita said, attempting to sound positive. Her words were greeted with a general groan. 'More officers have been drafted in to help and we'll be meeting new members of the team this afternoon,' she added. 'So let's get going and make sure all our records are up to date so they can be brought up to speed without any unnecessary faffing around.'

'None of us have been faffing around,' Naomi objected.

'If we'd apprehended Alice's killer straight away, we wouldn't be looking into another girl's death,' a constable muttered, voicing what everyone was thinking.

'It's only two weeks since Alice was killed. We've barely had time to start looking into it,' Geraldine protested mildly.

Binita barked at them that they knew what needed to be done. Reminding them to ignore the hyperbole in the press, she left the room. With two deaths in barely two weeks, the media had gone into a predictable frenzy, with lurid accounts of the two murders, accompanied by familiar reports of police inaction.

'They think we can perform miracles and for some reason choose to sit around doing nothing,' Ariadne said.

'They should try doing our job. There's a lot more to it than sitting on our arses churning out bullshit,' Naomi agreed.

Muttering and grumbling, the team went off to pursue their allocated tasks. The woman who had discovered the body had been too upset to give a coherent statement. According to the constable who had spoken to her, she just kept repeating, 'She was dead. I could see she was dead.'

Several hours having passed, Geraldine drove to the woman's house off Low Ousegate to speak to her at her home, where she would hopefully feel more relaxed than at the police station. It was important to gather as many details as they could about the crime scene as quickly as possible, before the witness started to forget what she had seen, or her memories became confused. As the first person on the scene, she might have spotted something that had escaped the notice of the scene of crime officers, or had disappeared by the time they arrived, perhaps blown away on the wind.

Janet Morley was in her sixties or early seventies, with short brown hair turning grey at her temples. She opened the door and peered out over half-moon glasses. After squinting at Geraldine's identity card, she let her visitor in without a word. To Geraldine's relief, the woman appeared to have recovered from her traumatic experience, at least sufficiently to speak sensibly.

'I'm really sorry about earlier,' Janet said, with a slightly embarrassed smile. 'It was such a shock, I'm afraid I rather went to pieces. She was just lying there on the ground, not moving. She was wet and she wasn't moving. I knew at once she was dead.' She shuddered.

'I'm sorry if this reminds you of something you'd rather forget all about, and I do appreciate your reluctance to dwell on the experience, believe me, but we need to find whoever did this. If there's anything you can remember, anything at all, however trivial it might seem to you, we really would like to hear about it.'

Janet nodded solemnly. 'Yes, of course I understand. What do you want to know?'

Geraldine knew better than to put any ideas into the witness's head by asking leading questions. 'Tell me exactly what you saw. Anything you can remember.'

Now that she was able to relate what had happened, Janet's account was quite lucid. She had crossed Ouse Bridge and reached Low Ousegate when she saw the body lying at the side of the pavement.

'Can you tell me what time it was when you found her?' Geraldine asked.

Janet shook her head. 'I'm afraid I can't say exactly, but it would have been about two or three minutes before I phoned the police. Maybe not as long as that. I made the call as soon as I realised she was dead.' She shuddered again and lowered her gaze.

'I know you've already spoken to my colleague, but I just want to go over this again, now you're not quite so flustered.'

Janet nodded. 'I understand,' she murmured. 'I was in a bit of a state earlier on.'

'You made the call at five to seven in the morning,' Geraldine said quietly. She didn't ask what Janet had been doing out on the street so early, instead letting the question hang in the air between them.

'I know it was early,' Janet said. 'I woke up about half past five and couldn't get back to sleep so I got up to make a cup of tea but I'd run out of milk. There's a Tesco Express round the corner that's open from six so I decided to pop out. I really wish I'd stayed in bed now. I mean, I know it wouldn't have made any difference to that poor girl, but at least I wouldn't have been the one to find her.'

'Why didn't you call us straight away?' Geraldine enquired. 'That's not a criticism,' she added quickly, 'we just want to know what happened when you discovered her. Why did you wait? According to what you just told me, it might have been two or three minutes before you called for an ambulance.'

'Well,' Janet hesitated. 'I called as soon as I could, as soon as I recovered from the shock. I think I panicked for a moment. It's not what you expect to see when you're going out to buy milk. I think I just stood there for a moment, looking around, hoping someone else would come along to help.'

'So then you phoned the emergency services?' Geraldine prompted her.

Janet nodded. 'I asked for an ambulance as well as the police, although I knew she must be dead. She was just lying there on the wet ground.' She frowned. 'Who was she? What happened to her?'

'Did you see anyone else nearby?' Geraldine enquired, ignoring Janet's questions.

Janet shook her head. 'You mean an evil-looking villain wielding a knife? No, no one like that. No one at all, actually.'

'Did you notice anything unusual?'

'Apart from a dead body on the pavement? No, nothing.'

Exhorting Janet to contact her if she remembered anything else, however seemingly irrelevant, Geraldine thanked her and took her leave.

'Do you think it's safe on the streets?' Janet asked anxiously as she opened her front door for Geraldine to go. 'The papers are saying all kinds of things, and now this is the second woman who's been murdered. Is it true what they're saying, that there's a serial killer on the loose, hunting for his next victim?'

'The papers like to exaggerate and catastrophise,' Geraldine replied evasively.

'How can you catastrophise murder?' Janet retorted a trifle sharply.

She was right, Geraldine thought, as she reached her car. Murder was by definition so terrible, it should be impossible to exaggerate its horror. Only people who dealt routinely with murder could come up with the idea that it might be overhyped. Driving away, she wondered if she had become so accustomed to investigating murders that she had become inured to their true and devastating personal significance.

31

'I REALLY HATE TO say this to you,' Jonah said to Geraldine when she walked into the mortuary and greeted him, 'but I was hoping I wouldn't be seeing you again so soon. Much as your presence lights up this wretched place, I would be lying if I said you were a welcome sight.'

'I assure you the feeling's mutual,' she replied. 'I don't want to come here any more than you want to see me here. As much as I enjoy your company, let's just say this isn't exactly my favourite place to visit.'

'If it's not the place that keeps you coming back here, then it must be me,' Jonah cried out with a theatrical flourish of a bloody glove. 'We both know we can't hide our feelings forever. But we can't go on meeting like this. What if my wife finds out? You have no idea what that woman is capable of. I wouldn't want to end up here, at the other end of an autopsy, with a cleaver stuck in my head.'

Geraldine laughed. 'You forget I've met your wife,' she said. Jonah's wife had arrived to pick him up one day when his car had broken down. 'She certainly struck me as violent. Quite the thug,' she added, recalling a gentle and retiring woman with a shy smile. Jonah nodded. 'She assures me that's how she survives caring for geriatric patients.'

'Well, you can tell her she has nothing to worry about. It's not you I've come to see, it's her,' she replied, laughing at him before gesturing at the corpse lying between them on a slab. 'Her name's Lauren Stokes. She was twenty-four years old.

What can you tell me about the cause of death and, I hope, about her killer?'

She looked at Jonah gravely. He was no longer smiling.

He heaved a loud sigh. 'At the risk of sounding repetitive, this poor girl was stabbed in the heart with a long blade that had been recently sharpened.' He looked up, his eyes troubled. 'I'm afraid it's looking like exactly the same MO as Alice. Not only that, but it looks as if the same weapon could have been used in both attacks, or at least two blades that have very similar dimensions. Once again, there are no defence wounds, which is going to make your job more difficult. We've scraped under her fingernails and you'll know straight away if we find anyone else's skin cells or any other traces of DNA on her, but there's nothing so far.'

'The medical officer at the scene figured time of death was between nine in the evening and midnight on Saturday, so was she drunk or high?'

Jonah shook his head. 'She had a relatively insignificant amount of alcohol in her blood, and she wasn't intoxicated or otherwise mentally incapacitated as far as we can tell. The tox report isn't back so the presence of a drug we haven't picked up on yet remains a possibility. Of course, we'll let you know if we find anything. But—' He broke off with a helpless shrug. 'I'm sure you've searched the area for the murder weapon but unless it's been found near the body, I'm guessing you'd be lucky to find it now.'

'We'd better be lucky then,' Geraldine replied grimly. 'Is there anything else?'

'Oh yes,' Jonah said. 'There is something else that might be of interest to you.'

Raising one of the dead girl's arms, he indicated a number of small round red blotches, some fairly bright, others barely visible, on the underside of the dead woman's upper arm.

'And here, and here,' he added, indicating similar marks

on both the inner thighs. Seeing Geraldine's puzzled frown, he went on. 'These are cigarette burns, inflicted over quite a protracted period of time.'

Carefully he turned the girl on her side and pointed to series of marks and fading scars on her lower back.

'Evidence of deliberate ill treatment,' he said. 'There's nothing that would be visible when she was dressed.'

'So are you saying there's evidence of sustained injury inflicted before she was killed?' Geraldine asked.

'Yes, inflicted on several occasions, possibly as recently as a few months before she died. And there's this.' He pointed out a few very faint small grey smudges on the victim's shoulder and side. 'From the spacing and dimensions, these could be marks left by fingers. It's hard to see how else they could have been made.'

Geraldine studied three small grey blotches on Lauren's arm, and stifled a sigh as Jason gently laid the body on her back. Lauren was handled more gently now she was dead than she had been in life.

'Poor girl,' Geraldine murmured, more to herself than to the pathologist who nodded, staring sadly at the dead girl.

'Also this,' he went on, indicating a sizeable bruise on her shin. 'She could have knocked herself there, but these ones look as though she'd been hit before she died.' He indicated a couple of large discoloured areas on her buttocks.

They discussed the chances of Alice and Lauren having been stabbed by the same killer. The only other possibility seemed to be if the second attack had been carried out by a copycat killer. Silently cursing news-hungry reporters, Geraldine tried to remember what details of Alice's death had been reported in the media. Meanwhile, her colleagues were busy hunting for any connection between Alice and Lauren. If they had both encountered, and rejected, a man with a history of violence towards women, that might provide the police with a strong lead. While such conjecture was unavoidable, it was never going to lead to anything conclusive. They had to work from evidence, not speculation, and it was probably going to take some time. Unlike the challenges faced by fictional detectives on the television, real-life murder investigations were not always easy to resolve.

'Is there anything you can see that might possibly link these two recent victims?' Geraldine asked. 'I mean, we're looking into any connection between them while they were alive, but is there anything about the nature of these two attacks that might help us?'

Jonah looked at her shrewdly. 'You're asking me to confirm whether or not this was the same killer, aren't you?' he said.

Geraldine didn't answer straight away, and Jonah stared at the dead body in silence. 'Well?' she prompted him at last. 'What do you think? Tell me your gut instinct, off the record. Are we looking for one killer here, or two?' She didn't finish the thought aloud, but they both knew where it was heading. Should they be fearing, or even expecting, another attack?

'If this wasn't the same killer in both cases, I'd be surprised,' Jonah replied. 'This is nothing more than an educated guess, so don't quote me, but I'm fairly certain the same knife was used in both attacks. If it wasn't the same knife, it was two that matched in size exactly.'

The discussion continued at a briefing back at the police station.

'Maybe a certain style of knife was aggressively marketed shortly before Alice and Lauren were killed, in which case it's plausible two killers independently bought the same knife,' Geraldine suggested. 'But it would be a coincidence and I don't think it's likely.'

Since the second killing, reporters on local television had been excitedly running the story throughout the day, and now the national press had become interested.

'And that's not counting the posts on social media.' Binita fumed.

Geraldine scanned a series of reports online. Most were melodramatic and generic, but one account in particular was disturbingly precise about the time and nature of Lauren's death. A little digging revealed the author of the post to be a nephew of Janet Morley. She must have given him a few details that had not been in the public domain but were now, thanks to her indiscretion. There was no such detail available about Alice's death which had not attracted as much attention, being the first. Geraldine shuddered to think of the reaction that might erupt were there to be a third such murder on the streets of York. Before that was even a possibility, the killer had to be stopped. But they were no closer to making an arrest.

32

The investigating team had established that a corner shop close to Lauren's house sold cigarettes. It closed at nine on Saturdays. That suggested the murder might have occurred shortly after nine, assuming Lauren had gone straight home after going to the shop, which might not have been the case. They had been unable to trace any of Lauren's family members, although there was mention on her social media of her having a toxic mother with whom she had fallen out. She claimed to be in a relationship with a man called Danny. This time some ferreting around produced the name Danny Brent, a man who turned out to live at the same address as the victim. Naomi had been researching Danny's history. She told them he had been involved in a number of minor skirmishes, several of which had resulted in cautions for assault and brawling, but he had never been accused of anything that led to a custodial sentence. The most serious punishment he had attracted was six months community service as a teenager.

'It was pub scraps. Nothing criminal, but he's definitely no stranger to violent affray,' she added. 'He seems to have learned his lesson after his community service, or at least learned to keep himself out of trouble. He attended a series of AA meetings in his twenties, but that didn't last long.'

'Was he always fighting with other men?' Geraldine asked thoughtfully.

'Yes,' Naomi replied. She spoke confidently, but avoided meeting Geraldine's eye. 'The scraps were always with other men and always over some petty provocation. From witness reports, and what we've managed to gather from our enquiries, it was mostly macho posturing. "You looking at me?" kind of arguments. One man he fought with accused him of looking at his girlfriend, or it could have been the other way round. It was that kind of spontaneous provocation when he was drunk. Nothing more significant than that. But from the frequency of these incidents, it seems he either enjoyed fighting, or had serious anger issues.'

'Or both,' Ariadne pointed out. 'Is there any evidence he ever abused his girlfriends?'

'No, but he could certainly be violent,' Naomi replied.

'These brawls and scraps,' Geraldine said, 'they were when he was a teenager?'

'Yes.'

'Is there any record of any violent encounters more recently?'

'No.'

'And there were no weapons involved?'

'Did he ever use a knife?' Binita added, following Geraldine's train of thought.

'No, there's no evidence of that. And no reports of him ever using a knife,' Naomi replied. 'The general consensus seems to be that he lost his temper easily and was involved in fist fights and general drunken brawling. All we know is that he was in fights with other men when he was a teenager, when he'd had too much to drink, but he never used a knife and so far as we know was never violent towards women. I'm not sure this is painting a picture of a likely suspect here.'

'He was living with the victim,' Geraldine pointed out.

'And the post mortem identified signs of physical abuse on the victim, inflicted before she was killed.'

They all agreed that certainly made him a person of interest. Binita made it clear that questioning him was a priority. Geraldine took a colleague with her when she went to find him the next day. Sam Cullen was a relatively new recruit who had recently transferred from uniform to detective work. Despite his lack of experience, he had proved himself sensible and resourceful on several occasions when he had worked with Geraldine, and she appreciated his enthusiasm. With his blond hair and easy-going manner, he reminded her of Ian when she had first met him. Ruefully, she admitted to Ariadne that Sam made her feel old.

Danny wasn't answering his phone and the manager at the betting shop where he worked told them he hadn't come into work that day, so they drove straight to the house in Fetter Lane where Lauren had lived with him. They parked a few houses along from the slightly run-down property where Danny was now living alone. The paintwork on the window frames was flaking and the front door looked shabby. Above them, the sky was unremittingly grey; rain had been threatening all morning but had not yet begun and the street was deserted. Everything around them seemed to be on hold, waiting for something to happen.

As though in tune with the stagnant atmosphere of the street, no one came to the door when Sam rang the bell. They drove into town and parked near the betting shop where Danny worked in case he had now turned up. There were already a few people in there, watching the screens and shuffling papers. No one was talking and no one looked up when they entered. Geraldine went straight to the counter and asked quietly for the manager. The gawky young man behind the counter asked if there was a problem. Having introduced herself and assured him there was no trouble in store for the betting shop, Geraldine repeated her request to speak to the manager. With a worried frown, the young man scuttled off and returned with an innocuous-looking middle-aged man in black-framed spectacles who looked like a minor civil servant or a bank teller.

He gave Geraldine a wary glance. 'Who's asking for the manager?'

When she introduced herself, he straightened up and flicked an invisible speck from his shoulder. Instructing his colleague to carry on, he led Geraldine into a stuffy room at the back of the shop. She followed, nodding at Sam to wait in the betting shop in case Danny appeared. The office was a cramped space with a few battered filing cabinets, a small scratched wooden desk and one upright wooden chair.

'I thought Danny would get himself in trouble sooner or later,' the manager said, as he perched on a stack of boxes and gestured towards the one chair behind the desk.

She sat down and enquired what he meant by that.

'Nothing illegal or he wouldn't be working here,' the manager replied quickly. 'He's a good lad, but—' He broke off and heaved a sigh.

'What kind of trouble are you talking about?' she repeated.

'It's just that he gets himself into fights, that's all,' the manager replied cautiously. 'He came in with a black eye recently and we've seen him come into work with a split lip, bruised jaw, you name it. What I mean to say is, he gets a few knocks, but he always jokes that we should see the other fellow. He wouldn't have lasted long in most jobs but here, well, no one here minds here, so it isn't a problem. It doesn't do any harm, to be honest, to have someone working here who looks like he can handle himself. Not that we ever have any bother here, but you never know.'

'Does he often get in trouble?' Geraldine asked.

The manager shook his head. 'He's not a bad lad. When all's said and done, he's decent and reliable, when he's here. When he's sober. He just can't hold his drink, that's all. What's he done now? He hasn't gone and killed someone, has he?'

'What makes you say that?'

'Well, it must be pretty serious this time, if you're after him.'

'What has he told you about the fights he's been in?'

'Nothing. He never tells me anything and it's not my business. I don't like to pry.'

'He must have said something.'

'Pub brawls, that's all he says. Some blokes can't hold their booze and Danny's one of them. But if you're looking to talk to him, I'm afraid I can't help you. He never turned up for work today. And before you ask me, I've no idea where he is. I can supply you with his address, but I'm guessing you already have that?' He paused to shake his head. 'Whatever he's done, it's the drink. I'm sure he never meant to cause any trouble. I wouldn't have had him working here if I thought he was untrustworthy. He's a decent guy. I can vouch for that. One of the best we've had here.'

Something about what the manager said didn't seem to add up, and Geraldine wondered whether he was deliberately lying to her.

33

Having drawn a blank at the betting shop, they returned to Fetter Lane. While they were waiting, Geraldine rang the bell at the neighbour's on one side and Sam tried on the other side. An old woman answered the door when Geraldine rang.

'Yes?' the old lady asked. 'Can I help you? You'll have to speak up because I'm a bit deaf.'

'I'm looking for Daniel Brent,' Geraldine said loudly.

'I'm sorry? What was that?'

Geraldine raised her voice even more. 'We're looking for Daniel Brent. He lives next door.'

'I'm afraid I don't know who lives next door.'

The neighbour shut her door. No one answered when Sam rang the bell at the house on the other side. Geraldine tried shouting through Danny's letterbox.

'Danny, if you're in there, you might as well come out now, because we're not going anywhere.'

They continued knocking and shouting for a few minutes. Eventually, just as they were about to give up, the door opened to reveal a slender young man slouching against the wall in a narrow hall. With a little care he could have been very attractive. Mirrored sunglasses added an air of glamour to his appearance, but he was unshaven, his bare feet looked dirty and his crumpled sweatshirt was inside out. Geraldine noticed an unpleasant odour as she stepped forward to address him.

'Are you Daniel Brent?'

'Danny,' he replied gruffly. 'It's Danny.'

His cheeks looked flushed and Geraldine wondered if he had been crying. In silence she held out her identity card and he leaned forward, apparently studying it.

'What do you want?' he asked, straightening up. He might have glanced at Sam, sizing him up, but it was difficult to tell with his eyes hidden behind dark glasses. 'I've already spoken to one of your colleagues and I've got nothing else to say to you. Nothing at all. Can't you leave me alone?'

'I'm afraid we have a few more questions we'd like to ask you, so I'm going to have to ask you to accompany me to the police station. Right now,' she added as he began to close the door.

'It'll have to wait. I'm not feeling well,' Danny muttered.

'My boss said right now,' Sam told him, putting one foot against the door to hold it open.

'Do you like being told what to do by a woman?' Danny sneered.

Ignoring the pathetic jibe, Sam stepped over the threshold and took Danny carefully by the arm to escort him to the waiting police car. Grumbling that he had to get his keys and shoes, Danny pulled away. Sam accompanied him into the house. Geraldine waited impatiently and after a few moments the two men reappeared and they set off, with Danny complaining vociferously about police harassment of a grieving man. He continued complaining all the way to the police station, while Geraldine and Sam listened without responding. When they were finally seated in an interview room, Geraldine asked Danny to remove his sunglasses. He refused. She repeated her request more firmly and he asked, somewhat belligerently, whether he needed a lawyer.

Geraldine inclined her head. 'That is your right,' she said noncommittally.

Leaving Danny with a uniformed constable, she explained to Sam that she was hoping the enforced waiting might rattle Danny. In any case, as a suspect he was entitled to representation. While they were waiting for the duty brief to arrive, she went on, it also gave her colleagues time to dig further into Danny's relationships and investigate contacts of his friends on social media. All they needed was one person linking Danny and Alice, however tenuously, and the net would begin to close around him. It would take only one party where they might have been introduced, one holiday where they could have encountered one another, one friend of a friend who might have introduced them, and his defence would begin to unravel. But so far they had not come across any connection that might prove they had known one another, or even met.

'Why not just ask him?' Sam wanted to know. 'They could easily have met without there being any record of it online.'

'In which case he could easily deny having known her. And it never does any harm to surprise suspects. Disturb their complacency and they're more likely to let something slip, however careful they are. Given time and opportunity, most people end up incriminating themselves.'

'So your plan is to let him do our job for us?' Sam grinned.

'That's what we're hoping.' She smiled.

An hour later they were seated in an interview room, facing Danny and the lawyer. Geraldine had given Sam clear instructions to watch the suspect closely and listen carefully without speaking.

'Wouldn't you be better off with Ariadne or Naomi, or someone else more experienced than me?' Sam had asked. 'I'm not going to be any use to you in there, am I?'

'You're there to learn. How else are you going to gain experience?'

Danny reluctantly accepted that he couldn't keep his sunglasses on indefinitely and he removed them to reveal he was sporting a black eye. Sam let out a low whistle. Geraldine didn't react but she made a mental note to reprimand her young colleague after the interview. It would be a useful lesson for him. He had to learn to remain impassive regardless of what came up.

'Perhaps you'd like to begin by telling us how you got that injury,' she said pleasantly. 'For the benefit of the tape, Daniel is going to give us an account of how he got his black eye.'

The suspect mumbled about his bruise being none of her business. 'And it's Danny,' he added sullenly. 'My name's Danny.'

Geraldine suppressed a smile. If she could rile him, he might blunder. But the lawyer was on to her straight away and leapt in to preempt any further subtle needling of his client who, he insisted, had nothing to hide.

'He was involved in an unfortunate incident in a pub last Wednesday evening,' he piped up quickly, in a voice devoid of expression.

Geraldine refrained from pointing out that Danny's girlfriend had been killed three nights later. 'He must have been upset and in pain,' she said instead, 'and easily provoked. That's not a good idea, for a man prone to violence.'

Danny began to remonstrate, but the lawyer raised a hand and he fell silent, biting his lip and glowering. 'My client refutes the accusation that he is a violent man,' he said smoothly. 'He was the victim in this altercation, assaulted by a complete stranger with no provocation from my client.'

Geraldine made a show of glancing down at her screen. 'In your statement, you claimed you were involved in a fight in a pub in Micklegate on Wednesday evening.'

Danny shrugged.

Without a pause, Geraldine asked Danny how he knew Alice James.

'Alice James? Alice James?' Danny repeated. 'That name rings a bell. Wait a minute,' he cried out suddenly, his eyes widening in alarm, 'isn't that the name of the girl that was stabbed? It's all over the news. And before you ask me, I didn't know her, I never met her. I never heard her name until I read about her in the papers. I'm guessing you think there's a link between what happened to her and what happened to Lauren?' When Geraldine didn't respond he went on to insist that what happened to Lauren had nothing to do with him. 'I wasn't even there. I keep telling you, I was at home.'

'Where were you early Tuesday morning two weeks ago?' Geraldine asked abruptly.

Danny glanced at his lawyer who shook his head slightly, murmuring a few words under his breath.

'No comment,' Danny said uncertainly, and the lawyer nodded, looking relieved.

'Is there a reason why you are unwilling to help us?' Geraldine enquired mildly. 'It was a simple question. Where were you before you went to work on Tuesday morning two weeks ago?'

Danny hesitated and leaned across to whisper to his lawyer who asked for a break so he could confer with his client. At her side, Geraldine heard Sam let out an impatient sigh, but she had no grounds for refusing the request. Sam scowled as they left the interview room, his petulant expression making him look very young. For a moment, Geraldine had forgotten how inexperienced he was.

'If only we'd spoken to him before that bloody lawyer turned up, he might not have had his story prepared about his black eye. We could have had him right where we wanted him. But now we've lost that opportunity.'

'Let's wait and see what happens next,' Geraldine replied. 'And learn to control your emotions if you want to keep your job. You were out of order reacting the way you did when Danny removed his sunglasses.

Sam drew in a deep breath and nodded. 'I'll be more careful. It was just a bit of a surprise.'

'You need to keep your feelings to yourself when you're talking to a suspect.'

He nodded and promised he would control himself in future. She wondered if he would be able to keep his word and smiled sympathetically. Sometimes keeping feelings in check was one of the hardest parts of the job.

'Tuesday two weeks ago?' Danny echoed, when they reconvened. 'We were away.'

'Away?' Geraldine echoed, with a faint sinking feeling. She glanced at Sam whose face was an impenetrable mask.

Danny nodded. 'We had a few days in Scarborough. A holiday.' His face contorted with grief and for a moment Geraldine thought he might burst into tears. 'It was a holiday, just the two of us. We went to Scarborough for a holiday. She'd never been there before. We were there Sunday to Friday and – and we had some good weather. We didn't know it would be the last—' He broke off and dropped his head in his hands.

'Where did you stay?' Sam asked, his voice expressionless.

Somehow Sam's lack of sympathy appeared to galvanise Danny, who looked up. His eyelashes were dry and he looked composed. He gave them the name of a B&B in Scarborough, seemingly keen to share the information.

'Tell us again where you were last Saturday,' Geraldine said, hoping Danny's emotional state might prompt him to make a blunder.

'My client has already made his statement,' the lawyer intervened. 'He was at home, waiting for his girlfriend to return from the shops with his cigarettes.'

'I should have gone myself,' Danny muttered.

'Why didn't you?' Geraldine asked.

He shrugged miserably. 'She offered to go. She wanted me to rest, because of this.' He indicated his swollen eye. 'I was in pain.' He lowered his head and was silent, lost in thought.

Geraldine waited.

'I loved her,' he murmured at last.

'Crime of passion, was it?' Sam asked flatly, as though to demonstrate how emotionless he could be.

Danny shook his head. 'I don't know. I wasn't there.'

34

The interview over, Sam repeated his complaint that the lawyer had interfered with their questioning of the suspect.

Geraldine nodded thoughtfully. 'So you're thinking we might have caught him at a disadvantage and forced a confession out of him if the lawyer hadn't been there to stop him talking.'

'You've got to admit it's possible,' he replied. 'He could have been handed to us on a plate. It was a good plan, but we wasted the opportunity to catch him out when he was on his own and vulnerable.'

'It's also possible waiting for the brief could have bought us enough time to find a connection between Danny and Alice. A man prone to physical violence who's connected to both victims would have been easier to rattle. On balance, I thought that would be a useful pressure point for us to use. Whatever story he was planning to concoct to explain away his black eye, he could do that for himself. Even a lawyer would struggle to argue that away. But if we could have hit him with his connection to both victims, he would have found it difficult to weasel his way out, lawyer or no lawyer. That was the approach I chose to adopt.'

Sam frowned. 'It didn't work, did it? Anyway, I just think my approach would have been better, that's all.'

'You were interested in getting him flustered. So am I. A flustered man is more likely to cave in. I agree, my approach was a gamble, just as it would have been a gamble to try and pressure him about the fight without allowing him to have a lawyer present, but we were right to avoid any possibility of a complaint about mishandling an interrogation. We need to be careful to work by the book. In any case, as soon as he felt worried, he would have demanded a lawyer be present anyway. There's no guarantee anything we try will work. We just have to choose our strategies with care. It just didn't work, that's all.'

'And you still think it was the best idea? Without even listening to my suggestion?'

'Sam, I'm not getting into the game of competing with colleagues over who has the best idea. We work as a team. What works, works. What doesn't work, doesn't work. But we're in this together. If you're not going to be a team player, you're not going to stay in this job for long.'

Sam looked genuinely shaken by what she had said. Clearly chastened, he hurried to apologise for having appeared insubordinate and promised it wouldn't happen again.

'You're the boss,' he said.

'Yes, and please don't forget that again,' Geraldine said severely. 'But I think I owe you an apology too,' she added, seeing how crestfallen he looked. 'I'm sorry if I made you think for one moment that your ideas aren't valued. Our ideas are what make us successful. So don't stop thinking about what might be the best thing to do and don't stop sharing your thoughts. I'm always ready to listen to you. I want you to know that. Now, we've got lots to do. We need to see if that story about a pub fight checks out and find out whether Danny really was in Scarborough when Alice was killed. '

They were pinning their hopes on finding no evidence to substantiate Danny's explanation of his black eye and no proof that Danny had been away from York when Alice was attacked. In the meantime, Danny was once again locked in a cell awaiting the results of further enquiries. An officer in Scarborough was despatched to the B&B to question the landlady. It didn't take long to establish that Danny and Lauren had stayed there during the week of the first murder. They had gone out to eat on Monday evening but had returned to the B&B at ten, and as far as the landlady knew they had not gone out again before breakfast at eight on Tuesday morning. She had a ring camera on the outside of her property which confirmed that no one had left the building between eleven on Monday evening and seven thirty on Tuesday morning, and Danny had not gone out until after ten.

Although no one could vouch for Danny's whereabouts at the time of Lauren's murder, he had an alibi for the Tuesday morning when Alice had been attacked. Geraldine reviewed the two post mortem reports, trying to establish to her own satisfaction that both women had been definitely been attacked by the same killer. It seemed fairly certain they were looking for just one killer, even though the newspapers had started ranting about a copycat killer.

'How many more women are going to suffer random violent attacks on the street?' one reporter asked in a histrionic article.

Media attention was something else Geraldine was careful to discuss with Sam, who was not used to coping with this kind of pressure. She assured him it was common for journalists to exaggerate and misrepresent the truth, and even to lie to the public about a crime they were reporting. In the meantime, they needed to follow up Danny's claim that he had received his black eye on Wednesday evening in a pub brawl and not in the course of a fight with Lauren early on Saturday. As soon as the pub in Micklegate Danny had mentioned opened its doors, Geraldine and Sam walked in. The interior was run-down yet not unpleasant. In some ways, it felt more welcoming than many refurbished bars Geraldine had visited. They walked up to the bar and asked for the manager. The girl behind the bar smiled and enquired if she could help.

'I'm afraid I would like to speak to the manager,' Geraldine said.

The girl told them the manager wasn't in but would be arriving later.

'Perhaps you could help us,' Sam said, before Geraldine had time to introduce herself.

He grinned at the girl behind the bar and she smiled back. Geraldine kept quiet, watching. Sam told her his first name, without explaining who they were or why they were there. The barmaid leaned against the bar and told him her name was Shelley.

'Shelley,' he repeated, still smiling at her. 'Nice name.'

Geraldine looked down, hiding a smile of her own at Sam's blatant attempt to charm the girl with a friendly approach.

'The thing is,' Sam went on, lowering his voice confidentially, 'Someone told us there was a bit of a ruck here the other night.' He paused. 'Wednesday night. Were you here then?'

Shelley nodded and straightened up, suddenly wary. 'I was working on Wednesday,' she replied, 'but who are you? Why do you want to know?'

Sam sighed. For a worrying moment, Geraldine was afraid he was going to invent an unnecessary tale about being a friend of Danny's, but with a glance at Geraldine he pulled out his identity card.

'We just want to find out what happened, that's all. Did you see the fight?'

Shelley hesitated before nodding again. 'There was a bit of a barney,' she admitted. 'But we didn't see anything because they took it outside. I'd have gone to watch but I couldn't leave the bar,' she added with a sigh.

'Who was fighting?'

Shelley admitted that she hadn't really seen what had happened. All she knew was that two men had been fighting. She had heard shouting and jeering from onlookers and then the brawlers had moved out into the street. When Geraldine asked the barmaid whether she could recall anything about the two combatants, Shelley shrugged.

'Did you notice whether either of them had fair hair?'

Shelley frowned. 'I can't remember. I didn't really see much.'

It wasn't unusual for arguments to break out in bars. Danny might have been involved in a fight on Wednesday. Equally, he could have witnessed a pub brawl, or even just gambled on one having broken out, and used it as an explanation for his black eye. Shelley insisted she couldn't tell them anything else. To their dismay, she told them the CCTV in the pub wasn't working. A few minutes later, Sam was thanking Shelley for her help and he and Geraldine were leaving the pub, disappointed.

'We have no evidence he was in a fight on Wednesday and we can't prove he sustained an injury while struggling with Lauren on Saturday night,' Geraldine said as they drove away. 'Don't look so glum. You handled that well in there. It's no reflection on you that the barmaid didn't see anything, and we're no worse off. Now we have to press on.'

'Just because he didn't kill Alice doesn't mean he definitely didn't kill Lauren,' Sam replied.

'You want it to be Danny, don't you?' Geraldine commented. 'You want to find him guilty.'

'Danny, Rob, whoever, I just want to nail the bastard who did this,' Sam replied. 'But given the cigarette burns on her body, yes, I think Danny has to be her killer. It stands to reason, doesn't it?'

'Possibly. But we still have to find evidence he killed her. And there's no point in being certain it was the wrong suspect. That just wastes time and energy. Now, let's get back and see what else we can dig up. And let's see if we can confirm definitely that Rob was in the area when Lauren was killed by looking at any CCTV we can find.'

But she was beginning to think they had not yet found the right suspect. And that meant the killer was still at large, with a knife, and possibly looking for his next victim while they floundered around following false leads and searching in the wrong places.

35

ALL THE NEXT MORNING, Geraldine kept a surreptitious eye on Naomi. However closely she observed her, she couldn't decide whether her young colleague was looking unusually stressed or not. Geraldine was reluctant to ask Ariadne for her opinion again. She didn't want to make her interest in Naomi seem too obvious, for fear of being considered odd, as though she was stalking her colleague. Although she was worried, there was very little she could do without drawing attention to her concern. She toyed with the idea of sharing her misgivings with the detective chief inspector, but was afraid of alienating Naomi if she did anything that could be interpreted as interfering. In the meantime, the investigation into the two murders was ongoing. Having already lost Rob as a suspect, the whole team was disappointed at the apparent confirmation of Danny's story that he had been given a black eye on Wednesday evening. Despite the absence of definitive proof, they had shared a tacit assumption that he had been given his injury in the course of an attack on his girlfriend late on Saturday night. That would have all but resolved the case against him.

'Of course, none of this actually proves he's innocent,' Ariadne said. 'He could still have killed Lauren on Saturday night, even if he did already have a black eye. The one doesn't necessarily have anything to do with the other. And we haven't established beyond any doubt that he didn't get his black eye on Saturday night,' she added. 'It seems plausible he was hit in the course of a pub brawl, but isn't it a bit of a coincidence, his being injured in a fight just three nights before his girlfriend was murdered? Are the two incidents really completely unrelated, as he claims?'

'Maybe his injury infuriated him,' Naomi suggested. 'It would have been a painful reminder of a fight he had lost and that could have made him more likely to lose his temper with Lauren.'

'It might explain why she went out to get his cigarettes for him,' Geraldine replied thoughtfully. 'He might not have found walking around and talking to strangers very comfortable.'

Several of the team remained convinced Danny was guilty, at least of Lauren's death, while others thought he was probably responsible for killing Alice as well. Nevertheless, without any evidence to justify keeping Danny locked up, they had to let him go. Geraldine went to the custody suite herself to give him the good news. She found him sitting on his bunk, leaning forward and staring dully at the floor. He didn't look up when she entered his cell and didn't seem particularly pleased on hearing he was being released. When Geraldine warned him not to leave the city, he didn't remonstrate as so many other suspects did.

'Where would I go?' he asked lethargically. 'She's gone and I'm on my own now. What's the point of going anywhere? I'll be on my own wherever I am.'

Even bearing in mind that he was grieving for Lauren, somehow Geraldine had the impression Danny was holding something back.

'Danny,' she said gently, taking a step towards him. 'Is there something you're not telling us?'

Instantly he looked guarded and shook his head defensively for no apparent reason, which only served to make her even more convinced that he was hiding something.

'If you are thinking of sharing something, now might be a good time, before you walk out of here,' she suggested hopefully.

He shook his head again. 'I've got nothing to say to you,' he replied, with a sudden burst of energy. 'I don't know what you're talking about. You told me I'm free to go so I'd like to leave now.' He said all that without once meeting her eye and then stood up, still staring at the floor.

With a sigh, Geraldine led him out to fetch his possessions: shoes, wallet and keys. He collected them morosely from the cheery custody sergeant, before trailing after Geraldine to the exit. On the point of leaving, he turned to her with a fraught expression on his face. For the first time, he looked straight at her. One of his eyes was still bruised, but was able to peer at her through a slit between swollen lids, while his uninjured eye stared at her earnestly.

'You will get the bastard who did this to her, won't you?' he said. 'She didn't deserve to die, not like that. She was a good person. A really good person. She always did her best. Please, don't let him get away with it. I want to see him go down for life. Don't let him weasel his way out of a murder charge.' He frowned, and winced because the movement clearly caused him some discomfort. 'They're saying this is a mugging that went wrong, like her death was some sort of accident, like no one meant for it to happen, but she was stabbed. How could that be an accident? Are they going to try and say it was her fault, that she provoked the attack? How can they say that? She was—' He broke off, unable to carry on.

'We'll do our best to make sure justice is done. That's our job.'

Danny shuffled out, shoulders hunched, looking thoroughly miserable. Geraldine wondered if his grief might be mixed with guilt. It had been difficult to read his expression with his face swollen out of shape on one side, but her overall impression had been that he was grieving. His plea for them to find Lauren's killer had seemed genuine, but she had learned to take nothing for granted. She knew from years of experience investigating murders that desperate people and psychopaths could be very convincing when they lied. As always, evidence was key, and that was what they still needed to find.

Taking Sam with her, Geraldine visited the newsagents where Danny said Lauren would have gone for his cigarettes. It was possible the shopkeeper might have seen someone hanging around, even perhaps following Lauren. They found the corner shop and drew up outside. The interior was dimly lit. Ignoring the jars and boxes crammed on dusty shelves, Geraldine went straight to the counter where a short man in glasses was waiting to serve her.

'Yes?' he asked.

She held up her identity card and he leaned forward to peer at it before straightening up, blinking nervously.

'I haven't reported anything recently,' he murmured. 'I don't need—'

Geraldine interrupted him, holding up a photo of Lauren. 'Do you recognise this woman?'

The shopkeeper nodded uncertainly. 'I think so,' he replied cautiously. 'Why?'

'Can you remember serving her last Saturday night, some time before midnight?'

He shrugged. 'I close at nine on Saturdays,' he said.

Geraldine nodded. 'Can you remember her coming here on Saturday evening?'

He nodded again. 'She bought cigarettes. Several packets. I don't remember how many.' He paused, looking worried. 'Is this the girl from the news? The one whose body was found? I said to my wife, "I think I've seen her in the shop!" I thought I recognised her, you see.' He was suddenly animated, then fell silent, probably anticipating Geraldine's next question.

'Why didn't you report this to the police as soon as you recognised her?'

He shook his head. 'I wasn't sure. She was here for such a

short time and I'd seen her before, many times. I could have been confused about her coming here on Saturday. I wasn't sure enough to come forward and say she was here on Saturday. She might not have been. It could have been another evening. She was here quite often, you see, and I have many customers coming in and out all the time, just popping in to make a purchase. I wasn't sure.'

It didn't make much difference, as the cigarettes found in Lauren's bag had already corroborated Danny's story, although that didn't give him an alibi for the time of her murder. But, for what it was worth, the shopkeeper had confirmed that he closed at nine. On her way back to her desk, Geraldine spotted Naomi walking towards the canteen and, on impulse, followed her. She decided against questioning her about her bruises again and instead determined to focus on the case, all the while watching Naomi for any signs of undue distress. Naomi took a seat at an empty table and began studying her iPad. Grabbing a coffee, Geraldine joined her before her colleague noticed her approach.

'How's it all going?' Geraldine enquired, taking a seat beside her.

Naomi looked up and Geraldine thought she looked tired.

'What did you say?' Naomi asked, clutching her iPad in front of her, like a shield. Geraldine noted her defensive posture and tried to ignore it. She didn't want to misinterpret Naomi's behaviour, imagining all kinds of sinister motivation that didn't actually exist. Naomi appeared reluctant to engage in conversation, but was probably just interested in what she had been studying and keen to return to her screen.

'So Danny's gone,' Geraldine burbled on. 'For now at least. What did you make of his story about the fight in the pub?'

Naomi shrugged. 'It seemed to check out. The barmaid corroborated that there was a fight.'

'Well, it's possible he was involved,' Geraldine agreed,

before proceeding to outline her reservations, all the while watching Naomi's response.

'So you're saying you think it could be a coincidence, his having a fight in a pub that week and getting a black eye, at around the same time Lauren was attacked?'

'I'm saying it's possible.'

'Anything's possible,' Naomi conceded, 'and I suppose we don't know for certain he was hit in the face during a scrap in the pub. We know there was a brawl of some kind, but he might not have been involved in it at all. He could have just witnessed it. And even if he was in a fight a few days before the murder, it's still possible Lauren gave him a black eye when he attacked her a few days later and he's using the pub fight to account for his injury.'

'So do you think he attacked Lauren?' Geraldine asked her.

Naomi hesitated before blurting out, 'Honestly, no, I don't think he did.'

'But you just argued that it's possible.'

'Well, anything's possible,' Naomi replied irritably. 'The point is, we just don't know. And, as you're always so keen to tell us, we have to be wary of believing unsubstantiated suspicions.' She glared at Geraldine as she was speaking and it was clear she was referring to more than the case against Danny. 'And now, if you don't mind, I'd like to get back to work.'

With difficulty, Geraldine restrained herself from asking Naomi whether she was all right. Instead, she stood up and returned to her desk, feeling uneasy. Naomi definitely didn't seem like her usual self and Geraldine didn't know why, but she was convinced her colleague's hostility had something to do with her brother's arrival in York.

'What's up?' Ariadne enquired as Geraldine sat down. 'We've had suspects who turned out to be false leads before now. We just have to keep looking. For all we know, it could be someone we've already come across. Is something wrong?' she asked when Geraldine didn't answer. 'You look like you just lost a pound and found a penny.'

Geraldine grunted. 'It's not me you should be worrying about.'

Ariadne looked puzzled. 'What's that supposed to mean?'

But Geraldine merely shrugged and turned back to her screen, her thoughts elsewhere. She wasn't ready to be explicit, but she knew something was amiss.

36

SITTING BY HIMSELF IN the empty flat was almost too depressing to bear. He kept looking round, expecting to see Lauren's pale face staring at him. Every now and then, fury overwhelmed him as he remembered that she had gone, forever, and he was alone. And it was all his fault. If only he had gone to buy his own cigarettes instead of agreeing to let her go out in his place, they would be together now. Instead, he had allowed her go, leaving him to sit around at home on his own, on the sofa, with his feet up, watching the telly and growing increasingly frustrated with her for taking so long. And now, he would never see her again. They might as well never have met. He had managed to hold his feelings in all the time he was at the police station, doing his best to block out their alternating hectoring and cajoling. He hadn't even lost his temper when they had made it obvious they thought he had attacked Lauren himself. But they had no evidence. Any of his DNA they found on her body was easily explained away since they had lived together and had been together before she was killed. He smiled uneasily, thinking how close he had come to being arrested. At least he was free, even if he was alone.

Slumped down on the sofa where he and Lauren used to sit side by side watching telly, he reached out and punched the empty seat beside him. Now that he was home, there was no longer any need to control himself. He abandoned himself to his temper and worked himself up into a rage, hitting the cushion until the seam burst and a shower of disintegrating fragments of orange sponge spurted out, spilling over the carpet. His anger spent, he fell back on the sofa, feeling numb. Gazing around, he became aware of a stale odour in the room and fumbled in a packet for a cigarette to get rid of the smell. Lighting up reminded him that Lauren had gone out that fateful night to buy his cigarettes. He wanted to turn the clock back so he could tell her to stay indoors. The cigarettes had been for him. He should have been the one to go out in the rain for them, but she had insisted. She hadn't deserved to die like that, on the street, left out in the rain like a bag of rubbish. He should have treated her with more respect.

Without Lauren, empty years of life seemed to stretch out in front of him like a desert, purposeless, and there was nothing he could do about it. She was gone and she would never come back. She had sacrificed her life to serve his wishes and he had sat back and let her do it. She had been an angel, willing to do anything for him. He would never find anyone to replace her. His loss hit him like a punch in the guts and he felt tears gather in his eyes. For the first time in years, he cried for himself and his lonely future. Gazing around at dirty plates and empty cans, and saucers overflowing with cigarette butts, he needed Lauren to clear up, but she wasn't there. No one cared. There was no one there to help him. Seizing a plate, he flung it across the room. It shattered as it hit the floor, scattering crumbs over the carpet. In a frenzy, he hurled another plate and another

He doubted he would be able to sleep that night, lying in a cold, empty bed, his thoughts spinning in circles. At the moment, the police seemed resolved to charge him with murder. He had to do something to divert their attention to a different suspect. There had to be someone they could investigate. If Lauren had a past boyfriend who had been violent, so much the better. Lying in bed, he tried to recall everything she had told him about her previous boyfriends, but she had always been reluctant to talk about the past, and he couldn't remember what little she had said about other boyfriends. For the first time, he regretted not having paid her more attention. It could have helped him now.

In the morning, not knowing what else to do, he went back to work. The manager's startled expression changed quickly to a smile of welcome, but not before Danny had noticed his surprise. Clearly he hadn't been expecting Danny to turn up. Danny wondered if he had blundered in coming back to work so soon and whether that was how an innocent man might normally behave right after his girlfriend had been murdered. The police had let him go, but until someone else was arrested, he was still at risk. The detective had made that clear. Appearances were important. Whatever else happened, he had to make sure he did nothing that might make him look guilty.

'Danny, my boy,' the manager called out to him and stopped, uncertain what to say. Red in the face, he was clearly embarrassed at having to deal with a potentially emotional situation. 'It's good to see you back. How are you—' He hesitated. 'I was sorry to hear about – you know. Sorry.' He hesitated before falling back on his first greeting. 'It's good to see you back. We've been struggling a bit here. You know how short-staffed we've been and we're already way behind schedule. You know how it is. We're always up against it. The boss is completely unreasonable. At least we're well paid,' he added, with a wonky grin. 'Could be worse.' He stopped, realising his comment had been crass under the circumstances. 'That is, what I mean to say is, we are being well paid for a day's work here.'

Danny nodded slowly. He hadn't really been listening to the manager burbling on about work. What he had noticed was how awkward the man had been, but that was understandable under the circumstances. He would have struggled to know what to say if he had been in the manager's shoes.

'That's okay,' Danny said. 'Let's just get to work. I – that is – I mean to say, it's better not to talk. About anything, I mean. There's nothing to say anyway. She's—' He broke off and heaved a sigh. 'Tell me what you want me to do today and let's get started.'

The manager nodded, mumbling again that he was glad to have Danny back. Suddenly brisk, he directed Danny to the job he was to work that day. They were both relieved. It was easier to talk about work than delicate situations packed with emotional issues. Danny threw himself into his work, obsessively tidying the slips and checking the pens were all working whenever he wasn't busy with a customer. After a flurry of activity over lunchtime, the shop quietened down, but when his colleague suggested he stop for a break, he shook his head.

'You go on and take another break if you like,' he said. 'I'll carry on here.'

With a shrug, his workmate left him alone. They weren't busy, and Danny was able to manage without any difficulty. As long as he could keep himself occupied, he was able to keep his mind off what had happened. The worst of it had been when he had gone to view her body. He still couldn't bear to think about that. No, the worst of it was knowing he would never see her again. No, the worst of it was remembering how he had let her go out to buy his cigarettes. If only he had gone himself, this wouldn't have happened and she would still be at home now, waiting for him at the end of the day. With a struggle, he switched his attention back to the shop which was empty apart from one man who was flicking through a bundle of betting slips. He looked as though he was searching for a slip that would bring him good luck, even though they were all exactly the same. Danny shrugged. He had seen plenty of punters going through the same pointless routine.

Having watched the man select a slip and fill it out, Danny waited for him to bring it over to the counter. The man looked quite old, perhaps in his late seventies, and he kept his eyes on the floor as he shuffled over. Even when he reached the counter, he didn't look up. Used to people doing their best to avoid attracting attention, Danny took no notice of the man's shifty behaviour. The customer's handwriting was difficult to decipher, and Danny queried what he had written.

'Me hands shake,' the old man said apologetically.

Danny nodded. He was fairly confident the poor script was deliberate. It was a common enough trick. Sometimes punters tried to hand in an ambiguous betting slip, thinking it would give them a chance of winning on more than one result. They thought they were being clever, but they never got away with it. Danny's colleague returned, having taken an extended lunch break.

'I figured you might want some time to yourself,' he muttered sheepishly.

He didn't add that with Danny working through lunch, they would still meet their target for the day, but they both understood that was the case.

'I owe you one,' his workmate added, slightly shamefaced. 'You've done more than your fair share today. In fact, if you want to knock off early—' He shrugged, without pressing the point.

'Don't worry about it,' Danny assured him. Going home to an empty flat was the last thing he wanted to do. 'I appreciate you giving me some space. I'm not in the mood for sitting around and chatting right now.'

'Yeah, well, I figured you'd want to be left alone,' the other man said quickly.

Danny turned away, scowling; he was going to be alone for the rest of his life.

37

MARIA WAS DOING HER best to put Rob and everything to do with him out of her mind. Despite her decision to forget about him, she felt a frisson of excitement every time she passed a tall man with short fair hair on the street in case it was him. It never was. She had finally broken down and confided to her sister that she and Rob had split up. Her sister had been surprisingly sympathetic and, like Maria's employer, had reassured her that there were plenty of eligible men in the world, it was just a question of finding the right one.

'What if there isn't a right one for me?' she had asked, despising herself for sounding so plaintive and needy. 'I don't want to be single forever.'

'There is,' her sister had replied. 'He's out there somewhere.'

'What if I never meet him, or anyone else? I don't want to end up on my own, a shrivelled and bitter old spinster like Great Aunt Sofia.'

Even as she was speaking she knew it was a ridiculous thing to say. She was only twenty. Great Aunt Sofia was four times her age. But her sister hadn't made fun of her for being so pathetic. On the contrary, she had been really patient and supportive. If anything, that had made Maria feel more emotional than before. She was glad her sister couldn't see her. In a way, she felt closer to her than she had when they were growing up in the same house, even though they were now living hundreds of miles apart.

'You're being so kind,' she murmured and felt like crying

when her sister replied, 'We're family, aren't we? I'm your sister.'

Aware that it would improve her job prospects if she returned to Spain speaking fluent English, she made a renewed effort in her English class. Even the studious Chinese girl seemed happy to be her partner again for pair work, and the tutor commended Maria for her effort. Apart from feeling anxious in case the police wanted to speak to her again, she was content with her life. A couple of the other girls liked to go out in the evening, drinking and dancing and chatting up men, and she took to going out with them, enjoying herself far more than she had with Rob. This was the life she had come to England to experience. Initially she had been disappointed not to find a job in London, but York turned out to be an exciting city.

Once the class was over, she trailed out with the other students who dispersed in different directions until she was sitting on her bus by herself. A stout woman heaved her bulk into the seat next to Maria who turned and gazed out of the window at a grey street trundling by. Whenever she was on her own with her thoughts, worrying memories surfaced. Even being with Jason was better than nothing. The pavements were busy and every other person she passed looked like Rob. She sighed. Although she had no wish to resume their relationship, forgetting about him was proving more difficult than she had anticipated. She sat on the bus in a daze, hardly noticing the other passengers. She closed her eyes and tried to wipe the memory of Rob from her mind. Preoccupied, she missed her stop. It would be just as quick to walk back as wait for a bus going in the other direction, so she set off on foot. It wasn't a bad thing as walking helped to clear her mind, and she had plenty of time to get back before she had to collect Jason.

As she turned off the main bus route, she nearly didn't notice him standing on the corner of her road. She struggled to control her emotions as she realised he must be waiting for her. That could mean only one thing: he was missing her. He turned slightly and caught sight of her staring at him. She almost broke into a run as she approached him, but he stood completely still, as though rooted to the pavement, and glared at her. She hurried towards him, eager to reassure him that she wasn't angry with him. On the contrary, she was in two minds over whether to admit that she had been missing him too, but when she reached him, he spoke first.

'I've been waiting for you,' he said.

The words were innocent enough, yet they sounded like a threat.

Taken aback, she muttered that she was on her way home from her language class and needed to get back and complete her chores before her employer returned. Fatuously, she concluded with a polite greeting she had recently been taught. 'I hope you're well.'

Rob's scowl darkened, and he snapped at her to keep away from him. 'I won't put up with your behaviour.'

'What do you mean?' she stammered. The pavement seemed to tremble beneath her feet as she stared at him.

'I know you went to the police spreading lies about me. You won't get away with it.'

'Are you going to kill me?' she whispered, terror flooding through her as she registered what he had said.

His voice was cold, but his eyes were blazing and she could see he was shaking with fury. 'Tell the police you lied about me. Tell them you were angry with me for dumping you. Make any excuse you like, only tell them you lied to them deliberately to get me in trouble. If you don't, I won't be answerable for my actions and you won't live long enough to regret your stupidity.'

Maria was so scared she didn't know what to say. Before she could recover from her shock, Rob turned on his heel and strode away, leaving her shaking. She could barely manage to hold back tears and had to force herself to walk towards the house. Scolding herself for overreacting, she forced herself to keep going. But Rob's words echoed in her head: 'I won't be answerable for my actions… you won't live long enough to regret your stupidity.' His meaning seemed clear. Too frightened to go back to the police to tell them Rob was threatening to kill her, she cast about for some other way of finding help, but there was no one she could turn to for protection.

She went home and tidied up automatically, before collecting Jason from school. After that, she seemed to be waiting interminably for her employer to come home. At last, she heard Julia's key in the door.

'I need to go home,' she blurted out as soon as Julia walked in. 'I cannot stay. I call the agency tomorrow and say I go home as soon as I can. I'm sorry. You are very kind but I must go home.'

'Good lord,' Julia burst out. 'Whatever's happened? It's not that boyfriend again, is it?'

Maria shook her head, but she was crying too much to speak. 'He's not my boyfriend,' she blurted out at last.

'Maria, we need to talk about this. If there's a problem at home I can let you take time off, and we'll manage without you for a short time. But you can't just walk out altogether without giving me any notice. The agency will have to find a replacement and that's going to take time. I need someone here to collect my son from school.'

Maria shook her head vehemently. 'I do not want to talk. I am leaving. I am sorry but I must go home. I must leave England at once.'

It was the only way to escape the danger.

38

Lisa was doing her best not to dwell on what had happened to her niece, but it wasn't easy. During the day she had Tom and Daisy to keep her busy, but in the evening, when she was accustomed to sitting down and putting her feet up, painful memories crowded in on her. It didn't help that early evening was the time when Alice often used to call in and spend time with her, drinking tea and chatting about her day. Lisa still caught herself listening out for the doorbell to ring, expecting to open the door and see Alice on the doorstep. She used to tell her to use her key, but Alice insisted on ringing the bell like any other visitor. It wasn't only the evenings that Lisa was finding difficult. Every morning she had to open the door to Geraldine. She felt an uncomfortable jolt on seeing her because, even without a word being exchanged, the sight of Geraldine reminded her of the investigation into her niece's murder. It was difficult to restrain herself from asking whether there had been any progress.

Nothing could bring Alice back, but it would give her some satisfaction to know her niece's killer was behind bars. Actually, they deserved to suffer a fate far worse than prison after what they did to Alice. Reading about the incident in the news, Lisa was furious at the suggestion that it was a mugging that had gone wrong, as though Alice's death had been some kind of accident, when in reality it had been the result of a vicious attack by a psychopath who didn't deserve to live. Lisa wasn't a violent person, but if she could get her hands on the inhuman monster who had killed Alice, she trembled to think what she might be capable of doing to him. She had to stop herself from fantasising about seizing a hammer and hitting the killer as hard as she could, again and again, venting her almost unbearable rage, or grabbing a knife and thrusting it into his heart. Such thoughts were unhealthy and she struggled to suppress them. But she couldn't control her nightmares.

She took Tom from Geraldine and hesitated. She had promised herself she wouldn't mention Alice to her again. She had already overstepped the mark by asking her to speak to Alice before tragedy had struck. Geraldine was the mother of one of the children Lisa looked after and that was the extent of their relationship. Questioning her about the case was inappropriate. But she couldn't help herself. The words seem to burst out of her mouth of their own volition.

'Is there any news?' she asked breathlessly, almost against her will, and immediately regretted having raised the subject.

'News?' Geraldine hesitated. 'I'm sorry, I know it sounds harsh, but I'm afraid I can't discuss the investigation with you. We're doing everything we can.'

Lisa knew Geraldine was not strictly allowed to talk about Alice's murder with her, but she was on the investigation team and obviously knew more than she was sharing. Desperate to know more, Lisa asked Geraldine bluntly whether the police had found out who killed her niece. There was no possible ambiguity about what she meant. All the same, Geraldine didn't answer straight away. When she did, her words were sympathetic, but she was frowning.

'I'm really sorry,' she said. 'I know you and Alice were close, and this whole experience must be unbearably painful for you, but I'm afraid I can't discuss an ongoing investigation, not even with someone who was related to the victim. I promise you we're doing everything in our power to bring the killer to justice, and you will be informed as soon as there is anything we are able to pass on to you. I'm really sorry I can't say more.' With that, she turned away.

'No, wait,' Lisa cried out.

Geraldine paused and looked back over her shoulder.

Lisa shrugged. 'It's nothing,' she mumbled.

'We're doing our best,' Geraldine repeated helplessly before she walked away.

Wretchedly, Lisa shut her front door. 'What does your mummy know that she's not telling me?' she whispered to Tom, who was squirming to be put down. She smiled at him chuckling in her arms.

'Mamam,' he burbled, waving a fat little fist at her as though he wanted to punch her. 'Mamam.'

'Yes,' Lisa replied. 'Mamam. What is mamam doing while you're here?'

'Mamam,' he repeated, pursing his lips and blowing out his cheeks.

Tom's antics made her smile, and she carried him indoors and placed him carefully on a playmat. He was almost ready to crawl and he could manage to roll over so she couldn't leave him unattended for longer than a few minutes.

'Come on, mischief,' she said gently, after tickling him for a few minutes. She lifted him up and put him in his playpen with a few soft toys to entertain him. 'I've got to clear away my breakfast. You stay there and don't go getting into any trouble while I'm gone. No trying to escape, you hear me? Mummy told me you climbed out of your cot the other day, you naughty little thing.'

Leaving Tom distracted by a fluffy pink elephant that jingled when shaken, she went to the kitchen. As she stacked the dishwasher, she wracked her brains trying to recall everything Alice had told her about Rob, but her memories were vague. She turned her attention to the one occasion when she had met him. He might have said something incriminating, if she could only remember what it was. She closed her eyes and tried to recall everything about the meeting. She could clearly remember her impression of him, but why had she taken against him? He must have let something slip to arouse her suspicions. It wasn't like her to dislike people for no reason. She preferred to give people the benefit of the doubt whenever possible.

Although nothing had been said, there was no doubt in her mind that Alice had flinched when Rob had raised his hand in front of her. With children, that was often a sign they were expecting to be hit. Rob had only touched his hair and it had been over in a split second, but the incident had been enough to make Lisa suspect that Rob was a violent man who had physically abused her niece. If only she could convince Geraldine of his true nature, she would feel she had done what she could for her niece. It was frustrating that she had no way of proving what she had witnessed. Nevertheless, she resolved to approach Geraldine again and do what she could to persuade her that Rob was guilty.

39

Geraldine always felt a twinge of guilt when she left Tom with his childminder and drove away. As she headed to work, she recalled her conversation with Ian the previous evening.

'I can't imagine you ever being content to stay at home with him all day every day,' he had told her. 'Admit it, after six months on maternity leave you were pleased to go back to work, weren't you?'

She couldn't deny it.

'It wasn't just that you were tired,' he had added. 'You were bored stiff.' He smiled kindly. 'There's nothing wrong with that. Do you think you're the only successful career woman who's been bored, being stuck at home all day with a baby? Don't beat yourself up over it and stop feeling guilty about needing the mental challenge of working. It's natural.'

'Natural?' she had retorted wretchedly. 'What's natural about a mother not wanting to take care of her own child?'

'Just because you're a mother doesn't stop you being the person you always were,' he had replied firmly. 'You're a detective.'

As soon as she arrived at the police station, Geraldine's concerns about Tom and her own abilities as a mother vanished, and she became completely absorbed in her job. It was like flicking a switch as she stepped into a different life, one she was comfortable with. She was passionate about her job and Ian was right when he said she was good at it. As for Tom, she would just have to stop feeling guilty about leaving him with Lisa and do her best to make her time with him count. All the so-called experts on childcare talked about spending 'quality time' with infants and that was what she planned to do. She would play with him and have fun with him and they would enjoy their time together. Feeling positive, she set to work reviewing her case notes.

Naomi came into the office and Geraldine went straight over to her to ask her how she was feeling. Naomi looked up and nodded at her before replying that she was fine, but her smile looked stiff and her voice was stilted. She turned abruptly back to her screen and Geraldine walked away feeling as though she had been dismissed. Her good mood punctured, she returned to her desk where she continued her examination of statements given by the different witnesses who had reported finding the two bodies. Looking for any details that might confirm or disprove the theory that they were searching for one killer, she failed to find anything significant.

Her morning was discouraging, so she was pleased to hear that Danny had come to the police station and was asking to speak to her. Closing her screen, she hurried to the interview room where he was waiting for her. She noticed at once that his shirt was crumpled and his jeans were grubby. His eyes were slightly bloodshot and he looked exhausted, as though he hadn't slept for days.

'It was Lauren's former boyfriend,' he blurted out. 'He used to beat her up.'

'How do you know?'

'She told me.'

'I'm afraid anything Lauren told you is hearsay. It can't be accepted as evidence.'

'But he killed her,' Danny said.

'What makes you say that?'

'Stands to reason, doesn't it?'

Geraldine hesitated. 'Why are you telling me this now? You haven't mentioned it before.'

Danny shrugged. 'I just got to thinking who might have done it,' he replied. 'I've been wracking my brains and it suddenly hit me. I'd go and sort him out myself, given half a chance, only I don't know who he is or where to find him. They'd know at the shelter where she was staying before she came to live with me, but I can't go there and ask. They'd never talk to me, especially not now after what's happened. They're bound to think I did it.'

'Why would they think that?'

'Because I'm a man. No other reason. And I was her boyfriend. Of course they're going to blame me.' Geraldine noticed how his voice rose in vexation and his fists clenched.

She took down the details of the shelter and told Danny she would look into his accusation.

'And you'll give me the bleeder's name when you find out who it is?' he asked. 'I'll see to it he gets what's coming to him.'

Geraldine reminded him mildly that he himself had been indignant when he had been suspected without any evidence.

'I've told you I'll look into it,' she went on. 'Leave it with me.'

'You tell me who he is, if you don't want me coming after you as well,' he snapped.

'Go home, Danny, and don't issue any further threats or I'll have you charged.'

'Charged? I can talk, can't I? What is this? A police state? I'm telling you, I'm going to sort him out.'

'If you persist in using threatening language, I'll have no choice but to charge you with intent to harass.'

'What are you talking about? You're going to charge me for sorting out the bastard who killed my girl? No court is going to agree to that.'

'You'll be charged under the Public Order Act. Threatening a person unknown, not to mention threatening a police officer. Drop it, Danny. Go home and leave this to us.'

Growling imprecations, Danny left.

Geraldine took Naomi with her to the shelter where Lauren had gone before she met Danny. It was an opportunity for Geraldine to talk to Naomi away from their colleagues. She decided to proceed cautiously, and as they walked to the car she began by discussing the case.

'I was so sure Rob was guilty,' Naomi said miserably, 'until his alibi checked out. Then we all thought it had to be Danny and I was really hoping he would turn out to have killed them both, with it seeming to be the same weapon that was used on both of the victims, but now he seems to have an alibi as well. We might as well not have bothered spending so much time investigating Rob and Danny because for all the work we did, we're still in exactly the same place we were when we started.'

Naomi had a lot of strong qualities which should have made her perfectly suited to a career as a detective, but she was far too easily disheartened when her theories were disproved. Recalling being similarly impatient when she was younger, Geraldine empathised with her. Naomi needed to control her emotional response when things didn't pan out the way she hoped. But Geraldine had other matters she wanted to discuss. Once they were both sitting in the car, she broached the subject that was uppermost in her mind.

'Naomi, I don't want to overstep the mark, but I think there's something you're not telling me.'

'I've no idea what you're talking about. If this is about my brother, I'd appreciate it if you'd stop interfering in my family affairs.'

Geraldine didn't want to fall out with her colleague. If Naomi refused to talk to her, there was not much she could do about it. She resigned herself to accepting Naomi's refusal to confide in her, and they drove the rest of the way in stony silence.

40

THE SHELTER WAS LOCATED centrally in the city in a red brick block with black railings around it. From the outside the building looked well maintained, with smart signage and windows that had the appearance of being recently installed. The two officers entered a well-furnished foyer where they were met by one of the shelter's managers who had agreed to talk to them. Jeanie was casually dressed in faded jeans and a loose sweatshirt, her hair untidily caught up in a ponytail, but her manner, although friendly, was businesslike. Geraldine had the impression she was dedicated to her job and probably very efficient.

'We are a Christian charity,' she told them, smiling easily with the clear conscience of someone who knows they are doing a worthwhile job and doing it well. 'We do our best for our clients and most leave us in better shape than they're in when they arrive. Misfortune can strike anyone,' she continued. 'Some of our residents are struggling with addictions and we offer appropriate support, but many are just the victims of bad luck and poor choices. We never give up on anyone.'

She seemed set on continuing with a public relations speech, but Geraldine interrupted her.

'We know you do a fantastic job,' she said, 'but we've come here to ask you about a specific person, someone you helped some months ago. Can we ask you to consult your records?'

'I don't think that will be necessary.' Jeanie smiled. 'I know all of our residents. That sounds like a boast, until you know there aren't actually that many of them. Who did you want to enquire about?' Her smile faded. 'I hope this isn't someone who's committed a crime while they were under our care. We do our best, but we can't be responsible for their actions when they're not physically under our roof.'

Geraldine explained they were looking for some information about Lauren Stokes.

'Lauren? Oh yes, that poor girl.' Jeanie sighed. 'We were all saddened to read about what happened to her. I hope you've managed to find her assailant. He's clearly in need of help. Was it drugs?'

Without addressing Jeanie's questions, Geraldine explained that they were trying to trace anyone who had known the victim, in particular any boyfriend she might have had before she arrived at the refuge.

'Boyfriend?' Jeanie repeated, sounding slightly puzzled.

'Yes, any man she might have been seeing.'

Jeanie sighed. 'You'd better come to the office. We can talk more easily there.'

They followed the manager to a small office on the first floor. She closed the door and gestured to two upright plastic chairs while she went to sit behind a small desk.

'Lauren had dealings with a lot of men,' she told them. 'She was a sex worker before she came here. We don't judge anyone here. Everyone who turns to us has suffered for their misfortune and poor decisions. We are none of us spotless.'

'So was there a pimp?' Naomi asked. 'What can you tell us about him?'

'Her pimp died,' Jeanie replied. 'That's why she came to us. She was scared of continuing her work without his—' she hesitated before adding, 'his protection. And then, of course, she met her boyfriend and left us to go and live with him. At first we all thought it was a very positive outcome for her, and then we heard she was dead. We remember her in our prayers.'

Geraldine sat forward. 'What can you tell us about how her pimp died?' she asked.

'An overdose. It was Lauren who found him.' She shook her head. 'Poor girl.'

'And when was this?' Geraldine asked, although it was clearly impossible he could have killed her.

'Before she came to us, and that must have been over a year ago. It was in the spring when she came to us, spring last year.'

'When she was working on the street, did she have any particular clients?' Naomi asked. 'Any men she saw regularly?'

'I doubt it. From what she told us, she didn't know who they were and they didn't know her, or care to. She was much better off here with us. She managed to stay off drugs and alcohol, although she drank when she wasn't here.' She sighed. 'We can't watch our clients all the time. An operation like ours runs on trust, but we can't expect people to undergo a complete transformation straight away. It takes time, but we like to think we make a difference. Our clients leave us in a far happier and healthier state than they are when they arrive. Is there anything else I can help you with?'

Jeanie told them Lauren had been a loner, who had not made friends with any of the other residents. She had stayed in her room most of the time, seeing no one.

'That's why we were pleased for her when she met her boyfriend in a pub and he asked her to move in with him. She was over the moon about it.' She smiled sadly. 'I don't suppose he was the one who killed her?'

When Geraldine enquired why the manager had thought he might be, she just shrugged.

'No reason,' she replied. 'I mean, he never came here. We never met him. It's just the first person you think of, isn't it, when something like this happens? Most murders are committed by people who know their victims, aren't they, although the journalists are saying it was a mugging, or a serial killer? It's impossible to know what really happened and I don't suppose you're going to tell me.'

I couldn't tell you even if I wanted to. We're as much in the dark as you, Geraldine thought miserably.

'Well, that was a waste of time,' Naomi complained when they were back in the car.

'Poor girl. What a miserable life,' Geraldine replied. 'What was it the manager said? Bad luck and poor decisions. It's frightening to think how one bad decision can ruin a life.'

'One bad decision followed by another bad decision followed by another bad decision,' Naomi replied with surprising bitterness.

Geraldine wondered if she was still thinking about the case.

'Naomi, is there something on your mind?' she asked.

'The case.'

'I mean, is there anything else bothering you?'

'No, and I wish you'd stop pestering me.'

Geraldine was too taken aback by Naomi's aggression to respond, but she was more convinced than ever that something was wrong.

41

THE NEXT DAY, NAOMI came over to Geraldine and asked to speak to her.

'I owe you an apology,' she said, looking shamefaced, before Geraldine could say anything. 'I was rude to you yesterday and probably insubordinate as well. I'd understand if you want to give me an official warning.' She hung her head.

'You might have been curt with me yesterday, but now you're being ridiculous,' Geraldine replied, suppressing a smile of relief that Naomi was ready to talk to her. 'And it's probably me who ought to be apologising for intruding on your privacy. What you choose to do in your own time is none of my business, unless it impacts on your work. I shouldn't have pried and I was out of order doing so. I was just worried you had a problem, that's all. I'm speaking to you as a friend, rather than as your senior officer,' she added.

'You're right, I did have a problem,' Naomi admitted, with a sigh. 'It was nothing to do with work, except that I clearly didn't do a very good job of hiding my feelings, so in a way I suppose it did impact on my performance here.'

'I don't think anyone else noticed,' Geraldine assured her. 'But you still don't want to talk about it?'

'There's nothing to talk about, not any more. He's gone,' Naomi replied.

'Gone?' Geraldine echoed.

'He didn't stay long.'

Geraldine hesitated before saying that she wasn't quite sure who Naomi meant. Although she understood perfectly well, she wanted to hear what Naomi had to say.

'I'm talking about my brother. He came to stay with me. You met him, remember? When you came round.'

'Yes, your brother,' Geraldine repeated, nodding and wondering how far she could continue the conversation without becoming intrusive again. 'It's nice that you could spend time together.' She paused, feeling her way. 'How long was he staying in York?'

Naomi shrugged. 'He wasn't with me for long, just a fortnight, but in the end he had to leave.'

Geraldine continued the conversation in as even a tone as she could muster, but it didn't escape her attention that Naomi's brother had come to stay with her in York shortly before Alice was killed and he had left soon after the fatal attack on Lauren. She couldn't help wondering if this was a coincidence and whether the possible significance of this time frame had struck Naomi.

'Where did you say he lives?' she asked.

'I didn't,' Naomi replied, becoming cagey again.

'So where does he live?'

'Where does he live?' Naomi repeated, her expression suddenly fraught. 'Honestly, I've no idea. I don't know that he lives anywhere, not permanently anyway. That's why he didn't want to leave, but I couldn't let him stay any longer. I know he's my brother, but I couldn't cope with him. He's very – erratic.' She paused, before adding in a low voice, 'I had to ask him to leave.' She gazed anxiously at Geraldine. 'He has a problem and it was too much for me. I couldn't control him.' Her face twisted in misery. 'I don't know where he can go now. I thought I could help him, but—' She broke off and shrugged. 'I guess I overestimated my own strength. I thought, with all my training, I'd be able to handle him. I should have done better. We used to be close, when we were growing up, but he's changed. I hardly recognise him any more.'

'So what caused him to change?' Geraldine asked. 'Was it drink? Or drugs?'

Naomi shrugged. 'Both,' she admitted miserably. 'He's worse when he's drunk. The thing is, I should have been able to help him. That's why we're in this job, isn't it? So we can help people. And I couldn't even help my own brother.' She sounded close to tears. 'I told him to go back to our parents, even though they'd thrown him out.'

'Our training doesn't always do anything to help when we're emotionally involved in a situation,' Geraldine said sympathetically.

'You manage to keep your personal issues and your work life completely separate.'

Geraldine thought about her recent panic when she had thought Tom was ill and shook her head. 'It might look that way, but believe me, I'm an emotional mess half the time.'

'Isn't that what being professional means, looking as though your troubles don't affect you even when they do?'

Geraldine looked at her young colleague for a moment. 'You know about my twin sister?' she asked. 'She was an addict, but she went into rehab and she's not been using for a while now. Admittedly it's been hell, but people can change and get through all kinds of adversity and come out the other side.'

'You didn't give up on your sister, did you?' Naomi said.

Geraldine shook her head again. 'No. There's a difference though, because we don't have parents to fall back on so I'm the only family she's got. You did the right thing, encouraging your brother to go to your parents for help.' She paused. 'He was violent, wasn't he?'

Naomi nodded without looking at Geraldine.

'And your black eye, was that him?'

'It was an accident,' Naomi muttered. They both knew that wasn't strictly true.

'You're not helping him by trying to cover up for him,' Geraldine said gently. 'Colluding with him to pretend nothing's wrong, or abandoning him to deal with his problem alone, isn't helping him to get the support he needs.'

Naomi bristled. 'Don't preach to me,' she said. 'Do you think we haven't tried to persuade him to get help? AA, rehab, counselling – my parents offered him every intervention under the sun. They even tried to get him to have acupuncture for his addictions. Acupuncture. Can you imagine? At least he's used to needles.' She laughed mirthlessly.

Geraldine gazed at her young colleague, feeling helpless. 'I had to really pull out all the stops to get my sister into rehab, but we got there in the end.'

'Well done, you, for saving your sister,' Naomi said sourly. 'You're obviously better at all this than I am.'

'It wasn't easy and it took a long time,' Geraldine admitted. 'And it took a lot of persuading. In the end, I think she felt too guilty not to at least try.'

Geraldine didn't describe how she had risked her career and possibly her life by impersonating her identical twin whose life was being threatened by a drug ring. She didn't tell Naomi that she had been arrested as a result of her actions and consequently demoted and forced to leave the Met. She also held back from mentioning that she had been supporting her twin financially and had threatened to stop paying her rent if she had refused to go to rehab. It had taken a combination of guilt and fear to finally persuade her twin to comply, but it had been worth it in the end.

'If your brother can't fight for his own survival, maybe he can find the strength to do it for your sake?' she asked, remembering what her sister had endured.

Naomi shook her head. 'He thinks we'd all be better off

without him.' She didn't add that he was right, but Geraldine suspected that might be what she was thinking.

Before Geraldine had a chance to ask Naomi outright where her parents lived and whether her brother had returned to them, Ariadne joined them and they went back to discussing the case. Ariadne was as peeved as Naomi at having lost two credible suspects.

'It's irrelevant that they seemed credible,' Geraldine said wearily. 'We're talking about two innocent men who happened to be in relationships with the victims of a killer.'

'Hardly innocent,' Naomi said. 'They both have a history of violence.'

'Which is what made them such credible suspects,' Geraldine replied. 'But that's neither here nor there. We know they are both innocent of murder, however badly they behaved, and we're going to have to look elsewhere to find our killer. Let's hope the murder charge will scare Rob and Danny into being more careful about how they treat women in future. Now, we need to get back to work, because while we've been focusing on investigating the wrong suspects, the real killer is still out there, quite possibly looking for his next victim.'

Keen though she was to find the killer, Geraldine desperately hoped it wouldn't turn out to be her colleague's brother. She wondered if Naomi was thinking the same.

42

'How could you be so stupid? Seriously, Rob, what were you thinking of, getting in a fight like that when you're being questioned by the police? The police, for Christ's sake! Aren't you in enough trouble already? What's wrong with you?'

Rob shrugged and ran his undamaged hand through his hair, making a mental note that it needed cutting. He didn't need any more aggravation. His life was in enough of a mess as it was.

'It wasn't my fault,' he said, hoping to shut her up. 'He just started on me. What was I supposed to do?'

But his sister hadn't finished. 'It wasn't your fault? No, it never is your fault, is it? What if you'd injured the guy? I mean, seriously injured him? You could have killed him.'

'Well, I didn't. And I wasn't going to. It was a disagreement, that's all. Nothing happened. I just twisted my wrist. He was fine. I was the one who ended up like this.' He held up his bandaged hand and winced. 'So what's your problem?'

'What's my problem? You're the one with a problem. You could have seriously hurt him and then what would you have done? What if he'd had a brittle skull and you'd killed him? Do you want to get yourself locked up?'

Rob blocked out the noise of his sister's ranting as he followed her out of the hospital.

'He started it,' he protested finally as they drove off. 'What was I supposed to do? Just stand there and let him knock me down without making any attempt to defend myself?'

'The point is,' his sister said slowly, with exaggerated patience, 'you're in trouble with the police. You need to get that through your thick skull. They think you killed your girlfriend, for Christ's sake. You can't get in any more trouble for being violent. You were involved. And as for who started it, that's just your word against his, isn't it? And who are the police going to believe? Not you, that's for sure.'

'Well, it isn't my fault if some nutter attacked me for no reason,' he muttered crossly. 'I told you, he started it. He said I was getting in his way and when I didn't move, he came at me. What was I supposed to do?'

'You should have moved out of his way. But you couldn't do that, could you? No, it's never your fault. Bad things just happen to you. Poor Rob. Always the innocent victim, every bloody time.'

'A little sympathy from my own sister would be nice. I'm the one who was injured, not him. And the police don't suspect me. They only questioned me because she was seeing me.'

'Seeing you? It was more than that. You were living together.'

He didn't answer, and they drove the rest of the way in silence. The lawyer had assured him the police would soon be done with him, but it was still hanging over him, because you could never be sure with those tricky bastards. Everyone knew the police lied but no one did anything about it. There was a chance he could go down for murder. And that bitch, Maria, hadn't helped either. Just thinking of how she had betrayed him made his uninjured fist clench. His sister dropped him at Alice's house and left, still muttering angrily.

That afternoon he went to work. Despite his distress and his physical injury, he had to crack on. Apart from anything else, he needed the money and was afraid they would dock his wages if he didn't show up.

'I wasn't expecting to see you today,' the foreman said,

looking at him in surprise. He glanced at Rob's bandaged wrist. 'You're no use to me with one hand.'

'It's not broken, it's only a bit bruised,' Rob told him, waving his hand and wriggling his fingers while forcing a cheery grin. 'It's nothing. See? I can still move it fine. If I wasn't wearing a bandage you wouldn't even know it was injured. It's only there to protect the skin, that's all. There's no real damage done.'

The foreman grunted. 'Come back when you're fit to work.'

'You can't send me away. This is my job. I can't manage on no wages.'

The foreman scowled at him, arms crossed. 'I know how that happened,' he said, nodding at Rob's hand. 'And I'm telling you now, I've got no room for troublemakers here. If you want to go getting into fights, you do it in your own time. You don't go getting into fights on my site. I run a tight ship here and we work as a team.'

Rob sighed. He had heard the speech before and waited for the foreman to finish before explaining that he hadn't started anything. One of his workmates had set on him for no reason. The foreman had heard the same story from the other man, and he shook his head.

'I'd be better off getting shot of the pair of you,' he said.

Rob tried an appeal for sympathy, blinking and trying to look appealing. 'Give us a break, Kev. I lost my girl.'

The foreman nodded. 'I know and I'm sorry about that, but it doesn't change the fact that you're no use to me one-handed. Go home and come back when you're fit to work.'

'You can't expect me to sit at home doing nothing just on account of a bruise,' Rob protested. 'I don't even need this bandage, but they put it on, just as a precaution they said, to remind me to be careful not to overdo it. I'm fine, really. And there must be plenty I can do here.'

'You can shift some of those bricks one handed, I suppose.

But you're on half wages until I'm satisfied you've got two good hands. And no more fighting.'

'It wasn't my fault,' Rob insisted. 'I keep telling you, he started it.'

Even his own sister was convinced he had picked a fight with one of his workmates. How could he expect the police to believe him when he told them he hadn't attacked Alice?

With a sigh, he went over to the pile of bricks that had just been unloaded and painstakingly began to stack them with one hand, muttering angrily about his pay being docked. It was going to be a long and tedious afternoon.

43

A WEEK HAD PASSED and still The Knife nestled in the cutlery drawer among lesser knives, forks and spoons. While it remained there, it posed an unnecessary threat. There was no good reason to hang on to it, but they had been through so much together, it would be a wrench to abandon it in the filthy waters of the river, as painful as burying a close friend. Of course, it had to be done. Reckless sentimentality couldn't be allowed to interfere with their carefully devised plan. Having reached a natural conclusion, there was no need for another victim. Yet every day The Knife stayed in the drawer, waiting to be needed again, its influence hard to ignore. Given the reckless delay, perhaps it was inevitable that another possibility would crop up. There was always another victim to claim.

They stumbled on their next victim by chance. It was fortunate The Knife had not been jettisoned yet because, irrational though it seemed, The Knife was germane to the success of their venture. They hadn't been looking for another victim, but Fate had thrown this woman in their path. No one was to blame if they took advantage of this final opportunity to right a terrible wrong. The hand of destiny had marked her out for death. Killer and Knife were merely its instrument.

The woman in question walked slowly through the shopping mall, blissfully unaware that she was being followed. In plain view, they were camouflaged by shoppers crowding the walkways and escalators, just another hooded figure carrying a backpack. If the woman had turned to look behind her, she would have seen only a throng of strangers manoeuvring their way between shops and cafés. Leaving the mall, she led them a short distance along the busy street to wait at a bus stop where a queue of people had already gathered in a ragged line. No one took any notice of one more anonymous person joining their number. No one knew The Knife was concealed between layers of jumpers inside an innocuous-looking rucksack at the back of the queue.

The woman took the bus to the top of her road. Only one other passenger alighted behind her, but she didn't appear to notice them follow her off the bus. Having discovered where she lived, it was simply a matter of holding out for a suitable moment. It might take several weeks of surveillance, mostly after dark, but they were used to waiting patiently for an opportunity to strike unseen. This was going to throw the police into a real tizzy. It would be the last time for a while, but having perfected their operation, they realised there was no reason to stop.

44

'There's someone here to see you, Ma'am,' the desk sergeant told Geraldine, who was engrossed in rereading post mortem reports on both the recent victims.

She sighed into the phone. 'Who is it this time?'

'She says she's Lauren's mother. She wants to speak to whoever's in charge of the investigation into her murder, although she didn't put it quite like that. She's very insistent. Verging on hysterical, in fact. What do you want me to do with her? I could send her away,' he added uncertainly.

There was a brief pause, during which Geraldine heard a shrill voice in the background.

'I'll be there in a moment,' she said.

Before going to meet Lauren's mother, Geraldine scanned the report filed by the officer who had informed the woman of her daughter's unexpected death. The mother had remained poker-faced throughout the visit and had not wanted anyone to support her. It sounded as though she had lost her self-control now. Geraldine steeled herself to face a grieving mother complaining about police inaction, as if it was their fault Alice was dead. If Alice had been killed by a random mugger, her mother would be unable to do anything to help them track down the attacker. But while it was still possible that Lauren had been deliberately murdered by someone she knew, it was important to pursue every possible lead. There was a chance Lauren's mother could give them a new insight into her daughter's life, which might assist the investigation into her death. Geraldine couldn't afford to overlook any potential source of information in an investigation that was proving so baffling.

'Mrs Stokes?' she greeted the woman who was standing in the reception area. 'I'm Detective Inspector Steel. I'm lead inspector on the investigation into Lauren's death. How can I help you?'

It was a crass question seeing as her daughter had been murdered, and the woman bristled, but it turned out she was objecting to the name Geraldine had addressed her by, rather than to the clumsy question.

'It's Miss Stokes,' the woman replied curtly, 'Miss Ann Stokes. I'm not Mrs Stokes,' she added, sounding scornful.

Having led Ann to an informal interview room, Geraldine invited her to sit down and studied the woman in front of her as she took a seat. Lauren was twenty-four when she died, which meant Ann couldn't have been more than mid-sixties, but she looked older than that. Her hair was white, her face was gaunt and wrinkled, and her veiny hands shook with what could have been Parkinson's. Her eyes had the despairing look of a woman who has been told she is terminally ill. She had nicotine stains on her fingers and a faint stench of stale tobacco hung around her, which could have explained why she seemed so jittery.

Geraldine spoke softly. 'I understand Lauren Stokes was your daughter?'

Ann didn't answer.

'I'm so sorry for your loss. Please accept my condolences.'

Still there was no response from the bereaved mother.

'When did you last see her?'

Geraldine hadn't intended to sound intrusive, but Ann reacted with a hostile glare. 'What are you accusing me of?' she demanded.

Taken aback, Geraldine concealed her surprise and explained that the police were keen to gather as much information as possible about Lauren. Anything Ann could tell them might help them to find her killer.

'So it's true what they're saying, you haven't caught him yet?'

'We're doing everything we can to bring your daughter's killer to justice.'

'Justice,' Ann scoffed. 'Is it justice when a daughter turns her back on her own mother? She did, you know. And if you ask me, she got what was coming to her,' she added in a bitter outburst. 'She was always no good, that one. I'm not a well woman. You'd think my daughter would have been there to help me, wouldn't you? Well, wouldn't you?'

Geraldine hesitated. She almost felt sorry for the woman sitting opposite her, but at the same time she couldn't help wondering what kind of a mother Ann had been. There was a malicious gleam in her eyes as she launched into a tirade against her daughter, complaining about how she had walked out of home without even stopping to say goodbye, and had failed to contact her mother even to ask after her health, which, as she was sure Geraldine could see, was not sound.

'You'd think my own daughter would have wanted to stay at home and look after me, wouldn't you? With all my ailments, you'd think she would have put aside a few hours a day to take care of me.'

Geraldine didn't answer.

'And now she's gone and got herself killed,' Ann added, as though Lauren had deliberately got herself murdered just to spite her mother.

Geraldine waited for a moment before speaking quietly, as though Ann hadn't levelled such an outrageous accusation against her daughter. Shock and grief could prompt unexpected responses from the bereaved, and irrational anger against the deceased wasn't unusual.

'Your daughter's death was a tragic accident,' she said gently.

'We haven't yet established what happened to her, but we haven't ruled out the possibility that she was killed by someone she knew.' She leaned forward. 'Can you think of anyone who might have wanted to harm your daughter? Anyone who might have had a grudge against her?'

'Apart from me, you mean?' Ann snapped. 'And before you ask, it wasn't me. Look at me. Do I look like someone who could overpower anyone, even if I wanted to? Although, if you ask me, she got what she deserved. What kind of woman abandons her poor, sick mother?'

Aware that she was clutching at straws, Geraldine tried another line of questioning. 'What about her friends? Might they be able to shed any light on what happened?'

Ann shook her head, but she was beginning to look helpless rather than angry. 'I don't know that she had any friends. If she did, I certainly never met them. I told you, I haven't spoken to her in years. She had a friend at school called Ella, but that was a long time ago. I wouldn't be surprised if she didn't have any friends at all after she abandoned me. If she could do that to her own mother, what sort of a friend was she going to be to anyone?'

Ann thought it was unlikely Lauren had kept in touch with her school friend, and couldn't remember the girl's full name.

'Did you ever meet her boyfriend?' Geraldine enquired, after noting down Ella's name.

'Which boyfriend?' Ann replied sourly. One of her hands began to shake violently in her lap and she slapped her other hand on top of it with an irritated grunt. 'She never said anything to me about any boyfriend, but she was always running around with different men. She liked them to slap her around. That was one of the reasons we argued, but we never had what you might call a close relationship. Not like a mother and daughter. No relationship at all to speak of. How's that for a daughter?'

'When did you last see her?'

'The day she walked out of the house, without a word, was the last time I saw her. You would think she would have been in touch to see how I was. For all she knew, I could be dead.'

It took a while, but eventually Geraldine was able to ascertain that seven years had passed since Lauren had left home when she was barely seventeen. Ann had heard from her only sporadically since that day, when Lauren had asked her for money.

'Last I heard, some bloke had taken her in off the street.'

'What was his name?'

'How should I know? She just called up one day, out of the blue, and told me some bloke had given her a home. More fool him, I said.'

'Did you make any attempt to find her?' Geraldine asked.

'It was up to her to come back to me,' Ann replied tartly. 'She was the one who walked out, not me. And if you think you can blame me for what happened, you're wrong. I did everything I could for that girl, brought her up single-handed, always worked to put food on the table and clothes on her back. But as soon as I fell sick and couldn't hold down a job, she was off. Thought she was better off without me. She was only ever interested in me for my money. Once that ran out, so did she.'

Ann's voice was hard and her expression bitter. Geraldine wondered if her resentment of her daughter had started only after Lauren had left her, or whether it had been a contributory factor in their estrangement. She continued to question Ann, but it was apparent that she knew next to nothing about her daughter's recent life. She didn't know Danny's name and was unable to say who Lauren had associated with for the past seven years.

'I'm sorry I couldn't be more help,' Ann muttered awkwardly as she clambered to her feet. 'I hope you catch him, whoever he is.' She hesitated. 'She was an ungrateful bitch, but she was my daughter, when all's said and done.'

There was nothing maternal in her tone. Nevertheless, Geraldine understood that despite her anger with her daughter, she was grieving for her. Gently, she promised Ann she would contact her as soon as they made any progress with the investigation, before she showed her out.

45

Without mentioning her suspicions to anyone, Geraldine set out to track down Naomi's brother, Charlie. She managed to trace Naomi's parents without too much trouble and decided to start by checking if Charlie had followed his sister's advice and returned to the family home. Mr and Mrs Arnold lived only about ten miles from York in the market town of Tadcaster. It was a pleasant drive along a good road, and she would normally have enjoyed the journey through open farmland. The sun shone from a clear blue sky; it was a while since she had left the confines of the city, but her destination dampened her mood. The thought of telling Naomi about her visit after the event hung over her, making her question whether she was being foolhardy. All too soon she arrived in the brick and stone town of Tadcaster. Passing an attractive old church, she approached a large Victorian brewery with an ornate tall stone chimney and entered the sadly rundown main street. With several empty premises and no trees, it was a depressing sight. As if in sympathy with the atmosphere of neglect, the sun vanished behind a bank of cloud, making the scene appear even more grey and dilapidated than before.

Geraldine found the address she wanted and drew up outside a decent brick-built semi-detached property. There was a small neat patch of grass beside the path leading to the front door. She rang the bell and the door was opened almost at once by a worn-looking woman whose resemblance to Naomi was noticeable. Having established that the woman was Naomi's mother and with Geraldine's identity explained, she enquired about Mrs Arnold's son. The woman's jaw dropped.

'Charlie?' she murmured. 'What has he done?'

Geraldine hastened to reassure her that Charlie wasn't in any trouble and hadn't committed a crime, as far as she was aware.

'Why do you want to see him then?' his mother replied, squinting suspiciously at Geraldine.

Neither of them mentioned Naomi, but Geraldine assumed Mrs Arnold knew she worked with her daughter. Just as she was beginning to regret having gone to Tadcaster without bringing Naomi, or at least telling her colleague about her proposed visit, Mrs Arnold invited her to go in. She led Geraldine into an open-plan, L-shaped living area, furnished as a lounge at one end, with a dining table and chairs at the other. French windows looked out on a small back garden overlooked on three sides by other houses.

'Please,' Mrs Arnold said, gesturing to an armchair. 'Sit down and tell me what you want with Charlie. Perhaps I can help you.'

Geraldine took a seat and Mrs Arnold sat opposite her. Carefully, Geraldine explained she was trying to find Charlie as she thought he might be able to help her with an ongoing investigation she was pursuing. Mrs Arnold nodded and admitted that her son had mixed with some undesirable characters. She seemed to accept what Geraldine had said without question. When Geraldine pressed her for Charlie's whereabouts, her response was disappointing. Mrs Arnold thought he was staying with his sister, Naomi.

'She's a police officer too,' she added. 'A detective.'

Geraldine was slightly surprised to discover that Naomi had never mentioned her name to her mother, but then she remembered Naomi's flash of resentment when talking about her parents and wondered if she actually saw much of them at all. It was not her place to pry into Naomi's relationship with her mother, so she merely nodded in a noncommittal way and repeated that she was looking for Charlie.

'He was staying with his sister, but he's not there any more,' she explained. 'He left her just over a week ago.'

Charlie's mother was clearly taken aback. 'Well,' she responded tartly, looking put out and not a little embarrassed, 'it seems you know more about my son's movements than I do. I thought he was still staying with Naomi.' She hesitated before asking, slightly plaintively, where Charlie was now. 'He never tells me anything,' she added, sounding resigned now and no longer resentful.

'I was hoping you would be able to tell us where he is,' Geraldine said.

'You could ask his sister?'

'She thought he might have come here.'

Mrs Arnold shook her head and muttered that was typical of Charlie. 'He'll tell us one thing and then go and do something completely different.'

'Does he have any friends he might have gone to stay with?'

'Friends?' Mrs Arnold snorted. 'I'm sorry, but I really couldn't tell you their names, any of them, even if I wanted to. He fell in with a bad crowd and that was the end of any relationship I ever had with him, my own son.'

The front door slammed. Just for an instant, Geraldine hoped Charlie might walk in, but Mrs Arnold said her husband was home. As she was speaking, a huge ball of black fur bowled into the room and hurled itself at her, panting, tail wagging furiously. If she had been standing up, the dog looked large enough to have knocked her over. She laughed.

'This is Benny,' Mrs Arnold said. 'Don't worry, he's harmless, but he's very friendly and he'll want to come over and say hello.'

The dog turned and bounded over to Geraldine, his tongue hanging out. He barked once, which Mrs Arnold explained was for attention, so Geraldine petted him and a moment later he trotted away from her and lay down at Mrs Arnold's feet. She beamed and commented on what a good dog he was. As Geraldine was politely agreeing, the door opened again. Mr Arnold's entry prompted another burst of excitement from Benny.

'He only saw me a moment ago.' Mr Arnold laughed and then checked himself on seeing Geraldine.

Like his wife, his expression darkened on hearing that Geraldine was enquiring about Charlie. He shook his head and told her that they had no idea where their son was.

'We haven't seen him for months,' he said.

There was no point in Geraldine staying any longer so she stood up and thanked them for their time. 'If Charlie turns up, or if you hear from him at all, please let me know.' She handed Mrs Arnold her card and took her leave.

The visit had been a waste of time. Not only that, she still had to disclose to Naomi that she had been to see her parents without discussing it with her first. Geraldine had been afraid Naomi might warn Charlie about her visit if she knew about it in advance. On reflection, Geraldine wondered whether that had actually been wise, as it was going to be obvious she hadn't trusted her colleague. She considered phoning Naomi to be sure she spoke to her before her parents could tell her about the visit, but she decided it would be best to tackle the situation face to face. As she drove the short distance back to York, she hoped she would have a chance to speak to Naomi before her parents could. She still wasn't sure what she was going to say and hoped Naomi would understand her decision.

46

Geraldine returned to the police station towards the end of the afternoon. As soon as she arrived, Naomi strode over to her desk. She had obviously spoken to her mother, and she accosted Geraldine furiously.

'Why didn't you say anything to me before you went rushing off to question my parents?' she hissed, flushed with anger.

Geraldine mumbled awkwardly about not wanting to embarrass Naomi in front of her parents. 'I thought you would insist on coming with me and I didn't want them to think you were involved.'

'That wasn't your decision to make. You should have spoken to me first.'

'I wanted to speak to your brother, not you,' Geraldine reminded her.

'Why did you want to speak to him? You suspected him, didn't you, without a shred of evidence, just because he happened to be here in York at the time the murders took place. Talk about clutching at straws. If you'd spoken to me first, you'd never have gone rushing off like that.'

Geraldine was taken aback. Not wanting to openly admit that she suspected Charlie was violent towards Naomi, she mumbled that it was a coincidence him being here just at the time two women were killed and she was keen to eliminate him from the enquiry.

'Do you think he was the only person to visit York at that

time? In any case, that doesn't explain why you went sneaking off to look for him without talking to me first. You might as well admit that you didn't trust me not to tip him off about you going to look for him. What did you think? That I'd cover up for him if it turned out he was the killer? I suppose it didn't occur to you that I would have brought him up as a suspect myself if there was any chance he had been responsible for killing two women? Is that really what you think of me?'

Geraldine sighed. 'I thought there is a chance he was responsible and you could be shutting your eyes to that possibility because you're emotionally involved with him.'

Naomi shook her head. 'I'm not shutting my eyes to anything. I know better than anyone what my brother is like and what he's capable of doing, and I know he didn't kill Lauren. Even if it wasn't impossible for him to have done something like that, the fact is he was fighting with me that night. Do you think I'd forget something like that? Or make it up to give him an alibi? That's why I threw him out. I told him he had to go first thing in the morning. But he wasn't out of my sight all evening when Lauren was killed, and he didn't actually leave until midday on Sunday, when she had already been dead for hours, so it couldn't have been him. In any case, Charlie might lash out when he's high, or drunk, but that's what it amounts to. He lashes out. And most of the time he misses, because he's too drunk to hit his target. There's no way he could have attacked someone without them showing some signs of having defended themselves. And as if that's not enough to convince you your theory was implausible, Charlie's too high most of the time to plan one murder, let alone two. You should have asked me instead of running off to my parents to look for him and upsetting them for no reason, when I could have told you he's not guilty.'

'Do you know where he is?' Geraldine asked.

'No, but even if I did, I wouldn't tell you. Not now. Because unless you don't believe a word I've said, you would accept that there's no need for you to know where he is. So there it is. I'm not going to help you look for him. And if you don't trust me, well, that can work both ways.' Naomi turned on her heel and stalked away.

Geraldine nearly leapt to her feet and followed her, but she decided to leave Naomi alone to simmer down for a while. Eventually, she would have to acknowledge that, mistaken though Geraldine had been, she had acted in a way that she had judged necessary at the time. If Naomi couldn't bring herself to see that, then they might struggle to work together again.

'What's wrong?' Ariadne asked Geraldine, coming over to her desk. Geraldine shrugged and didn't even look round. 'Come on, I can see there's something on your mind. Do you want to talk about it?' Ariadne moved forward to stand beside Geraldine.

'Is it that obvious?'

'Probably not to most people,' Ariadne replied, 'but I know you too well for you to try and fake it in front of me. You can tell me about it, if you want to talk to someone.'

All at once, Geraldine felt a wave of relief. Grateful to share her misery, she admitted that she had fallen out with Naomi.

'With Naomi?' Ariadne repeated in surprise. 'What happened?'

'It's too complicated to explain, but I behaved crassly and made her think I don't trust her. Of course I do, but now she's lost all respect for me and will probably never trust me again.'

'I'm sure what you did can't have been that bad,' Ariadne said.

Geraldine shrugged. 'I prioritised the investigation over her feelings. I make no apologies for that, but she's the best sergeant – one of the best, that is,' she corrected herself quickly, with a glance at Ariadne, 'one of the best colleagues I've ever worked with, and it's going to be difficult to rebuild the trust we had.'

They both knew how crucial it was for members of the team to have complete trust in one another. In potentially dangerous situations it could mean the difference between life and death.

'Why don't you tell her what you just told me?' Ariadne asked.

'She's not going to listen to me.'

'You could at least try,' another voice chimed in. 'Maybe I'm more understanding than you think.'

Geraldine whirled round to see Naomi standing behind her.

'Much as I'm enjoying listening to you flatter me behind my back, I think I've heard enough,' she said with a faint smile. 'I dare say you were doing what you thought was best and I suppose it's fair enough that you were hoping to spare my feelings if it turned out Charlie was involved in some way.'

Ariadne looked baffled. 'Who's Charlie?' she asked.

'Don't expect Geraldine to tell you,' Naomi replied, before Geraldine could answer. 'She might not trust you to keep quiet in front of me.'

'I thought you'd accepted my apology?' Geraldine reminded her.

'All right,' Naomi agreed.

'Let's leave it that we had a disagreement but it's over now.'

Geraldine saw her own relief reflected in Naomi's smile.

'Come on then, team,' Geraldine said, 'we've got a killer to track down.'

47

NAOMI SPENT THE FOLLOWING day searching online for any mention of Lauren's friend. All they knew about her was her first name, Ella, although even that could have been just a nickname. Lauren was on Instagram and Facebook but she wasn't active on either. She had set up her accounts while she was still a teenager and had a flurry of activity for about a year, but she had hardly posted anything online since leaving school. She had very few connections, none of whom were called Ella. Despite extensive searching, Naomi could find no one with that name on Lauren's social media accounts, and it seemed the two girls had never connected online. Probably they had lost touch after they left school. In the absence of any other information, Geraldine decided to ask Danny, as there was a possibility he might be able to point them to any friends Lauren had associated with before her death. If her friends suspected Danny was guilty, then he was unlikely to want to help them find them, but she thought it was worth asking. At any rate, it could do no harm to try.

Geraldine called at the betting shop and found Danny standing behind the counter. She waited for a moment while he took a bet from an elderly man in a shabby raincoat before she stepped up to the counter. He looked up, and seeing who was facing him, gave a surly nod.

'I don't know what you want with me now,' he complained with exaggerated weariness. 'I've already answered all your questions. I've got nothing more to say to you. You've had your go at me and it's over. I'd like you to leave me alone from now on.' He glanced around the betting shop as though to emphasise that he was working and unavailable for further questioning. 'This conversation is over.'

'As long as we're still looking into what happened, it's not over,' she replied. 'The investigation remains ongoing, and we will continue to question you whenever we feel it's necessary.'

'Look, I would never have hurt Lauren, so can't you leave me alone to get on with my life and grieve for her without you harassing me all the time?' he replied in a low voice, leaning towards the window and staring at her. 'I've got work to do here.'

Quietly Geraldine explained what she wanted.

'Friends?' Danny repeated, looking bemused. 'You want to know if she had any friends?'

'Yes. Did you ever meet any of Lauren's friends?' Geraldine repeated her question patiently.

Danny shook his head, looking puzzled. 'No. I never met anyone and there was no one that I knew about. She did mention one girl, someone called Ella, but I never met her and, before you ask, I've no idea what her full name is, or where she lives. There was a woman at the shelter where she was staying before she moved in with me, but I don't know her name or anything about her. It's not that I wasn't interested in Lauren's life or anything like that,' he added defensively, 'it just never came up. She was a very private person. Now, I need to get on with my job.'

The betting shop wasn't busy, but evidently Danny couldn't or wouldn't give Geraldine the information she wanted. Ann had mentioned that Lauren had met her friend, Ella, while they were still at school, so Geraldine decided it would be worth making enquiries there. She went to the reception desk at the school Lauren had attended and explained what she wanted. The school secretary contacted the head teacher who came out to talk to her after a short delay. He smiled genially at Geraldine as he asked how he could help her. It was six years since Lauren had left the school, and he told her he had only been at the school for three years. While he was able to confirm that Lauren Stokes had been a pupil there and that there had indeed been a girl in her class called Ella Fletcher, he explained that had never met either of them himself. The school kept fairly detailed records of their pupils, but he suggested Geraldine might find it more helpful in the first instance to speak to his deputy head, who had been working at the school for longer than he had. She would almost certainly have known the two girls Geraldine was enquiring about.

The deputy head, Sonia Jackman, came bustling into the reception area a couple of minutes later. A stout middle-aged woman with a bouffant-style hairdo and a maroon suit, she gazed at Geraldine with an air of authority and announced that she could only stay for a few minutes. Just then a pupil walked past them and the deputy head pounced on the girl, demanding to know why she wasn't in a lesson. The girl started as though she had been ambushed and mumbled incoherently about having a doctor's appointment. Geraldine waited patiently, observing the deputy head.

'I've got a class in a moment,' Sonia explained, turning back to Geraldine when the pupil had accounted for her movements and gone on her way. 'Now, I understand you're here to ask about Lauren Stokes. We heard about what happened to her. What a tragedy. It's hard to believe.' She shook her head with a solemn expression and her hair waggled comically. Geraldine wondered if any of her pupils giggled when she moved her head around. 'Such a dreadful thing to happen to a young woman,' the deputy went on.

'Do you remember her?'

'Oh yes, I remember her well. I taught her,' Sonia said gravely.

'Can you tell me what you remember about her? I know it's a few years since she left school, but anything you can tell us might be helpful, especially details about who she might have associated with while she was here.'

Sonia narrowed her eyes and stared at Geraldine. 'You don't know who did it, do you?' She sounded disappointed. Somehow, Geraldine felt as though she was a pupil who had failed a test she had been expected to pass.

'What can you tell me about her?' Geraldine repeated firmly, determined to hang on to her own authority and find out as much as she could before the deputy head rushed away to teach.

'Lauren was a quiet girl, very reserved. To be frank, we were a bit worried about her being so withdrawn when she first joined the school. But she was never any trouble,' the deputy head added quickly. 'She was just very shy. Her parents were separated, I think, although I could be wrong about that. I'd have to check the records. At any rate, I don't think we ever saw her father.'

'What was her mother like?'

Sonia screwed up her face in an effort to remember. 'Possibly a little histrionic? But I could be confusing her with someone else. We see so many pupils over the years. I remember the ones I taught, but I don't remember all their parents. I have a feeling Lauren's mother wasn't very interested in her daughter's progress, but I'd need to check our records to be sure. She could have been overly fussy and interfering, or else uninterested in her child. Possibly both. You'd be surprised how inconsistent parents can be when it comes to finding out about their own children.'

'And what can you tell me about Ella Fletcher?'

A bell rang, prompting Sonia to glance at her watch. 'Ella Fletcher? Oh yes, I remember her. That is, I remember the two of them together.' She smiled. 'Lauren and Ella were inseparable. Ella was the reason we never intervened with Lauren. We thought as long as she had one good friend, there was nothing much to worry about. It's the loners, the solitary children, who are most at risk of being bullied.' She broke off with a frown. 'Not that bullying is a problem here, of course. I wouldn't want to give you the wrong impression of the school. We implement a zero tolerance policy when it comes to bullying. But Lauren was vulnerable, one of those pupils who seem to be a target for bullies. I know that sounds like victim blaming. It's not, but there's no getting away from the fact that some children are less mentally robust than others. Funnily enough, out of the two of them we thought Ella was the one most likely to need support because she'd grown up in care after being removed from an abusive father. But that makes some children emotionally resilient. Lauren was the opposite, of course.'

She glanced anxiously at Geraldine, who murmured a few vague words of encouragement.

'Anyway,' the deputy head resumed, 'Ella was a sensible girl, and we were pleased when she took Lauren under her wing and wanted to look after her. After they became best friends, Lauren seemed much happier and we felt she was no longer at risk of being bullied. Ella stood up for her, so we didn't need to. It's usually better that way, when problems are resolved among the children without our having to intervene.' She gave an awkward smile. 'I don't want to make it sound like we have a problem with bullying here, but it's a fact of life in all schools, however hard we work to try and eradicate it.'

'Like crime in society at large,' Geraldine muttered, more to herself than to the deputy head who raised her eyebrows.

'Please do contact us if you have any further questions,' Sonia said, as she excused herself and hurried away, leaving Geraldine to wonder how fragile Lauren had coped once she no longer had her best friend, Ella, looking out for her.

48

Having traced Ella Fletcher, Geraldine decided to pay her a visit before going home at the end of the afternoon. In common with her best friend from school, Ella lived in York, although unlike Lauren, she had not lived there continuously since leaving school. She was renting a flat in Amberley Street off Acomb Road. As she was living locally, Geraldine didn't phone ahead, so Ella had no idea the police would be calling on her. There was a slim chance she might be more relaxed and readier to talk freely if she hadn't been given time to prepare for the visit and become anxious about it. Geraldine had explained her reasoning to Sam, whom she had brought along for the experience of questioning someone who might conceivably be able to offer useful information. He had looked at her stoically. She had the impression he didn't agree with her reasoning, but he hadn't said anything. Geraldine hoped he had taken her earlier reprimand on board and wasn't going to sulk, and was pleased when he drove her to Ella's address cheerfully enough.

Amberley Street was a quiet road of small terraced houses with front doors that opened directly on to the narrow pavement. Several of the properties looked in need of restoration. Geraldine swore under her breath when it began to rain just as they pulled up. Climbing out of the car, they hurried to Ella's house where Geraldine rang the bell. There was no porch to shelter under and they waited in the light rain, huddled in their jackets. After a few minutes a small dark-haired woman came to the door. She could have been around the same age as Lauren.

'Are you Ella Fletcher?' Geraldine enquired.

'Yes. Why? Who are you?' the young woman asked with a faintly belligerent air. She looked at each of them in turn with a worried expression.

Having established the woman's name was Ella Fletcher, Geraldine quickly introduced herself and her companion. Ella appeared startled on hearing who they were, but she quickly recovered her composure and stared impassively at Geraldine. 'What do you want with me?' she asked, making no move to invite them indoors, even though it was raining.

Geraldine explained the purpose of their visit, and Ella admitted that she had been friends with Lauren.

'May we come in?' Geraldine asked.

Ella looked at her warily. 'What for?'

'Because it's raining,' Sam muttered.

'What do you want?' Ella repeated.

Geraldine reiterated that they were investigating what had happened to Lauren. 'You must have seen the sad news.'

Ella nodded. 'I read about how she was killed online,' she conceded. 'It's all over the news.'

'We know she was a close friend of yours at one time, and we would like to ask you a few questions about her. It might help us understand more about her life. We're questioning everyone who knew her,' she added reassuringly.

'You want to know about Lauren's life?' Ella repeated, frowning. 'I would have thought you'd be more interested in finding out about her death. What do you want from me?'

The rain had started falling more heavily, and Geraldine asked again whether they might go inside. With a shrug, Ella nodded and moved aside to let them in. Entering the hall, they picked their way through an assortment of shoes, empty packets left from deliveries and a bag with a logo of a local gym. Geraldine wondered if the rest of the flat was similarly untidy and whether Ella had wanted to keep them on the doorstep because she was embarrassed to let anyone see the chaos in her living room. Ella stood blocking the narrow hall, preventing them from going any further, muttering that she didn't want them dripping all over her living room. At least they were under cover, but the hall was narrow, and they had to stand in single file, with Sam hovering behind Geraldine who stood facing Ella.

'Lauren's mother told us you met Lauren while you were at school?' Geraldine began.

'Yes.' Ella nodded. 'That's right. We were at school together. We were best friends.' She hesitated, before adding angrily, 'I can't believe anyone would do that to her. It's sick.'

'Did you keep in touch with Lauren after you left school?' Geraldine continued.

Ella hesitated before answering. 'Yes, sort of. I mean, we were friends. Why wouldn't we keep in touch? Only we didn't see much of each other once she moved in with Danny.' Her voice took on a bitter tone when she mentioned Lauren's boyfriend, whom she had evidently disliked.

Geraldine waited for a few seconds in case she was going to continue, but Ella fell silent.

'What did you think of him?' Geraldine prompted her gently when it became clear that Ella wasn't going to say any more about Danny.

Ella shook her head. 'He was no good for her. He was really bad news.'

She glanced at Geraldine from under lowered lids, and Geraldine had the impression she was holding back from telling them everything she knew about Danny. This seemed promising. If she could only persuade Ella to open up, they might gather some useful information.

'In what way was he no good for her?' Geraldine asked.

Ella hesitated again. She appeared to be considering how much to tell them. 'I think he used to hurt her, I mean physically hurt her,' she mumbled at last, adding in a rush that he was a sadistic monster.

'That's a very serious allegation,' Geraldine said, hoping to tease more information out of her. 'What makes you say that?'

'She had a cigarette burn on her arm one time. She tried to cover it up but I saw it. She said he hadn't done that to her, but she was lying. He did it all right.'

'Did you witness him harming her?' Sam piped up, a little too eagerly.

'I witnessed her injury,' Ella replied stonily.

Geraldine tensed, hoping Sam hadn't pushed too hard, but suddenly Ella's composure fractured. Her face twisted with distress and tears spilled from her eyes. 'It's my fault she's dead,' she wailed. 'It's all my fault.'

Behind her, Geraldine heard Sam stir and she glanced back at him with a slight frown, warning him to be quiet.

'I tried to persuade her to leave him,' Ella blurted out. Listening to Ella, Geraldine remembered hearing how she used to protect Lauren from bullies at school. 'Why did she stay with someone who treated her like that?' Ella cried out, clearly distressed. 'She insisted I had the wrong impression of him and he would never hurt her, but I know what I saw. We argued about it the last time we met. I wanted to help her but she refused to listen. And now she's dead.' She stared at Geraldine, stricken. 'It's my fault she's dead. It's all my fault.'

'What do you mean?' Geraldine asked softly, scarcely able to credit what appeared to be a confession. 'How was it your fault?'

Ella's next words dispelled the impression that she had just admitted she was guilty of murdering Alice and Lauren. 'He must have killed her because she tried to leave him. But was that because of what I said to her? I pushed her to leave him.'

Geraldine reassured the distraught girl that she was not responsible for Lauren's death. Regaining her self-control,

Ella said bitterly that she couldn't understand why Lauren's boyfriend hadn't been arrested.

'He was a vicious bastard and now he's gone and killed her. Why isn't he behind bars? He needs to be punished for what he did. Prison's too good for him.'

The venom in Ella's voice only confirmed how attached she had been to her friend.

'We're really sorry for your loss,' Geraldine said gently. 'It was a terrible tragedy, and I assure you we're working round the clock to find out who did this to Lauren. We're investigating Danny as a possible suspect. How well did you know him?' She explained that any specific details Ella could give them about him might help them to build a case against him.

'I met him once. That was enough. I could see straight away what he was like.' Her eyes widened in an expression of alarm. 'Promise me you won't tell him I mentioned his name to you. I don't want that psychopath coming after me.'

Geraldine reassured Ella that they wouldn't mention her name to Danny. Even so, Ella flatly refused to go with them to the police station to make a statement. She clammed up and declined to say anything else. After a few more questions to which Ella replied only that she hadn't wanted to have anything to do with Danny and had tried to persuade Lauren to leave him, Geraldine and Sam left, stepping carefully over shoes and packaging.

'She was scared of Danny, wasn't she?' Sam asked as they climbed back in the car. 'Genuinely scared. And she only met him once.'

'She certainly seemed very nervous of him,' Geraldine agreed. 'She seems convinced that Danny killed her friend, so it's understandable she would be scared of him. But we know he couldn't have killed Alice. So unless by some incredible coincidence we have two killers using identical knives, he didn't kill Lauren either.'

Sam nodded. 'Unless he's lying. He could have drugged Lauren and slipped away to kill Alice without anyone else knowing.'

Geraldine shook her head. 'It doesn't add up. Jonah said some of those cigarette burns went back years. She'd only been with Danny for about a year and the burn marks seem to have stopped when she was seeing him.' She was convinced Danny could not have killed Lauren, but he might be able to provide them with a vital clue as to who did.

'I think it's time we had another word with Danny, find out what was going on. We need to bring him in, but before we do, we'll double check all the CCTV near the B&B where he and Lauren were staying when Alice was killed. His alibi seems to add up, but given what we've just learned, we're going to reexamine him from every possible angle under a very strong microscope. If there's the tiniest crack in his story, we need to find it.'

She broke off, aware that her voice was rising in exasperation, and pressed her lips together firmly. Apart from anything else, Sam had the makings of a first-rate detective, and she needed to set him a good example. If she allowed her frustration to overrule reason, she would be doing exactly what she had reprimanded him for doing.

'We'll get whoever did this,' she assured him, smiling fiercely. 'Wherever he's hiding, we'll find him.'

She fell silent, aware that she was trying to convince herself, not Sam. He nodded uneasily, and they drove back to the police station without talking, each of them absorbed in their own thoughts.

49

Geraldine had spent a frustrating day searching for information and wanted a break from work, but it was difficult to stop thinking about Alice and Lauren, puzzling over who might have been responsible for both deaths. All the leads they had found so far had led nowhere. At the time of Alice's death, Danny had been in Scarborough and Rob had been with his friends. Ruling them both out for the attack on Alice meant that the team no longer had a likely suspect for either of the two murders. Not only that, but they were still no closer to finding a killer who had already struck twice. For all they knew, the perpetrator might be busy stalking his next victim, even as they were hunting for him. It was a horrifying thought. When the time came to go home, Geraldine found it difficult to drag herself away from her desk, but she could no longer stay late at work whenever she felt like it. She had other responsibilities, on top of her work, now that she and Ian had a baby. Determined to put her work out of her mind for the evening, she went home.

'How was your day?' Ian asked her, smiling as he reached to embrace her.

In spite of her intention to keep her problems to herself, she found herself blurting out her work issues to Ian, who listened patiently and empathised with her frustration.

'And now we don't have any leads to follow up,' she concluded wretchedly. 'We'll have to start looking further back in the history of the two victims and see if we can find an ex-boyfriend or something similar to investigate, because at the moment we don't have anything to go on. Either we're looking for one killer, or by some strange coincidence two fatal incidents occurred within a mile of each other, carried out by killers using identical knives.'

She shook her head. She wasn't sure if Ian was still listening, but she carried on anyway, turning over possibilities aloud, mainly for her own benefit. She only stopped talking when Tom woke up and began to yell.

'I'm sorry,' she muttered, with an apologetic smile, when she returned to the living room with a pacified Tom snuggling in her arms. 'I didn't mean to bore you with it all. It's not your case and it's not as if it's even very interesting. Two victims, one killer, no leads. That's all there is to say, really.'

Ian smiled as he reached out for Tom. 'Don't be daft,' he told her. 'Of course I'm interested in anything that affects you.'

'I'm sure we'll get to the bottom of it,' she said, feigning a confidence she wasn't feeling.

'I never doubted that for a second,' Ian replied, his attention on Tom who was giggling at being tickled.

Watching them, Geraldine smiled and offered to make dinner. Leaving Ian playing with Tom, she went to the kitchen to see what she could find to eat. She and Ian had both been busy and neither of them had been shopping that week. Resorting to scrabbling through what she could find in the freezer, she landed on some breaded fish and a packet of frozen chips.

'How does fish and chips grab you?' she called out.

'I thought you were going to be cooking?' he called back.

'From the freezer. That counts as cooking, doesn't it?'

'Fair enough,' he laughed, adding that fish and chips sounded good.

Humming to herself, Geraldine put two generous portions of fish in the oven before spreading chips on a tray to go in once the fish was defrosted. As she laid the table, she contemplated how her life had changed since Ian had moved in with her, and even more so since Tom had come along. Before her son was born, she would have been at her desk right now, working her way through witness accounts and suspects' statements, searching for a clue to unlock the mystery and solve the case. Instead, she was busy at home, feeding the baby and preparing dinner for herself and Ian. Recently, they had decided to eat in the kitchen in the evenings, instead of in front of the television. Geraldine wanted to set Tom an example by eating at the table, even though he was still too young to understand what was happening, and Ian agreed with her. He thought it would be good for him to hear adult conversation as well.

'He's already trying to talk.' Geraldine said, as they sat down at the table together.

As she spoke, Tom started to burble and she and Ian both laughed.

'I think he understands a lot more than we realise. We'll soon have to avoid talking about work,' she added. 'It really helps to talk things through with you, but we won't be able to do that for much longer when Tom's in the room. We don't want to traumatise the poor child.'

They had finished eating and Tom was fast asleep in his cot when the phone rang. Geraldine was about to clear the table, but hearing who was calling, Ian offered to stack the dishwasher. Grateful for the reprieve, Geraldine settled down in the living room to chat to her adopted sister.

'Geraldine, how are you? We haven't seen you for such a long time. How's Tom? Is he walking yet? And how's Ian?'

'We're all fine. Tom's not walking yet, but he's trying, and he's trying to talk as well, making all sorts of sounds. He's discovered he can blow raspberries.' She laughed. 'What's the latest with you?'

Listening to Celia chattering about her own family, Geraldine felt her attention wander. With an effort, she forced herself to focus on what her sister was saying. Having gone through all her family news, Celia enquired about Geraldine's work. Geraldine sighed, but she couldn't share any details of the case with her sister. She mumbled about work being busy and Celia laughed.

'What's new? But seriously, Geraldine, you're not overdoing it, are you? You can't keep going like you used to, not now you've got Tom waking you up at night.'

Geraldine sighed. She and her sister had engaged in this conversation several times before, and the exchange often felt uneasy. Having given up work to devote herself to running her home and raising her two children, Celia struggled to understand why Geraldine had wanted to return to work so soon after Tom was born.

'He's not even one yet,' she had protested.

But Celia had never been keen to go out to work, even before she was married. She had flitted from one uninspiring job to another, regarding work as something to be endured for the sake of the extra income, and had happily handed in her notice as soon as she had fallen pregnant with her firstborn, Chloe. That was seventeen years ago, and she had made no effort to look for another job since then. Geraldine believed her when she claimed to be perfectly content to potter about at home. Bringing up two children and looking after the house and garden seemed to keep her fully occupied, even though she had a cleaner and a gardener. Geraldine, by contrast, had always been focused on her career and couldn't imagine being satisfied with a life of comfortable domesticity.

'I don't know what you mean when you say you need the challenge of working,' Celia had countered, when Geraldine had tried to explain her feelings. 'Bringing up children is enough of a challenge for anyone.'

Geraldine had always felt it was unfair that Celia felt entitled to take the moral high ground in such discussions, frequently finding fault with Geraldine's choices. She never came right out and said she thought Geraldine and Ian should have married before Tom was born, and Geraldine should have given up work altogether, but she implied it. Celia was, of course, entitled to think that Geraldine should marry and stay at home to look after Tom. If Geraldine had been completely satisfied that she had made the right choice for Tom, she would have dismissed Celia's criticisms without a second thought. But she felt ambivalent about leaving Tom with a childminder, and listening to Celia's veiled concern only pricked her conscience. She knew Celia meant well so she let her talk, confident it wouldn't be long before she left off commenting on Geraldine's life to resume talking about her own family. With a teenage daughter and a toddler, she had plenty to say, and Geraldine was pleased to be distracted from her own situation as she listened to Celia's misgivings about Chloe's friendship with a boy.

'You mean she's got a boyfriend?' Geraldine interjected when Celia took a breath.

Celia sighed. 'She's too young to get involved with a boy.'

'Remember what you were like at seventeen?'

'That's what worries me.'

'It's only natural she'd be interested in boys at her age,' Geraldine reassured her, not for the first time. 'You wouldn't want her to end up like me.'

Celia sounded surprised. 'What are you talking about? What's wrong with you?'

Geraldine was surprised in her turn. 'Well, I'm not married, for a start.'

'So what?'

'I always thought you disapproved of me being single and a mother.'

'If you wanted to get married, you would. But, in any case, that's hardly the point. You're not seventeen. And you're a successful career woman,' Celia added, sounding a little wistful.

Geraldine resisted retorting that she didn't feel very successful, with an unidentified killer at large. Most failures at work had financial consequences. In her job, failure put innocent lives at risk.

50

CASTING AROUND FOR ANOTHER lead, Geraldine studied the pathologist's reports into the two murders carefully before speaking to Jonah again.

'Geraldine,' he greeted her when he came to the phone. 'To what do I owe this pleasure? It's always lovely to hear your voice. Why don't you call me more often? There's no need to be coy with me. You know I'm counting the hours until I hear from you again.'

Geraldine couldn't help laughing at his nonsense, even though she knew she ought to discourage him from addressing her in such inappropriate language. She had all but given up trying to warn him that he was going to get himself in trouble one day by flirting with a woman who didn't appreciate his banter. He seemed to have no concept of political correctness.

'When you work with the dead, you realise ideas about gender and ethnicity are meaningless,' he replied, when she warned him about using language that some people might find inappropriate or offensive. 'Once you open people up, you find we're all the same inside. We all deteriorate with age just the same. I should know. Remove a few organs and appendages, and the odd irregularity, and there's not much difference between one cadaver and the next.'

'I'm talking about the living, not the dead. These days, people are easily offended. Not everyone's going to appreciate your humour.'

'Doing a job like mine, I'm entitled to seek a little light relief from time to time.'

'Yes, but some people won't see your joking around as light relief,' she replied.

'I refuse to let anyone dictate what I may or may not find amusing. If anyone challenges my right to a little harmless fun, they can try doing my job and see how they feel then.'

'You are incorrigible. I'd hate to see you getting in hot water but I'm really afraid it's only a matter of time.'

'Everything's only a matter of time. None of us are here forever. You and I face that reality more often than most people. What's wrong with trying to lighten the mood a little?'

With an exasperated sigh, she scolded him for being deliberately obtuse before explaining the reason for her call. She added that she had studied his report but wanted more details about the timing of Lauren's past injuries.

'Ah yes, those troublesome cigarette burns,' Jonah said, his levity gone. 'There may have been other injuries as well, which are less clear-cut. There's evidence of possible broken ribs in the past and a broken wrist. But there's no ambiguity about those cigarette burns. They leave a very distinctive scar.'

'Yes, I saw that in your report. My question is, what do you mean by "over the years"? Specifically, how long ago might the earliest cigarette burns have been inflicted?'

There was a pause. When Jonah replied, he sounded uncharacteristically hesitant.

'That's really very difficult to say.'

'Off the record, what's your opinion?'

'Possibly as long ago as five or six years, but that's just an educated guess. It could be ten years depending on the severity of the burn. Some of the scars were made quite recently. I can't really be more specific than that. Whoever did that to her was a sadistic bastard,' he went on, becoming animated in his anger. 'Are you thinking whoever did that also killed her? It seems likely, doesn't it? I hope you nail him soon, whoever it was. Such monstrous cruelty almost beggars belief. Between you and me, I don't suppose a sick pervert like that is likely to just stop. What's hard to stomach is that the poor girl put up with such abuse for so long. Poor, sad thing. One of life's victims, I suppose.'

Geraldine nodded, although Jonah couldn't see her. The deputy head at Lauren's school had said very much the same thing. She pondered the phrase, 'one of life's victims'.

'I'm not saying she was in any way culpable,' Jonah added quickly. 'Please don't run away with the idea that I'm victim blaming. Nothing can possibly excuse that kind of torture. There's no other word for it. And for what? Some sadistic satisfaction? To exercise control through fear? There's no way to look at it other than to say it's unhinged. And I dare say the killer will weasel his way out of a custodial sentence by putting up a defence of insanity,' he concluded bitterly.

Geraldine let him talk uninterrupted for a few minutes before she cut in to thank him for his help and say she had to go. She rang off quickly before he had a chance to start telling her how much he was going to miss her. He had given her something to think about and she needed to focus on it. But she could barely contain her excitement at this hint of a lead which had actually been right in front of her for a week. Someone had been burning Lauren with lit cigarettes. So far they had been assuming that was Danny. He was Lauren's boyfriend with a history of violence and he smoked. But the injuries had been inflicted over the course of several years, which meant the perpetrator was not only Danny. He might have picked up on the abuse and continued with it, but depending on when he had first met Lauren, it now appeared that someone else had been abusing her since before she and Danny had met. Geraldine recalled Ann's nicotine-stained fingers.

'You're not suggesting her mother was responsible?' Ariadne asked when Geraldine shared her idea with her colleagues.

Geraldine hadn't often seen her sergeant looking shocked, but she seemed shaken by the suggestion that Lauren's mother might have been viciously abusing her over a long period of time before killing her.

'Do you really think it could be her?' Ariadne repeated.

Geraldine shrugged. 'Right now, we don't know what happened, but it's a possibility. It's our job to find out if it could be true, however hideous it is. So let's have Ann brought in for further questioning.'

Naomi was occupied conducting research on the Home Office Large Major Enquiry cross-referencing system, looking for similar cases. With two victims having apparently been stabbed by the same person, it was possible there could have been more. If so, other unsolved investigations might offer information that would help in finally identifying the killer. So far, the only unsolved murder that bore any similarity to the two cases currently under investigation in York had happened nearly three hundred miles away, in Portsmouth, seven years earlier. There didn't seem to be anything to connect it to the York cases other than a single fatal stab wound to the heart and the absence of clues to the identity of the killer. But absence of evidence proved nothing.

Leaving Ariadne to arrange for Ann to be picked up, Geraldine went to the betting shop where Danny worked. Ignoring a couple of men who were seated at small tables studying screens, she walked past the gambling machines with their flashing lights and went straight to the counter where Danny was watching her approach.

'Have you found him yet?' he muttered in a low voice before she could speak.

She didn't answer directly. 'We're investigating what happened,' she said. 'Can I speak to you for a few moments?'

Danny glanced around, but the betting shop wasn't busy and no one was waiting to place a bet. Exchanging a nod with a colleague who was standing at another position at the counter, Danny gestured at Geraldine to meet him in the cramped office at the far side of the long counter. The door opened from inside a moment after she knocked and Danny admitted her. The air in the office seemed even staler than she remembered it, and she sat down awkwardly on the solitary chair while Danny perched on the edge of the scratched desk.

'We're looking into what happened to Lauren before the attack,' Geraldine said, as delicately as she could.

Danny kept very still as though he might crack if he moved a muscle.

'What can you tell me about Lauren's relationship with her mother?'

'Her mother?' he repeated. He looked uncomfortable and hesitated. 'Why don't you ask her?' he mumbled at last. 'I've got nothing more to say to you.'

Geraldine was convinced he was hiding something, but he refused to say anything else, claiming that he had never even met Ann.

'Lauren had severed ties with her mother,' he admitted, when Geraldine pressed him. 'She refused to even speak about her. Now, if that's all?' He stood up, suddenly brisk. 'I need to get back to work.'

'Did Lauren tell you much about her mother?'

'No, I just told you, she wouldn't talk about her.'

'Yet you know they were estranged?'

Danny sat back on the edge of the desk. 'All she told me was that she had walked out of her mother's house years ago and hadn't seen her since. And she said she didn't want to see her either. But she never told me why they had fallen out and I never asked. These things happen in families. It's not unusual,' he added sourly, leaving Geraldine to wonder about his own family history.

There was nothing more Geraldine could say. Urging him

to contact her directly if he thought of anything else about Lauren's mother, she left. The meeting hadn't been entirely unsatisfactory. She was now convinced that Danny was hiding something about Lauren and her mother. It seemed as though there might be some substance to Geraldine's suspicions of Ann, although why Danny would be reluctant to talk about it was puzzling.

'Perhaps he's embarrassed that he didn't know any more about Lauren's relationship with her mother,' Ariadne suggested when Geraldine discussed what Danny had said.

Geraldine had a feeling there was more to it than that. She just couldn't work out what might lie behind Danny's reticence.

51

Ann looked even more agitated than on the previous occasion she had faced Geraldine, possibly because this time Ariadne was also present to give the encounter a more formal appearance. Ann's eyes were slightly bloodshot, her hair looked greasy and her complexion had a greyish tinge. Compared to Ariadne, with her glowing olive complexion, glossy hair and bright eyes, Ann looked seriously unhealthy. Clearly she wasn't taking care of herself. The cuffs of her jumper were frayed and she fidgeted with one of them, picking at a loose thread. Geraldine wanted to warn her to stop pulling it before the sleeve started to unravel. Not in a position to afford to buy many clothes, she would probably be well advised to look after the ones she had. But it wasn't Geraldine's place to comment on Ann's wardrobe. She had more important matters to raise with a potential suspect in a murder enquiry.

'What's this about?' Ann asked, clearly perturbed. 'Why have you brought me here? Do I need a lawyer?'

'You have that right,' Geraldine replied, wondering what dark secrets Ann might be hiding. 'Although, if you are innocent of any wrongdoing, I can't see why that would be necessary.'

'I've heard,' Ann muttered and stopped. 'I've heard stories about what you do to people in here, pushing them to confess even when they've done nothing wrong.'

Geraldine gave what she hoped was an encouraging smile. 'We just want to talk to you about your daughter. This isn't a formal interview. You haven't been charged with any crime. There's no need to be frightened.'

Ann grunted and lowered her eyes, seemingly reassured, although her nicotine-stained fingers continued compulsively fiddling with her sleeve. Geraldine watched as a few more stitches unwound. 'What do you want to know?'

'Tell us about your relationship with Lauren,' Geraldine said.

Ann shrugged and was silent.

'She was your only child, wasn't she?'

Ann nodded.

'How would you describe your relationship with her?' Geraldine persisted.

'She was my daughter,' Ann replied, her voice devoid of emotion. 'My only child. I was her mother. What do you think?'

'Why did she leave home when she was seventeen?' Geraldine asked.

Ann shrugged but said nothing.

'You must have argued?'

'She had a boyfriend,' Ann snapped. 'She left home to live with him.'

The memory of Celia's concerns about Chloe flashed across Geraldine's mind and she resolved to call her sister again soon. She might even offer to speak to Chloe, although she wasn't sure what that could achieve.

'Teenage girls can be challenging,' she said gently.

Ann looked up at those sympathetic words, and Geraldine glimpsed a crafty expression on her face. Almost at once, she looked sad again, but the mask had slipped for an instant.

Perhaps worried she had revealed her true feelings, all at once Ann became voluble. 'I never wanted her to leave home. She was my daughter and I didn't want to lose her. But she insisted. She was seventeen and there was nothing I could do to stop her. I begged her not to go. I told her to stay at home. I said she was too young to go off like that. But one night she packed a bag and buggered off, leaving me all alone. It hadn't been easy for me, you know, bringing her up on my own. I did everything for that girl. And this was how she repaid me for all my years of sacrifice and going without so I could give her everything she wanted. She just left me for some good-for-nothing scum who didn't care that he was taking her away from me.'

Geraldine asked for details of the boyfriend Lauren had gone to live with, but Ann said she didn't know anything about him. She couldn't even tell them his name. She said she had seen him once, through the window, and thought he had dark hair.

'Where were they when you saw them through a window?' Ariadne asked. 'Can you remember where they were living?'

Ann shrugged. 'I spotted them in a pub in York. I can't remember which one. I was walking past and saw her, clear as I can see you now. I went straight in, but she'd seen me and pushed past me in the doorway as they left. She didn't even look at me, just hissed at me to stop stalking her because she never wanted to see me again. I wasn't following her, I just happened to see her.'

'Can you describe him for us?'

'I can't remember anything about him. I was looking at her. She looked terrible, high as a kite she was. Anyway, he chucked her out after a few months,' she added with a nod of grim satisfaction. 'Any fool could see that coming a mile off. And after that, I don't know where she went or where she was living.'

'How did you know he threw her out?' Geraldine asked.

'Because she came home asking for money.' Ann scowled. 'I told her I didn't have any to give her, which was true. She stormed off and never bothered to get in touch with me again, not even to ask how I was. I could have been dying and she wouldn't have cared. That's the kind of daughter she was. After all I did for her. All she wanted to do was run after men.' She stopped, seeming to recall where she was, and hung her head, muttering that she had nothing more to say about her daughter.

While the bad feeling between them didn't mean Ann had been guilty of abusing her daughter, if she had, that would explain why Lauren had been so keen to leave home. And if Ann had been injuring her, she might have gone on to kill her.

'She must have been a very difficult child?' Geraldine hazarded, hoping to draw Ann into confessing to having mistreated her daughter. 'And you brought her up all by yourself. It sounds as though you were a saint to put up with her.'

But Ann was not so easily manipulated. 'I did what any mother would have done,' she replied.

'What was that?' Ariadne wanted to know.

'I put food on the table and clothes on her back.'

'Did you love her?' Ariadne asked.

'Love?' Ann scoffed. 'Would you love someone who throws all your care back in your face and despises you for doing your best for them? But yes, she was my daughter so of course I loved her.'

Geraldine wondered if that was true. 'Lauren had some cigarette burns,' she said, changing tack without warning. 'She must have really upset you before she left, enough to make you want to retaliate.'

Ann started. 'Are you suggesting I did that to her?' She glared at Geraldine. 'You're disgusting.'

'But is it true?' Geraldine pressed her.

'Absolutely not.' Ann sounded genuinely affronted. Her cheeks flushed and she picked furiously at her sleeve.

'Do you have any idea who might have done that to her?' Geraldine asked.

Ann shook her head. 'You're sick,' she replied. 'That's a horrible accusation to make to a mother whose only child has just been murdered.'

Geraldine was unapologetic. 'We're just trying to get to the truth,' she replied quietly. 'We want to find justice for Lauren, and the only way we can do that is by discovering who killed her.'

'Well, you're not going to do that by throwing filthy accusations at the one person who ever cared for her. I'd like to leave now.' She stood up, staring balefully at Geraldine. 'You're sick, you know that? Sick. You deserve to rot in hell.'

Gazing at the suspect's distraught face, Geraldine wasn't sure whether Ann was looking outraged or scared by the accusation. Either way, she wasn't about to make a confession. With a shrug, she stood up as well.

'Please don't leave the area,' she said. 'We may want to speak to you again.'

With a snort of fury, Ann stalked out of the room without a backward glance.

Geraldine and Ariadne discussed the interview over a quick lunch in the police station canteen. Ariadne refused to believe Ann could have killed her daughter. Geraldine had to admit it seemed unlikely, given that they appeared to have had little contact for years. It was possible they had encountered one another by chance and argued, but so far there was no evidence to support that theory.

'We really are back to square one,' Ariadne sighed.

Geraldine was more positive. Ann had mentioned previous boyfriends and the killer might possibly be found among them, if they could only track them down. In the absence of any other contacts of Lauren's, she decided to talk to Alice's former flatmate again to see if she could help them find a connection between the two victims. Someone had to know what had happened. It was just a case of searching for the truth, however long it took.

52

IT WAS IAN'S TURN to collect Tom from the childminder, so on her way home from work Geraldine decided she might as well take a short detour and visit Hayley straight away. Having registered her decision, she drove to the restaurant on Fossgate, where she waited patiently for a few minutes to speak to a waitress, only to be told that Hayley wasn't working that afternoon. Leaving there, she hurried to the address further along on the same street where Hayley rented a flat above an antique shop. She found the right door and rang the bell. While she waited, she glanced at the shop which looked well maintained, with freshly painted woodwork and a display of smart and expensive-looking items in the window. There were a number of relatively small items: an old-fashioned black telephone with a rotary dial, a vintage typewriter, an old wooden barometer and a case displaying brightly coloured costume jewellery. The central exhibit was larger than everything else: a wooden grandfather clock with ornate carvings and a price tag of nearly two thousand pounds. Further back, she could make out various other items, none of them as impressive as those in the front. As happened with some people, the window proffered a speciously alluring impression of its contents.

To the side of the shop, set back from the pavement, the door to the flat above the shop looked shabby, its blue paint chipped and grubby. Geraldine rang the bell again and waited. She was about to give up and go home when she heard muffled footsteps approaching. Hayley looked slightly taken aback to see Geraldine on her doorstep, but she made no move to close the door.

'May I come in?' Geraldine asked, seeing Hayley looking at her uncertainly.

'Is this about Alice again?'

'Yes. If you have a moment, I'd like to talk to you. We think you might be able to help us with our enquiries.'

'Well, I don't think there's anything more to say,' Hayley replied. 'I've already told you everything I know. And we didn't really see anything of each other once she moved out. We didn't fall out or anything,' she added quickly, as though afraid she might become a suspect. 'It's just that we both worked and there never seemed to be time.'

'I'll only keep you a minute. We're trying to find out what happened to your friend. I'm sure you want to help us.'

With a sigh, Hayley stood aside to let her enter. 'I suppose you'd better come in, then.'

Geraldine followed Hayley up a narrow steep flight of carpeted stairs. At the top, they turned right to enter a square lounge packed with furniture that looked too large for the room. Two armchairs upholstered in different fabrics and a faded leather sofa were arranged around a tiled Victorian fireplace. It was a cosy place, if in need of decoration and new furniture. Hayley invited Geraldine to take a seat and offered her tea. Sitting down, Geraldine declined the offer of refreshment and repeated that she wouldn't be staying long. She just wanted to ask Hayley if she was able to supply the police with any information about Alice's past boyfriends.

'Are you talking about before she met Rob?'

Geraldine nodded. 'That's right. We're interested in finding a past boyfriend who may have held a grudge against her for leaving him. It might be a man who drank excessively or took drugs, or just someone with a bad temper, capable of extreme violence. I know this is a long shot, but we wondered whether you might have met any boyfriend she had while she was living here and if you could share with us whatever you know. Anything at all would be very helpful.'

Instead of replying, Hayley appeared to be thinking. Geraldine waited, but Hayley sat perfectly still, frowning. Eventually, Geraldine prompted her, this time posing her question more bluntly.

'Did you meet any of Alice's boyfriends?'

'Alice's boyfriends?' Hayley repeated, seeming uncertain how to respond. 'She – she had a few boyfriends,' she stammered at last. 'She was attractive. She met a lot of men.'

When Geraldine pressed her for details, Hayley shook her head and replied that she had never met any of Alice's boyfriends other than Rob. According to Hayley, Alice used to go out a lot. Geraldine remembered Lisa painting a very different picture of Alice's social life. It seemed she hadn't known everything about her niece.

'She was always going out,' Hayley said, without a trace of bitterness. 'Sometimes she stayed out all night. I didn't actually mind. It meant I had the place to myself in the evening and could watch what I wanted on the TV,' she added, looking slightly embarrassed by her confession. 'It's not that I wanted her out of the way,' she added. 'I liked Alice. We got on right from the start. She always seemed genuinely interested in me. She was like that. Anyway, everything worked out fine. We were perfectly happy until she met Rob and moved out. We were renting part of a house, but I had to move out as well when she left. I couldn't afford to stay there on my own and I didn't fancy starting all over again, sharing my flat with a stranger. And then this place turned up and it's perfect for me, just along the road from where I work. So there were no hard feelings between us when she moved out. I mean, I was disappointed, but we both knew it was going to happen sooner or later. We weren't going to be living together for the rest of our lives.' She smiled wistfully. 'It could just as well have been me that met someone, although realistically it was more likely to happen to her as she went out with so many men.' She paused. 'It might sound silly to say this, because she met so many men, but I think she lacked confidence. It was like she had to keep proving to herself that she was attractive. But I don't think it worked.'

'Was there any one in particular who lasted any length of time, or were they all very brief relationships?'

'You mean did she sleep around?' Hayley asked, with a scowl.

'I'm not making any judgements, I've just come here looking for information.'

'She had a lot of boyfriends,' Hayley said. 'I didn't meet any of them and I don't remember any of their names. She didn't bring them home and she never really talked about them. We didn't talk about men much at all,' she concluded sourly.

Geraldine had the impression Hayley didn't have many boyfriends, but that was of no interest to her. She needed to focus on Alice.

'What about girlfriends? Were there any girls she used to socialise with?'

'I don't know. We shared a flat but we lived separate lives.'

Geraldine held her breath. 'Did she ever mention meeting a woman called Ann?'

'No.'

'Or Lauren?'

Hayley shook her head. Geraldine pressed her, but Hayley couldn't tell her what she wanted to hear.

'Is there anything else you can tell me about Alice?'

Hayley sighed. 'She was a good person,' she said, echoing what Lisa had said about her dead niece. 'She didn't deserve to die like that. She was so young. I mean, something like that shouldn't happen to anyone. But she was nice. And she looked after herself. Physically, I mean.' She hesitated as though there was something else she wanted to say, but then she just shook her head.

Feeling frustrated, Geraldine went home and tried to put the case out of her mind, but it wasn't easy. She greeted Ian before going to the nursery to look at Tom who was snuffling contentedly in his sleep.

'He's only just gone down,' Ian murmured behind her. 'Let's not disturb him and I'll make us something to eat.'

Geraldine nodded, aware that if she hadn't wasted so much time going to see Hayley, she would have been home in time to see Tom. But if she missed seeing Tom one day, she would still be able to see him the following day. Lisa would never see Alice alive again.

53

THE FOLLOWING MORNING, WHEN Geraldine was dropping Tom off, Lisa detained her on the doorstep, wanting to know if the police had made any progress with the investigation into Alice's death. Geraldine found it hard to meet Lisa's anxious gaze and trot out the routine response that they were currently following several leads. All they had done was eliminate a couple of suspects, and it was misleading to suggest they had made any serious progress. Muttering assurances that the investigation team was making progress and she would tell Lisa as soon as she had anything definite to share with her, Geraldine hurried away.

In a briefing that morning Binita wondered whether the two murders could actually have been unrelated. It was true that the forensic team were confident the same knife had been used in both attacks. But it was possible Lauren's killer might have come across Alice's body before it was discovered by the witness who had reported finding it. Stumbling upon the corpse with the murder weapon beside it, he might have taken the knife and subsequently used it to kill Lauren. While the theory seemed unlikely, it was feasible.

'We might be tying ourselves up in knots trying to find a common killer for both victims,' Binita concluded. 'I think we should continue to investigate both murders, but pursue separate lines of enquiry. If we discover the two incidents are connected in any way, other than in the use of the same knife, we can look for one killer then. In the meantime, let's focus on each victim individually and see what we can come up with.'

With that instruction in mind, the team dispersed to focus on their allocated tasks.

Halfway through the morning, Geraldine looked up to see Naomi walking purposefully towards her. Naomi's face was curiously animated as though she had just made an exciting discovery.

'You have to see this,' she exclaimed as she drew level with Geraldine's desk.

Without a word, Geraldine nodded at Ariadne and they both stood up. They followed their young colleague to a desk where a grey-haired video images identification officer was seated at a monitor showing a grainy black and white image of what appeared to be the interior of a pub. The camera was pointing at an entrance.

'Play it again,' Naomi said tersely.

The video resumed and they watched a man come in through the doorway. He was wearing a bulky jacket and jeans, and appeared to be staggering slightly. As he entered the dimly lit bar he removed the sunglasses he was wearing and gazed around, blinking, before putting them back on.

'Focus on his face,' Naomi said. 'Let's see the frame where he's taken his sunglasses off. Show them what you showed me.' She sounded impatient.

The camera zoomed in on the man but as the image enlarged, his features became too distorted to be seen clearly.

'Wait a sec. I saved the enhanced image from earlier,' the video images identification officer told them. In stark contrast to Naomi, the grey-haired officer seemed very calm.

A still image appeared on the screen and Geraldine recognised Danny, sporting a black eye.

'When was this taken?' she asked.

The video officer told them the film had been taken on

Wednesday evening at ten, in a pub along Micklegate. It confirmed that Danny had a black eye before Lauren was killed early on Sunday morning.

'That doesn't mean he wasn't in a struggle with her on Wednesday before he went to the pub,' Naomi pointed out.

But they all knew the film bore out Danny's story. It was possible he had been fighting with Lauren on Wednesday and had returned to the argument and finished her off on Sunday, but that was pure speculation. It was equally possible Danny's black eye had nothing to do with Lauren at all, as he insisted. Other than the evidence of physical mistreatment there was nothing to suggest he had ever abused her, and they knew several of the cigarette burns had been inflicted before she had even met Danny, which suggested he might not be responsible for any of them. They urgently needed to trace her former boyfriends. Hayley hadn't met any of Alice's previous boyfriends, but they hadn't yet asked Ella who might have known more than she had so far shared about Lauren. There might even have been a boyfriend at school who had not been happy when they split up. She could have had a stalker for years, Ariadne suggested, her eyes alight with interest.

'Let's not get ahead of ourselves,' Geraldine advised her. 'But we do need to go and speak to Ella again.'

This time, Ella looked unconcerned as she invited them in, but Geraldine sensed there was something studied about her insouciance.

'What do you want to know?' Ella asked, smiling earnestly. 'I really do want to help you nail that bastard.'

'Who are you talking about?' Geraldine asked gently.

'Danny, of course. It was him, wasn't it? He deserves to be punished for what he did to her. I don't understand what you're waiting for. You should have arrested him already and charged him with killing her.' There was something pathetic in her insistence.

Assuring Ella that they would do everything in their power to bring Lauren's killer to justice, Geraldine asked her about any other boyfriends the dead girl might have had.

'Other boyfriends?' Ella repeated. 'I can't remember anyone apart from Danny. She never introduced me to anyone else and I don't think she stayed with anyone else for very long. I can't understand why you haven't arrested him,' she repeated irritably.

'Did you ever meet a nurse called Alice?'

Ella shook her head.

'Did Lauren ever mention someone called Alice to you?'

'No. I don't know anyone called Alice. Who is she? But what's happening about Danny? You can't just let him walk away, not after what he did. He needs to be locked up. You don't seem to understand, he's a dangerous man.'

'Did you think there was something not quite right about what she was saying about Danny needing to be punished?' Geraldine asked Ariadne as they drove away. 'Was she a little too emphatic? She seemed almost hysterical.'

'That's understandable. Her friend is dead and she thinks Danny killed her. I'd be pretty crazy about it if I thought someone was getting away with killing one of my friends.'

Geraldine sighed. 'Yes, I suppose you're right. Well, if Ella's right, then we're missing something.' She wondered if Lauren's cigarette burns had led them astray. 'Just because Danny wasn't inflicting one kind of injury doesn't mean he didn't kill her. We need to scrutinise his alibi more carefully. And perhaps if we put more pressure on him, he might confess. Let's go and question him, let's see if we can make him crack.' She frowned.

'You're not convinced it was him though, are you?' Ariadne asked.

Geraldine didn't answer. She was no longer sure what to believe in this case that seemed to be growing more confusing by the minute.

54

Hoping Danny was about to take his lunch break, Geraldine and Ariadne turned up at the betting shop. The scrawny young man who had been present on Geraldine's first visit was standing behind the counter. He raised his eyebrows and stared at them suspiciously but went off without a word when Geraldine asked to speak to Danny. A moment later the young man reappeared, nodding at them as he walked past them on his way back to his post behind the window. Geraldine was about to approach him again when the bespectacled manager arrived, strutting officiously across the shop floor.

'Now then, now then,' he said fussily, glancing around at a couple of gamblers who were glued to screens fixed on the far wall. He stepped closer and lowered his voice. 'How long is this going to continue? I have nothing against the police, you understand, nothing at all. I'm grateful to you and all your colleagues for the work you do, really I am, but you can't keep coming in here like this. It's going to start unsettling my customers. Unless you're here to place a bet?' he added hopefully, glancing around the shop.

Geraldine explained the reason for their visit and the manager's expression cleared. 'Danny's not in today. He's having a day off. He called up to say he thinks he's got the flu,' he added dismissively as though he didn't believe his employee was really ill. 'You should be able to find him at home. You have his address, I presume?'

With that, he spun on his heel and scurried away. Muttering her thanks, Geraldine left with Ariadne at her heels. The manager was right because they found Danny at home. He looked at them expectantly when he saw who was on his doorstep.

'Have you found out who killed her?' he blurted out, the words tumbling over each other in his eagerness. 'There's something I want to ask you.' His voice trembled. 'Can I have a moment alone with him? Just one moment.' His hands clenched at his sides and his expression darkened as he made his request. 'I've been thinking about this, and I want to look into his eyes and ask him why he did it. That's all.'

Geraldine shook her head. 'You know that's out of the question,' she replied. 'But we still need your help, Danny. Can we come in?'

His shoulders drooped as she spoke and he understood they had not yet caught Lauren's killer. Without speaking, he shuffled backwards to let them enter his narrow hallway. They followed him into a poky living room which stank of stale cigarette smoke and an acrid assortment of rank food smells. There was a sturdy-looking armchair, an upright wooden chair and a battered-looking sofa, all facing a large television which was blaring out an advertisement for toothpaste. Geraldine frowned at the screen and Danny silenced it, muttering that he wasn't watching anything, he just had it on to hear a human voice in the house.

'I miss her so much,' he said plaintively.

He sat on the wooden chair, leaving the upholstered seats for his visitors. Geraldine lowered herself on to the sofa which sank down further than she had expected on its broken springs. Ignoring her discomfort, she turned to look at Danny. Ariadne perched on the armchair, watching him.

'We want to ask you about Lauren's injuries,' she said.

He shook his head. 'I only know what I read in the reports online—' he began, but she interrupted him.

'Let me stop you right there. We're not talking about what

happened in the course of the fatal attack. Lauren had a number of scars from past injuries where someone had burned her with lighted cigarettes. We want to know who inflicted those injuries. Someone was stubbing cigarettes out on her body,' she repeated, leaning forward as far as she was able and looking him straight in the eye. 'Was that you?'

Danny didn't drop his gaze. 'I knew you'd be on to me about that sooner or later. To be honest, I thought you'd ask me about it before now. Yes, she had cigarette burns. I knew all about them. Of course I did. She was my girlfriend. I was trying to stop her. Check out the burn marks. You'll see none of them are recent.' He paused, and rubbed his eyes. 'She more or less stopped doing it when she was with me, but I had to keep an eye on her all the time. She had these dark moods.' He scowled. 'I tried to help her,' he muttered.

Hiding her surprise at what he had told them, Geraldine asked him to confirm that Lauren had been self-harming.

'That's what I just said,' he replied, 'and it's hardly surprising, given how that bitch of a mother treated her. It was emotional abuse right from the start. It's no wonder she had issues. I did my best to help her, but it was hard going. I admit, I lost patience with her more than once. She was just so pathetic. I don't know why I put up with her for so long.'

'Why *did* you put up with her?' Geraldine asked gently, sensing there was more Danny could tell them.

'She threatened to kill herself if I threw her out.'

'That must have been hard for you,' Geraldine murmured. 'So much pressure. You must have been relieved when she was killed?'

Danny looked up, his face turning red. 'I never wanted to see her dead,' he burst out furiously. 'I tried to help her.'

'Did you believe a word of that?' Ariadne asked as they drove away. 'I mean, how could she have been self-harming for years without anyone else knowing about it?'

'Perhaps other people did know.'

'Well, no one told us about it,' Ariadne insisted.

Geraldine looked thoughtful. 'Maybe they wanted to protect her.'

'How is that protecting her when she's dead?'

'I don't know, they could have been trying to protect her memory in some way.' Geraldine sighed. 'Anyway, we need to get to the bottom of this, find out if what Danny has told us is true.' She paused. 'He hasn't lied to us so far. Not that we know of, anyway.'

'That doesn't mean he's not lying now,' Ariadne said grimly. 'I don't know why you would believe a word he says.'

'Innocent until proven guilty,' Geraldine murmured.

'So you really think we should give him the benefit of the doubt?'

'That's the only choice we have at this stage,' Geraldine snapped. 'This isn't about my opinion, it's a question of seeing justice done, regardless of what we think. You understand that as well as I do, or you'd never have lasted so long in the job.'

Ariadne drove on in silence while Geraldine stared doggedly out of her passenger window, turning over in her mind everything she had learned about the cigarette burns. But there was something else Danny had told them that was hovering at the edge of her mind. She needed to get back to the police station, write up her notes and think.

'Jonah told us some of the cigarette burns could have been inflicted years ago,' she said at last, 'which means it's possible Danny is telling us the truth about Ann torturing her. But that doesn't explain the more recent injuries.' She frowned. 'It's plausible Danny took up where Ann left off, but it's equally likely he's telling us the truth and Lauren was self-harming all along. In any event, there's no point in charging him if an accusation could fall apart against a robust defence. Whoever killed these women, we have to make sure we have a watertight case against them. The balance of probabilities isn't good enough. We have to be sure.'

'I know, you're right,' Ariadne mumbled. 'It's just so frustrating.'

'You can say that again,' Geraldine replied fiercely. 'We won't let up until we have him behind bars where he belongs, whoever he is.'

Ariadne nodded. 'He's out there somewhere.'

'Don't worry. We'll find him.'

Geraldine hoped they weren't just mouthing empty words at each other. Talk was easy, especially when they could fall back on platitudes. Finding the truth was proving a lot more difficult.

55

Back at the police station, Geraldine compared her own and Ariadne's notes on everything Danny had said. All at once she frowned; one sentence seemed to stand out from the rest. She went to check her notes with Ariadne, who confirmed that Danny had told them Ann was ill. He had accused her of torturing her daughter, driving her to self-harm, and had accused her of being 'sick in the head.' That much Geraldine and Ariadne agreed on.

'But he also said she was physically ill,' Geraldine said. 'And that bears out what Ann herself told me.' She searched for her notes on her own interview with Ann. 'Here it is,' she said, barely able to conceal her excitement. 'She told me she's not a well woman, and she railed bitterly against Lauren for abandoning her when, according to Ann, she should have stayed to take care of her mother when she was ill.' She looked up at Ariadne. 'Don't you see what this means? There's no question about it. Ann's not well.'

Ariadne nodded uncertainly. 'That can't have helped,' she said. 'It seems pretty obvious she was deranged in some way, but she might also have been physically ill and that can make people short-tempered and unsympathetic. I'm not excusing her behaviour, if Ann really was cruel to her daughter. I'm just saying it makes it more credible that she might have been callous enough to harm her daughter or even drive her to self-harm.'

'We don't know what's wrong with Ann,' Geraldine said,

sticking to her train of thought, 'but I wonder if she could have been hospitalised at any point?'

'And whether she could have met Alice while she was being treated?' Ariadne said, picking up on Geraldine's idea.

Geraldine nodded. 'Could Ann be the link we've been missing between the two victims?'

They stared at one another for a second, overwhelmed by this possible lead that had been in front of them since they started to investigate Lauren's death. They weren't yet sure what it might signify, or whether it might actually point to Ann being guilty of murder, but it was a lead worth pursuing. Geraldine ran the idea past Binita and then asked Naomi to set up a team to look into Ann's medical history. In the meantime, Binita agreed that Geraldine and Ariadne should go and speak to Ann again. She, at least, must surely have known about her daughter's behaviour, however flawed she had been as a mother. And while they were there, they would subtly question her about any hospital stay. This was the first time Geraldine had seen Ann at her home, having questioned her at the police station on the previous two occasions they had met. Ann opened her front door, holding on to the door frame with one hand, as though she was unable to stand without support. Her red-rimmed eyes narrowed on seeing who was on the doorstep and she shook her head when Geraldine asked to come in.

'No,' Ann replied. 'You certainly can't come inside. The house is a mess. I can't receive visitors today. I'm not well enough to keep the place clean and tidy. It's not as if I have anyone to help me,' she added bitterly.

Ann's voice quivered and she was shaking visibly. Geraldine recognised her frayed jumper and wondered whether she had even changed her clothes since the previous day. A long thread of wool hung down, fluttering as her arm trembled, and she stank of stale cigarettes.

'We have just a few questions for you,' Geraldine said, trying not to inhale the stench. 'It will be easier if we come in. You'll be able to sit down,' she added solicitously.

Ann shook her head and, with a shaking hand, felt in the pocket of her cardigan for a packet of cigarettes. 'No. You can't come in. This is my home. I don't want you here.'

'Tell us about the cigarette burns on Lauren's body,' Geraldine said bluntly.

Ann took a step back and dropped the packet she was clutching. 'I told you, it wasn't me,' she cried out. 'I wouldn't have hurt her. She may have hated me, but she was my daughter. Do you even understand what that means?' Her eyes glared frantically at Geraldine.

'You never told us she was self-harming when we asked you about her, even though you knew we suspected you had been abusing her. Why did you keep quiet about what she had been doing?' Geraldine asked.

Ann shrugged her narrow shoulders and sighed. Grunting with the effort, she reached down and retrieved her cigarettes from the floor. Her hand shook as she put the packet in her pocket. 'They made me promise not to say anything about it,' she replied.

'Who made you promise that?' Ariadne asked, stepping forward.

'The counsellor who saw her at school said we mustn't break Lauren's confidence. She said it would be very damaging to her if I told anyone about it. Apparently it was a trust issue. Not that the counsellor lasted long. Lauren only saw her twice and it made no difference. They knew about it at the school but none of them did anything to help her. They said it was up to her whether she saw the counsellor again. She had to make her own decisions, they said, and we all had to respect her wishes, even though she was stubbing cigarettes out on her arms.' Her voice grew shrill with anger. 'And they said I could damage her if I told anyone. They insisted that what she was doing was confidential. As if keeping it a secret was more important than trying to help her.'

'Who told you not to tell anyone?'

'It was the deputy head, Mrs Jackman. Jackass more like. She should never have been put in charge of children. Bloody cow. She insisted it be kept confidential, but what difference does it make now? Lauren's dead, isn't she? And they didn't help her for all their self-importance, telling me what I could and couldn't do. I should never have listened to them. I should have had it out with Lauren myself. But they told me it was best for her if I kept quiet, and I was stupid enough to believe them.'

A single tear rolled down her wrinkled cheek and she lowered her head to stare at the floor.

'We understand you're not well,' Ariadne said.

Ann's head whipped up so abruptly, Geraldine was afraid she might have hurt her neck. 'Who told you that?' she asked.

'You told me yourself,' Geraldine answered. 'You told me you're not a well woman.'

Ann sniffed and mumbled that her condition was none of their business.

'I'm afraid in a murder investigation, everything is our business,' Geraldine replied gently. 'Do you want to tell us about your condition, or do we need to find out from your medical records?'

'So much for confidentiality,' Ann growled. 'It only works for some people, does it? All right, if you must know, they told me I had Parkinson's, but it turns out I haven't. And now they don't know what's wrong with me or why I shake like this.' She held out a trembling hand. 'I've been like this for years. Afflicted, that's what I am, and it's exhausting, shaking like this all the time. The time it takes between appointments, I'll be dead before they find out what's wrong with me. I've been waiting for another brain scan for months.'

'Have you ever been treated in intensive care at the hospital?'

'Intensive care?' Ann scoffed. 'I've never been given any care of any kind, intensive or otherwise. They never even kept me in overnight. Just left me sitting around waiting for X-ray after X-ray and scan after scan, and they still haven't got a clue what's wrong with me. All they say is that I should stop smoking. But how is that going to help, when they don't have a clue what's wrong with me?' She glared at Geraldine as though she was personally responsible for the health service. 'They don't even send me to the local hospital. I have to go all the way over to Leeds for my appointments. So why don't you bugger off to Leeds and ask them what the hell's wrong with me. And if you manage to find out, please let me know.'

With that, she shut the door in Geraldine's face.

Ann's parting shot sounded truthful, but Geraldine wanted to wait and hear what Naomi had discovered before reaching any conclusions.

56

Geraldine and Ariadne discussed what they had heard as they walked back to the car. Danny had told them Lauren had inflicted cigarette burns on herself, but it was possible he had made that up in order to protect himself. Ann had confirmed what he had said, but she hardly struck either of them as trustworthy. Ariadne suggested Danny might even have persuaded Ann to lie for him, perhaps paying her to back up his story. What was also plausible was that Danny and Ann had concocted a story about Lauren self-harming to cover up her abuse at both of their hands. They knew it was not uncommon for victims of childhood abuse to seek out similar relationships when they grew up. Geraldine was inclined to believe Danny, which suggested Ann was also telling the truth, but she had to admit it was slightly puzzling that Ella would have been quite so oblivious to what was going on. But, of course, issues could easily be concealed when people chose not to share them, especially if no one else was expecting to come across them. They seemed to be skirting around the truth without managing to see it clearly.

Leaving Naomi to look into Ann's medical history, Geraldine returned to the school to speak to the deputy head again, hoping to discover what had actually been going on with Lauren. She arrived as pupils were streaming out of the main entrance at the end of the school day. Making her way through a throng of noisy youngsters, she went to the reception desk and asked to speak to Mrs Jackman.

'I'll see if she's available,' the receptionist said, inviting her to take a seat.

Geraldine sat down on a soft chair opposite the desk. A moment later the receptionist called her over and told her that the deputy head was in a meeting.

'I'm afraid she'll have to leave her meeting for a moment to speak to me,' Geraldine said.

'She's in a meeting,' the receptionist replied doggedly.

'Very well, please take me to the meeting room.'

The receptionist frowned and shook her head. 'I can't do that.'

'Right now,' Geraldine added.

When the receptionist still didn't stir, Geraldine sighed. 'If you insist, I'll have to summon back-up to escort me to this meeting,' she said. 'You'll be taken to the police station and formally charged with obstruction,' she added, speaking loudly enough for anyone passing to hear. 'I'm afraid that is a criminal offence, but if you're determined to flout police authority, you'll leave me no choice. It's up to you.'

Pupils and a few members of staff were still leaving. One or two turned their heads in Geraldine's direction as she raised her voice.

By the time she had pulled out her phone, the receptionist was on her feet, exhorting her to wait. Geraldine went and sat down again, and a moment later the head teacher joined her. The receptionist watched them apprehensively through her glass partition.

'Now, now,' the head said, 'what's so urgent? Naturally we're keen to do all we can to assist you in your enquiries, but this is a school day, as I'm sure you appreciate—'

Geraldine interrupted him to say she wanted to speak to Mrs Jackman.

'I won't keep her long,' she added, 'but I would like to catch her before she leaves for the day. I could call on her at home, but she might have plans for the evening and, in the meantime, I'm here and I know she is too. So it would really be simpler and quicker all round if we could just talk here, right now.'

The head nodded and went over to speak to the receptionist who picked up her phone, scowling at Geraldine. The head waited with Geraldine and a moment later, Mrs Jackman came through the internal door to the reception area. With a glance at the receptionist, who was clearly eavesdropping, Geraldine asked if there was somewhere discreet where they could talk. Mrs Jackman nodded and led her through the internal door and along a corridor to an empty classroom. Finally able to question the deputy head, Geraldine began by asking her about Lauren's mental state.

'Her mental state?' the deputy repeated, suddenly wary.

'I think you know what I'm talking about, but if you'd like to check your records, we can wait.'

With a sigh, Mrs Jackman went over to the computer on the desk at the front of the classroom and began tapping at the keyboard.

'Let's hope this is working,' she said with a rueful smile. 'Ah, here we are. Yes, yes, Lauren Stokes. You know, we're all still in shock at hearing what happened to her. There are children here who remember her, although they were six years below her at school. And some of the staff who taught her are still here, myself included. We all have fond memories of her.'

'Can you describe Lauren's mental state while she was here?' Geraldine repeated.

The deputy head's dogmatic air faltered. 'Her mental state?' she echoed uncertainly.

'Yes. Did she experience any mental health problems?'

Mrs Jackman sniffed. 'The usual teenage angst,' she blustered. 'You know the kind of thing. A lot of pupils go through it in different ways.' She began to launch into a list of problems teenagers typically suffered, when Geraldine interrupted her.

'We're only interested in Lauren right now. If I want a summary of typical teenage problems, I'll ask an expert,' she said rudely. 'Was Lauren good at PE?'

Mrs Jackman looked surprised by the question. 'PE?'

'Yes. Can you check her school reports to see if she was good at PE?'

Frowning, the deputy checked the screen and then shook her head. 'There are no reports about her PE once she reached Year Ten. That's the year she started GCSEs,' she added helpfully.

'So her PE reports stopped around then?'

The deputy head pressed her lips together, as though she was reluctant to answer any further questions.

'Why was that?' Geraldine prompted her.

'I remember now. Lauren was excused from PE on account of a physical condition.'

'What condition was that?' Geraldine asked, although the deputy head must have realised the police knew about Lauren's injuries.

'We were concerned,' Mrs Jackman said, looking increasingly flustered. 'Lauren was frail. And a little underweight. And she was stressed about her exams.'

'So she never had to change into PE kit in front of other pupils?'

Mrs Jackman nodded without speaking, but her fraught expression answered Geraldine's question before she had posed it.

Geraldine pressed on. 'What about her appointments with the school counsellor?'

Mrs Jackman shook her head. 'I'm afraid that's confidential.'

'We don't require you to break any confidences at this

stage, although we might have to insist on that later on. I'm afraid you are not entitled to refuse to cooperate in a murder enquiry, if we consider your information is necessary to our investigation.'

Mrs Jackman stared at her without responding.

'You must have been aware that Lauren was burning herself with lighted cigarettes while she was in your care here?'

The deputy head stiffened for an instant, and then her rigid expression crumbled. 'I don't suppose I'm breaking any confidence seeing as you already know about it. And in any case, the poor child is dead. Yes, we knew about her problem. We did everything possible to support her while she was here. We liaised with her mother and insisted Lauren see the school counsellor, but she only attended two sessions and then refused to attend any more. We had to consider her wishes. We did everything we could to ensure she received the help she needed, but we couldn't act against her will. You can't force someone to accept help. They have to be willing to agree.' She paused before muttering, 'The counsellor didn't think she was suicidal. That would have been an entirely different matter, but we all thought she would grow out of it.'

Geraldine bit back a furious response.

'Who else knew about this?' she asked coldly.

'As far as I'm aware, no one else knew about it.'

'What about her best friend, Ella?'

'No, Ella didn't know about it. Lauren insisted on that and we were obliged to abide by her wishes. Besides, we were loath to do anything that might disturb their relationship. Ella was so good for Lauren, you see. We were all worried that learning about Lauren's self-harm might upset Ella and damage their friendship. We acted in Lauren's best interests.'

'So you're saying Ella didn't know her best friend was self-harming?'

'As far as I'm aware, no one knew about it, apart from

myself, the school counsellor and Lauren's mother. That was what Lauren wanted and we respected her wishes,' she bleated pathetically, her bombastic manner vanished.

57

Preoccupied by what she had learned, Geraldine collected Tom from the childminder. She was barely conscious of the cheerful noises he was making in the car on the way home. He had recently discovered he could blow raspberries and entertained himself happily as they sped along. She laughed at his delight, but inwardly her mind was racing, turning over what Sonia Jackman had told her. While Ian prepared supper, she bathed and fed Tom. As she chatted to him, her thoughts were on the case.

'So, would you like to talk about it?' Ian asked her later.

Tom was asleep, and they had finished supper and cleared up and were sitting on the sofa in the living room, supposedly relaxing for the evening.

'Talk about what?' she replied.

Ian shrugged. 'I'm asking if you want to talk about whatever's been buzzing about in that overactive brain of yours ever since you walked through the door this evening.'

He smiled at her and she felt a wave of love, mingled with relief at being able to talk through what was troubling her. They agreed it seemed unlikely, but not impossible, for Lauren to have concealed her self-harming from her best friend, if indeed she had been self-harming. Geraldine told Ian she had believed Danny when he told them he had tried to help Lauren. And besides, there had been no recent burn marks. That series of injuries seemed to have stopped since she had moved in with him.

'Lauren had other injuries, didn't she?' Ian asked. 'Whether or not she'd been self-harming doesn't mean Danny wasn't abusing her.'

'What I want to know,' Geraldine replied, 'is who is Ella protecting by pointing the finger at Danny? Or did she really not know Lauren was self-harming, in which case she might believe Danny killed her. She did seem shocked by having seen a burn mark on Lauren's wrist.'

Geraldine recalled seeing Ann picking at her own cuff and shuddered.

'Come on,' Ian interrupted her thoughts. 'You know this is all speculation. There's no point in going over old ground. Wouldn't it be better to leave it for now and wait until tomorrow and see what other evidence you can uncover? For the time being, let's put the TV on and forget about work until tomorrow. Can you do that?'

Geraldine sighed. 'Of course I can,' she lied, forcing a smile. It wasn't fair on Ian to expect him to put his life on hold on account of her perplexing investigation.

She struggled to focus on a spy series they were watching. There were dramatic scenes, but the plot was quite convoluted. Having once missed a twist in the story, it became almost impossible to follow. In the end, she abandoned any attempt to keep up with what was going on and sat quietly watching, more or less disengaged, while Ian remained glued to the screen. He didn't seem to notice her lack of attention or, if he did, he didn't say anything. Geraldine settled down and tried to watch the programme in a desultory fashion while her thoughts kept flicking back to Alice and Lauren. She had a niggling feeling that she had come across a connection between the two victims, but she couldn't see what it was.

The next morning, Ian took Tom to Lisa's and Geraldine went into work early to reread her notes on her meeting with Sonia Jackman. The constable tasked with looking into Ann's medical history had confirmed that she had never been treated in the hospital where Alice had worked, so they still had nothing to connect the two victims. Thinking back to Rob's statement, Geraldine remembered with a jolt that he had told them Alice often went to the gym before work and Lisa had also mentioned that Alice had joined a gym. Lauren's friend, Ella, worked at a gym. Geraldine wondered whether that was a coincidence, or if Ella could somehow be the missing link between the two victims. It was difficult to see how that might be significant, but it was a puzzling coincidence all the same. Meanwhile, they were focusing their attention on Lauren.

'Could Ella still be hoping to cover up Lauren's self-harm, by the putting blame on Danny?' Ariadne wondered. 'Danny and Ann seem to want to cover up Lauren's self-harm too, but isn't it a bit extreme for everyone to keep up the pretence now she's dead?' Ariadne frowned. 'There seems to be a bit of a conspiracy of silence all round.' She shrugged. 'I mean, it's hardly a state secret.'

There was only one way to try and find out whether Ella had been privy to Lauren's secret. Leaving Naomi to set up a team to look into Ella's history in the hope that might shed further light on recent events, Geraldine took Ariadne with her to speak to Ella herself. They drove straight to Amberley Street, hoping to catch Ella before she left for work, but she had already gone. The gym where she was employed was located in the town centre. Parking on the road was problematic, so they left their vehicle in a nearby car park and walked to their destination. They didn't talk on the way, each absorbed in her own thoughts.

The door to the gym opened into a spacious area where they saw Ella seated behind a large reception desk. Her eyes flickered in recognition when Geraldine approached, but she didn't stir from her position.

'We'd like to speak to you somewhere private,' Geraldine said quietly.

She half expected Ella to remonstrate, protesting that she was at work and couldn't leave her desk, but she merely nodded and picked up her phone to summon a colleague to cover for her on reception. A moment later a lithe young man joined her behind the desk and asked Ella what was wrong. She murmured to him and he nodded, glancing at Geraldine with undisguised curiosity.

'How long will you be?' he asked.

Ella shrugged. 'Ask her,' she replied.

'I'm afraid it will take as long as it takes,' Geraldine said.

The barrier opened to admit them, and Ella led them along the corridor to a small treatment room. In addition to a massage table, there were two bamboo chairs leaning against the wall. Ella perched on the edge of the treatment table, leaving the chairs for Geraldine and Ariadne. Once they were all seated, Geraldine asked Ella about Lauren's self-harming.

'Is that what he told you?' Ella spat out the words, her face reddening with indignation. 'It was Danny who said that, wasn't it? Of course it was. He would say that, wouldn't he? Anything to convince you it wasn't him. I suppose he told you how much he cared about her? Bastard. The man's a monster. You can't believe a word he says.'

Carefully, Geraldine explained that Lauren had been self-harming for years. 'You must have known?' she added gently, seeing Ella's sullen expression.

'No, I didn't know, and I can tell you why. Because it's not true, that's why. Surely you can see he's lying to you? That's what he's been doing, all this time. But he can't cover up what he did, not this time. He deserves to be punished.' She glared at Geraldine with a desperation that was almost manic. 'So go on, arrest him. What are you waiting for? Go on, you have to arrest him before he can hurt anyone else.'

'Very well,' Geraldine said carefully, rising to her feet. 'I suggest you accompany us to the police station to make a formal statement, telling us everything you know about Lauren's relationship with Danny.'

Ella nodded. 'That's more like it. The sooner the better, I suppose, if you think it might help. I'll come straight after work.'

'We'd like you to come with us right now,' Geraldine said. 'We may need to act swiftly.'

Ignoring Ariadne, who was staring at her in perplexity, Geraldine smiled encouragingly at Ella. 'I'll wait with you here while my colleague brings the car round.' She turned and nodded at Ariadne, who hurried away to fetch the car.

While they were waiting, Ella explained to her colleague on the desk that she had to go to the police station to make a statement. 'I'm an important witness in a police investigation,' she added.

'You'll have to clear it with Stella,' the young man said. 'You can't just walk out.'

'I'm afraid she can,' Geraldine interrupted him. 'Tell your manager to call the police station if she has any questions. Right now, we need to go.'

'Well, this all sounds very dramatic,' he replied, raising his eyebrows in mock horror.

Geraldine turned away from him without responding and escorted Ella outside.

As they were on their way to the police station, Naomi phoned Geraldine.

'I'll be with you in a minute,' Geraldine said quickly, before Naomi had a chance to say a word. 'We're in the car with Ella Fletcher. We're bringing her in to make a statement.'

'Make sure you speak to me before you start questioning her,' Naomi said before she rang off.

Hiding her impatience, Geraldine said nothing about Naomi's message while they were in the car. As soon as they reached the police station, she left Ella with Ariadne and hurried to find out what her colleague had discovered. She wasn't surprised to learn that Alice had been a member of the gym where Ella worked. It was possible the two victims had both known Ella. Geraldine was not yet sure how that would help her to prove the identity of the killer, but she thought she was beginning to glimpse a truth that was almost impossible to believe.

58

Ella smiled eagerly at Geraldine and Ariadne across an interview table.

'I can't tell you how pleased I am you want to speak to me again,' she said. 'It's about time that monster was dealt with. He's evil through and through. I'll do anything I can to help you. So, what do you want to know?' She leaned forward in her chair and lowered her voice, continuing in a conspiratorial tone. 'I always knew Lauren was vulnerable, right from the first time we met. The moment I saw her, I could tell she needed someone to protect her.'

'You could tell that just by looking at her?' Geraldine asked, carefully eschewing any hint of sarcasm.

Ella nodded. 'We were only eleven, but I could see it in her face. There was an air of fragility about her, you know? I could see it, even if no one else could. She was brittle as glass. Mentally, I mean. One unkind word and her chin would start quivering. She had no inner strength, but luckily she had me.' Exasperation flitted across her features, creasing her forehead and twitching the corners of her lips down. 'I warned her it would end badly years ago, when she started seeing that first boyfriend of hers, but she wouldn't listen. I should never have left her alone in York. Well, Danny's going to get his comeuppance now,' she concluded fiercely.

'You wanted to protect her, didn't you?' Geraldine asked, encouraging Ella to continue talking.

Ella nodded her head vigorously. 'Yes, exactly. I always

looked out for her, ever since we met. She shouldn't have moved on, not like that. She should never have trusted anyone else.'

'When Danny came along, he took her away from you,' Ariadne said quietly.

'Took her away from me? I hope you're not going to try and make this out to be something weird,' Ella said with a short bark of irritated laughter. 'We were friends, but I was never possessive over her or anything like that. I hardly ever saw her once we left school. There were other men before Danny. But I knew he was abusing her, burning her with cigarettes. I saw it for myself.'

'You witnessed Danny harming Lauren?' Geraldine enquired.

'I didn't sit and watch, if that's what you're suggesting. I'm not sick. But I know what he did to her. I saw the scar with my own eyes.'

Geraldine spoke very slowly and clearly. 'A scar caused by Lauren when she was self-harming?'

Ella's eyes narrowed suspiciously and she drew back in her chair. 'What are you talking about? Lauren wasn't self-harming. That wasn't what was happening. Is that what he told you?'

Geraldine explained that Lauren had developed a habit of giving herself cigarette burns, and Ella shook her head in disbelief.

'That's a terrible thing to say,' she cried out. 'Why are you lying like that, to me of all people? You must realise I was her friend. You're trying to make out he wasn't to blame. Do you really want to let him go unpunished? Look, I don't know what lies he's been telling you, but don't be fooled by him, not for one second. I knew Lauren. We were friends. She would have confided in me if she had any problems.'

'It seems she didn't tell you everything. She never told you she was self-harming.'

Ella shook her head. 'How can you be so blind? It's obvious

what's going on. Danny made that up to defend himself, but it's not going to work. Don't fall for his lies. You can't believe a word he says. I know what was going on, and I'll swear to it in any court of law.'

Ariadne told Ella that Lauren's self-harming had started when she was barely in her teens while she was at school. Ella shook her head when she was told the issue had been confirmed by Ann and the school, as well as Danny, and she scoffed at the suggestion that he had been trying to help Lauren.

'You're lying. You're lying. It was him. I know it was him!' Ella's cheeks flushed with anger and she stood up. 'I'm not staying here to listen to his lies. I know what I saw.'

'Sit down,' Geraldine said.

Ella hesitated and looked over at Sam who was standing stolidly by the door. He shifted his weight forwards and she sat down again, staring at her hands twisting in her lap and muttering darkly.

'I think it's time you told us about your stepfather,' Geraldine said quietly.

Ella's head shot up and she stared at Geraldine in shock for an instant, before she rallied. 'What the hell are you talking about now?' she demanded, her voice shrill with indignation. 'I'm here to tell you what I know about Danny, Lauren's boyfriend. That's why I'm here, to see him arrested for murder.'

Geraldine didn't answer straight away. She nodded at Ariadne who drew a document out of a folder and placed it on the table between them. Ella glanced down and gasped on seeing her own medical records in front of her.

'What's this?' she cried out in alarm. 'This is none of your business. It's confidential.'

'These medical records date back to your early childhood when you were hospitalised several times with broken bones before you were taken into care. Shall we talk about what happened to you?'

Ella stared at Geraldine, aghast. 'You have no right to go snooping into my past,' she said, shaking in her agitation. 'What happened to me has nothing to do with your investigation. Nothing at all. Keep your hands off my past. Now, what are you doing about Danny?'

Geraldine reached forward and tapped the file on the table. 'According to your records, you alleged that you were the victim of a violent stepfather. You reported him for beating you up, but the case never came to court due to insufficient evidence. You were judged to be an unreliable witness. You were only eleven at the time and it was your word against his. In the absence of any evidence of physical abuse, and with your mother unable or unwilling to confirm the accusation, the case collapsed. The reported allegation certainly looked flimsy. You suffered a fractured wrist and cracked ribs, but there was no evidence that your stepfather was responsible for your injuries. He claimed you accidentally fell down the stairs. Due to a breakdown in your relationship with your parents, you were brought up in care after you were removed from your family home.'

'That's a lie. The social worker made it up. My stepfather never touched me.'

'It's all documented. The hospital records, the social security reports, the care home, foster parents. It's all here, along with your statements accusing him of abusing you.' She tapped the file again.

Ella scowled. 'Oh all right, yes. It happened, just like I said at the time, only no one believed me. He was a monster. He should have gone to prison, but he died.' She suddenly banged on the table with a clenched fist. 'Do you know how that felt, knowing he'd escaped punishment? After everything he did to me, he got off scot-free.'

Geraldine nodded. 'So what happened, Ella? Tell us what you did.'

Ella hung her head and stared at the floor.

When Ella didn't answer, Geraldine went on. 'All right. Let's talk about Alice. We know you met her at the gym where you work.'

Ella bit her lip, but she didn't deny it.

'What happened? Did she confide in you, tell you about how Rob was hitting her, just like your stepfather used to hit you?'

Ella's face flushed with anger. 'She told me he hit her,' she muttered between clenched teeth. 'Not a lot, but that's how it always starts. And then it escalates. He had to be stopped. I told her to go to the police.'

'Only he killed her before she could report him,' Ariadne said. 'You must have known none of it was your fault. Even if you had come to us with your suspicions, there's nothing we could have done while Alice refused to come forward.'

'I don't follow what happened after you met Alice,' Geraldine said, raising her hand as a signal to Ariadne to keep quiet. 'You were, quite rightly, upset about Rob abusing her, and you must have been very angry with him. But why didn't you do anything about it? Why didn't you help her?'

'I begged her to go to the police, but she wouldn't listen and that meant he was getting away with it. I couldn't let that happen. Not again. He had to be punished for what he was doing to her.' Her expression hardened. 'Death was too good for him. It would have been over too quickly. He had to be punished, locked up to rot in prison for the rest of his life. If she hadn't been killed, he would never have got what he deserved. She had to die. It was the only way to see him get what he deserved.'

'You killed Alice in order to see Rob convicted of murder, so he would be punished,' Geraldine said softly.

'I had to save her from the pain he was causing her and see him punished for what he was doing to her. It was the only way,' Ella repeated earnestly.

'I'm not sure I understand,' Ariadne said. 'You wanted to see Rob locked up for abusing Alice, but to make sure that happened you killed her?' She frowned, struggling to believe what she was hearing.

'What about Danny?' Geraldine asked. 'Did you kill Lauren because you were desperate to see him punished?'

Ella nodded. 'Lauren was the reason I came back to York. I'd discovered what was going on, and it was only right to finish what I'd started by punishing the monster who was abusing my childhood friend. The others were just girls I met, but this was someone I knew.' She smiled. 'You can do what you want with me now, but Danny will always know Lauren was killed because of what he did to her. He'll have to live with that for the rest of his life. Locked in a cell, he'll have years to remember what he did.'

'You were on a mission to punish men who hurt women, but Danny was innocent.' Geraldine's voice sank to a low murmur. 'Lauren had been burning herself with cigarettes for years and Danny was helping her deal with her pain. Thanks to him, she had stopped harming herself for the first time since she was a child.'

Geraldine didn't add that Danny had probably been hitting Lauren. That would allow Ella the comfort of her insane fantasy that her actions had been justified. She didn't deserve that much compassion after what she had done.

'Lies, lies, you're lying,' Ella replied. 'I know you're lying.'

'You killed her. You killed them both, Lauren and Alice.'

'Yes, I killed them,' Ella gloated. 'And they weren't the only ones. I killed them so their abusers would be punished. Those men are vicious sadists who deserve whatever suffering they've got coming to them. They're going to be locked up for the rest of their lives.' She grinned.

'You're wrong, Ella. Danny's innocent. We have proof that Lauren caused her own injuries. I'm afraid the only monster is you.' Ella shook her head as Geraldine continued. 'You killed innocent women in an attempt to be revenged for the abuse you suffered at your stepfather's hands. But that was never going to resolve anything for you, was it? The deaths of your friends and the arrests you were hoping to see as a consequence, none of that was ever going to alleviate your suffering. Your stepfather's dead and beyond your reach. You can never be avenged for what happened to you, however many people you kill.'

'And you won't be claiming any more victims, you can be sure of that,' Ariadne added.

Geraldine nodded grimly. 'Your personal vendetta is over. If there's any justice in the world, you're the one who's going to be locked up for the rest of your life.'

Ella shook her head, her eyes wide with horror. 'No,' she murmured. 'No. I had to do it. Those men are monsters. They need to be punished for what they've done.'

'The only monster is the one inside your head, Ella, and the man who created it is dead and buried,' Geraldine said. 'If he could see you now, he'd be laughing at you.'

'No,' Ella howled. Her cry sounded inhuman.

Geraldine terminated the interview.

59

THAT AFTERNOON, GERALDINE HAD one last visit to make. Looking surprised to see who was on her doorstep, Lisa took a step back with an almost imperceptible shake of her head.

'Geraldine? I was expecting Ian to pick Tom up later,' she said, glancing at her watch and looking slightly flustered. 'Is everything all right? It's very early. Tom's still asleep.'

Geraldine assured Lisa that she was not there to talk about Tom. She had come to tell her the investigation into Alice's murder was concluded. Lisa's jaw dropped and she hurried to invite Geraldine in.

'Are you sure I won't be intruding?' Geraldine asked.

'Don't be daft. Come in, come in. I'll put the kettle on and you can tell me all about it.'

Geraldine followed Lisa into the living room where Tom was lying on a mat in a play pen, surrounded by a collection of brightly coloured soft toys. As she walked in, he opened his eyes sleepily and hit a red and blue fabric ball. He chuckled when it tinkled as it rolled over. The little girl Lisa looked after was busy cradling a doll and took no notice of the visitor, but Tom squealed with excitement when he saw Geraldine. His little legs kicked energetically, and he reached out towards her with his tiny fingers. She bent down and picked him up and held him close to her, feeling the warmth of his chubby body through their clothes. After a few moments, he wriggled and squirmed to be put down. She returned him to the playpen, where he immediately fussed to be picked up again. As Geraldine leaned towards him, Lisa came in with a tray of tea and biscuits and little Daisy dropped her doll and toddled over.

'Didit,' the little girl demanded. 'Didit.'

Laughing, Lisa lifted her into a high chair and gave her a biscuit and a drink, before propping Tom up in the playpen and handing him a rusk which he sucked on happily. Her two charges taken care of, Lisa handed Geraldine a cup of tea and only then sat down and looked at her expectantly. Geraldine noticed she was clutching a tissue and hoped she wouldn't break down in tears on hearing what had happened to Alice.

'So my poor niece was killed by some crazy woman she met at the gym?' Lisa sighed, dabbing her eyes with her tissue, when Geraldine had finished her account. 'It's ironic, isn't it? She joined a gym because she wanted to be healthy and ended up getting herself killed because of it.' She blew her nose and tucked the tissue up her sleeve. 'Poor Alice. She was such a goodhearted girl. All she ever wanted was to help other people. She was so happy when she was accepted on a nursing course and could devote herself to alleviating the suffering of her patients. If only more people were like her...' She broke off and heaved another sigh before thanking Geraldine.

'I know it doesn't change what happened, or soften the loss, knowing who killed her,' Geraldine said, wanting to comfort Lisa but feeling helpless. 'I wish there was something I could do to help.'

'We all do what we can,' Lisa replied gently, as though it was her place to console Geraldine, not the other way round. 'And you're wrong if you think you haven't done anything, because it does help to know who killed her. Somehow knowing what happened takes the anger away so I can grieve quietly.' She nodded. 'I can think about Alice now without feeling as though I want to scream and hit out.' She paused. 'So this Ella will be going to prison?'

Geraldine nodded. 'Prison or a high security psychiatric

hospital. That's for the courts to decide. But she won't walk free. You can be sure of that.'

Lisa nodded. 'She sounds like a very damaged young woman,' she said.

Geraldine was reassured to know Tom was being looked after by someone so compassionate. She wasn't sure she would be as forgiving herself, and she wanted Tom to grow up to be kind and understanding. They finished their tea in silence. It was early to be collecting Tom, but it made no sense to leave without him, so she stayed for half an hour, watching over him and Daisy while Lisa cleared away and did a few chores. Playing with the little ones was relaxing, and Geraldine was amazed to discover how responsive Daisy was to her suggestions.

'It's a completely different ball game once they start to talk,' Lisa agreed, when Geraldine expressed her surprise. 'Babies are a source of endless wonder and joy, but I think most people find them more interesting when they start to interact more meaningfully. It takes any relationship to a whole new level.'

Consumed with guilt at finding Tom boring, it had actually never occurred to Geraldine that she might not be alone in feeling that way.

'I mean, I love him, of course I do,' she told Ian later that evening. 'But, as you know only too well, spending all day every day at home with him just wasn't for me. I never thought most other people might feel a bit the same way. Even Lisa said she prefers it when they start to talk, and she chooses to spend all her time looking after other people's babies.'

'And your point is?' Ian asked, smiling quizzically at her.

She shrugged. 'I was just worried that I was unnatural, not wanting to spend all day every day with Tom. It might sound stupid, but I was afraid he might be scarred by it.'

Ian frowned. 'Now I really have no idea what you're talking about.'

'I mean, I was afraid he might be feeling rejected.'

'That's the most – well,' he corrected himself, 'that's one of the stupidest things I've ever heard.'

'Are you calling me stupid?' Geraldine replied, laughing. She drew herself up to her full height. 'I'm a detective inspector.'

'And a very successful one,' Ian added. 'I gather you just solved an almost impossible case.'

She smiled. 'Nothing is impossible. Life itself is a miracle.' As she spoke, Tom let out a yell. 'Speaking of which—' She laughed and started towards the nursery. 'We really must do something about his sleeping arrangements before he climbs out again,' she added as she hurried to pick him up before he could clamber out of his cot and hurt himself.

60

THE INCIDENT ROOM WASN'T large enough to accommodate every officer who had worked on the case, but without their uniformed colleagues the team of detectives all managed to squeeze themselves into the space. For a few minutes Binita struggled to make herself heard above the general hubbub of the assembled officers as they reminisced about the investigation. Geraldine leaned against the wall, scarcely listening to the voices chattering around her. A few phrases caught her attention, spoken by colleagues with particularly penetrating voices.

'…beginning to think we'd never get to the bottom of it…'

'…were all so sure it was Danny…'

'…who would have believed it was…'

'…never thought it would turn out to be a woman…'

'…just shows how important it is to be open-minded, not that…'

After a few moments, some officers began trying to silence the others, pointing out that the sooner Binita finished addressing them, the sooner they would be able to leave for the pub. Eventually they all settled down to listen to the detective chief inspector's traditional praise for their efforts. Once again, Geraldine paid scant attention. As her thoughts drifted to Tom and his childminder, a few phrases reached her. She heard Binita talking about 'solid police work' and 'unflagging determination'. Her senior officer's speech sounded rousing and appropriate, even though it consisted of a series of clichés. Geraldine resisted the temptation to scoff. Had she attained the rank of detective chief inspector herself, as she had once intended, she wondered how effectively she might have spoken on such an occasion.

In any case, Binita's oratory wasn't important. All that mattered was that a deranged killer had been apprehended before she could claim any more victims. For a moment, Geraldine closed her eyes, allowing herself to savour the sense of pride she always experienced at the successful outcome of an investigation. That was what made her job worthwhile, knowing she was helping to track down the guilty and protect the innocent. Thanks to her team, other potential victims of Ella's insane violence would now be safe. Even while Binita was talking, there might be a woman going about her normal life, walking along the street, doing her shopping, waiting for a bus, who would have been cruelly murdered by now had Ella not been apprehended.

It was stuffy in the incident room, and a stultifying smell of warm bodies recalled her to the present.

'I'll see you all in the pub later,' Binita was saying, smiling brightly.

A sigh of relief rippled around the room.

'I feel like I'm back at school and it's the end of term,' Naomi muttered to Geraldine, who chuckled.

They dispersed to make a start on the paperwork needed to tie up the case. With Ella's confession a conviction should be certain, but they couldn't afford to leave any discrepancies for a defence team to exploit. At the end of the day, Geraldine, Ariadne and Naomi made their way together to the local pub to join their colleagues for a drink as was customary at the successful conclusion of a murder investigation. It had begun to drizzle, and they walked quickly without speaking, with their eyes on the ground so they could avoid stepping in puddles. Most of the team had already left to go home or to meet in the pub for a celebratory drink.

Some of their colleagues were likely to stay on, or break up in groups to go into town for something to eat. Geraldine had never felt particularly sociable on such occasions. She was usually tired, her exhaustion accompanied by a feeling of emptiness whenever an investigation ended. At one time her preferred ending to such an evening was to go for a Chinese meal with Ariadne. Since Ian had moved in with her and Ariadne had married Nico, they had both taken to going straight home whenever they were finished at work.

'We should all go out for a meal one evening,' Geraldine said to her friends as they arrived at the pub.

Ariadne and Naomi murmured in agreement, but they all knew it was unlikely to happen, despite their best intentions. Ariadne was always keen to get back to Nico, and now that Tom was at home, Geraldine was less likely to go out in the evening after a day at work. Ian was collecting Tom from the childminder, so she was free to stay as long as she liked, but she was tired and wanted to get home before Tom fell asleep. It had been an unexpected bonus seeing him the previous afternoon and now the case was over, she intended to spend more time at home.

The bar was lively, with officers drinking and chattering while they waited for the detective chief inspector to arrive. Although Geraldine recognised all of her colleagues and had worked closely with many of them, she felt overwhelmed as she entered the bar. It was like walking into a wall of noise. She found a seat at a table in a corner of the room with Ariadne, leaving Naomi to fight her way to the bar. A temporary hush fell as the detective chief inspector entered and then the noise level rose again as the company resumed mutually congratulating each other on their success.

Geraldine made her excuses and left after one half-pint.

Ian was surprised to see her back home so early. 'I thought you'd be out late, carousing with your team after your brilliant performance.' He smiled, enjoying the success she was too tired to appreciate straight away.

'Something smells good,' she replied, suddenly realising how hungry she was.

'I left dinner in the oven for you,' he replied, holding his arms out to embrace her. 'I ate earlier with Tom.'

'Where is he?' she asked. 'I just want to see him before he goes to sleep. You're not going to bed yet, are you?'

'Is that an invitation?'

As they kissed again, they heard Tom cry out.

'I guess dinner can wait a few minutes,' Ian said. 'You go and see to him and I'll turn the oven off. It'll stay warm until you're ready.'

With a grateful smile, Geraldine hurried to the nursery to check on Tom. After spending the best part of a month preoccupied with a case, she was finally able to focus on her son.

As she reached down to lift him out of his cot, her phone rang.

Acknowledgments

Back in 2008, when I was writing Cut Short, I never dreamt my debut story would actually be published. How the goal posts move. My ambition to find a publisher for my first manuscript changed, and for a long time I hoped to write 20 books in the series. That seemed an unattainable ambition, yet now here we are, Geraldine and I, with her 23rd case completed. The next story is due to be published at the end of the year, and recently I signed a contract for two more books in the series. Having surpassed my goal of 20 titles in the series, would it be tempting fate to wonder how many more killers Geraldine will manage to track down before she retires?

I am indebted to Jamie Hodder-Williams and Laura Fletcher for their continuing faith in Geraldine Steel. It is a privilege to work with you and the team of experts at team at No Exit Press, Bedford Square Publishers. My thanks go to Anastasia Boama-Aboagye for her enthusiastic support with marketing, Polly Halsey for her invaluable help in production, Jem Butcher for his brilliant covers, Jayne Lewis for her highly skilled copy editing and Maureen Cox for her eagle-eyed proofreading.

My editor, Keshini Naidoo, has been with us from the beginning of the series and I am grateful for her unerring judgement. It was a lucky day for me and Geraldine when Keshini agreed to work with us.

My thanks go to all the bloggers and interviewers who have supported Geraldine Steel, and to everyone who has been kind enough to review my books. Your support is sincerely appreciated.

I am grateful to readers around the world for continuing to follow Geraldine's career. I really hope you continue to enjoy reading the stories.

My final word of thanks goes to Michael, who is always with me.

A LETTER FROM LEIGH

Dear Reader,

I hope you enjoyed reading this book in my Geraldine Steel series. Readers are the key to the writing process, so I'm thrilled that you've joined me on my writing journey.

You might not want to meet some of my characters on a dark night – I know I wouldn't! – but hopefully you want to read about Geraldine's other investigations. Her work is always her priority because she cares deeply about justice, but she also has her own life. Many readers care about what happens to her. I hope you join them, and become a fan of Geraldine Steel, and her colleague Ian Peterson.

If you follow me on Facebook or Twitter, you'll know that I love to hear from readers. I always respond to comments from fans, and hope you will follow me on **@LeighRussell** and **fb.me/leigh.russell.50** or drop me an email via my website **leighrussell.co.uk**.

To get exclusive news, competitions, offers, early sneak-peaks for upcoming titles and more, sign-up to my free monthly newsletter: **leighrussell.co.uk/news**. You can also find out more about me and the Geraldine Steel series on the No Exit Press website: **noexit.co.uk/leighrussellbooks**.

Finally, if you enjoyed this story, I'd be really grateful if you would post a brief review on Amazon or Goodreads. A few sentences to say you enjoyed the book would be wonderful. And of course it would be brilliant if you would consider recommending my books to anyone who is a fan of crime fiction.

I hope to meet you at a literary festival or a book signing soon!

Thank you again for choosing to read my book.

With very best wishes,

Leigh Russell

noexit.co.uk/leighrussell

About the Author

Leigh Russell is the author of the internationally bestselling Geraldine Steel series, which has sold over a million copies worldwide. Her books have been #1 on Amazon Kindle and iTunes with *Stop Dead* and *Murder Ring* selected as finalists for The People's Book Prize.

www.leighrussell.co.uk

@LeighRussell

NO EXIT PRESS
More than just the usual suspects

— CWA DAGGER —
AWARDED BEST CRIME & MYSTERY PUBLISHER

'A very smart, independent publisher delivering the finest literary crime fiction' **Big Issue**

MEET NO EXIT PRESS, an award-winning crime imprint bringing you the best in crime and suspense fiction. From classic detective novels, to page-turning spy thrillers and literary writing that grabs the attention. Our books are carefully crafted by some of the world's finest writers and delivered to you by a small, but passionate, team.

In over 30 years of business, we have published award-winning fiction and non-fiction including the work of a Pulitzer Prize winner, the British Crime Book of the Year, numerous CWA Dagger Awards, a British million-copy bestselling author, the winner of the Canadian Governor General's Award for Fiction and the Scotiabank Giller Prize, to name but a few. We are the home of many crime and noir legends from the USA whose work includes iconic film adaptations and TV sensations. We pride ourselves in uncovering the most exciting new or undiscovered talents. New and not so new – you know who you are!

We are a proactive team committed to delivering the very best, both for our authors and our readers.

Want to join the conversation and find out more about what we do?

Catch us on social media or sign up to our newsletter for all the latest news from No Exit Press.

f fb.me/noexitpress   **X** @noexitpress

noexit.co.uk